Secret Heart

Hearts of Three Rivers
#4

AMITY LASSITER

For Caleb

ACKNOWLEDGMENTS

Huge thanks to Zoe York who answered all my silly questions about babies and mothering because I didn't, at the time, have the experience to base it on.

To my beta readers and editor, Keriann, for being gentle and saying just the right things to prop up my fragile ego after such a long hiatus from publishing.

And of course, to my husband, who always seems to be able to walk the perfect line between pushing me and supporting me.

ONE

"YOU ARE A *lifesaver,*" Layla Sullivan said with a sigh of relief as she opened the door to Kerri Maddock.

The teen smiled back, holding her hands out. "I know."

Without hesitation, Layla handed over Mason. The baby's feet kicked in excitement as the girl held him to her chest, stepped into the house and closed the door behind her. Layla double checked for her keys and cell phone, patting her pockets before she grabbed her purse to check for her wallet.

"You're fine, *go,*" Kerri insisted, following her into the kitchen with Mason on her hip. The girl offered her a gentle smile.

How much harder would these last eight months have been without her? At this rate, she was sure the baby would grow up believing he had two moms, but she didn't trust anyone as much as Kerri.

"It's gonna be a late one," she said, wincing. As if she could just call in for no babysitter; she

1

needed this extra shift so badly she was convinced it had been divine intervention when she got the call. Danny hadn't given her much notice, but she'd been praying for some way to find the money to fix the thermostat on the car, which she was certain was on its last leg.

"I know. I brought my overnight bag; I'll just crash on the couch."

"Okay," Layla breathed, pressing a kiss to the infant's forehead and crushing the teenager in a hug. "Thank you. Be good, I love you, have fun."

Kerri lifted Mason's hand to wave. "Love you too, mommy!"

She checked the time on her phone once more and waved to her gurgling son, then shut the door behind her and took the two steps off her porch in one long stride.

At the car, Layla paused and checked her reflection, smoothing her hands down over the little pooch of belly she was still self-conscious about. The uniform at Danny's was white-t-shirt-painted-on-blue-jeans; that outfit looked cute on just about every spunky bartender except for one who had always been taller and bigger than the other girls, *and* was eight months post-partum. It seemed like she'd been hustling since the day Mason was born trying to provide a life for them, leaving little in the way of time for personal improvement. They were finally on somewhat of an even keel, but a missed shift or a mechanical failure could throw everything off balance, which was why she was thankful for small miracles and any extra shifts she could pick up.

She slid behind the wheel of her ancient Ford Fiesta and wasted no time getting to Danny's Bar, Three Rivers' favorite and *only* watering hole. There were a handful of cars in the lot—the after-supper crowd hadn't shown up yet, but there were a few die-hards that chose to drink their dinner. She wasn't judging; they always slipped her a couple crumpled dollar bills for her disinterest. She pulled into a spot near the service entrance and jumped out, jamming her keys into her purse as she jogged toward the door.

Danny Thatcher met her in the hall with an armload of beer headed for the coolers out front. "Thanks again, Layla. I'd have covered, but it's the missus' birthday and I gotta take her out on the town."

Smiling, Layla stashed her bag in the storage room and grabbed another box of domestic beers, following Danny out behind the bar. "No problem. You know you can call me anytime, Danny."

"I call you *every* time, Layla." The older man laughed and shook his head.

"I appreciate it," she said, taking a moment to covertly survey the patrons and the state of their drinks. A couple of regulars had parked at stools at the bar and she nodded a greeting when she caught their eyes. The bar job meant good money and she was in need, but it had the beneficial side effect of upgrading her social status from the equivalent of leper to the equivalent of hobo. Those in the community who might not have given her the time of day before now at least made polite small talk while she poured their drinks.

"I know, sweetheart." Danny squeezed her shoulder, and she felt her hairpin trigger tears pricking her eyelids. Danny Thatcher had been kinder to her than he needed to be, especially since she'd discovered she was pregnant and going through it alone. In a town where not everybody afforded her that kindness, he'd become something of an aspirational father figure to her. Her own family hadn't stood by her as steadfastly as her employer had, and that was saying something...about the character of all involved.

"Now you get gone. Don't keep Rita waiting. I've got this."

"I'm loading the cooler!" Danny protested. "Give me twenty minutes."

"Fifteen," she quipped back, then turned to greet a Tuesday night regular. "Hey, Dell."

Ten minutes later, Danny had finished loading the cooler, facing bottles on the back of the bar, and refilled her ice tray. Layla turned to her employer. "Okay, you. Out. For real."

"All right, all right," Danny said, laughing, and gave Layla a quick hug. "You're the best."

"You know it."

Planting her hands on her hips, Layla drew in a breath, inhaling the smell of whiskey and old polished wood. She felt more at home behind the bar than she did in most other places these days. It had been a steep learning curve, but six months later, she had a handle on just about any problem that might cross her during a typical shift, including her brother, sitting at the back with a couple of his buddies. She nodded to him the same way she nodded to the other regulars because that was about all Jimmy Sullivan was to her anymore—a regular at her bar. The bell over the door sounded at the entrance of another patron and Layla's next breath hiccupped in when she turned.

Though she hadn't seen it in almost eighteen months, she would have recognized that face anywhere.

"Nate Montgomery," she breathed out again, a silly little quiver moving in her belly when she remembered the last time she'd seen him. It had started in this very bar, but under entirely different circumstances. And had ended with something entirely different than this meeting would.

"Layla Sullivan." A slow smile drew across his features. Despite his somewhat disheveled appearance, it was handsome as ever. He'd put on a bit of weight, in a kind of mature, grown up way. And he'd grown a beard—in the years they'd known one another, she'd never seen him anything but clean-shaven—but it suited him. His hair hadn't seen a trim in quite a while, either. She knew, because she'd always paid attention to the handsome younger Montgomery brother, this was out of character. But either way, he looked happy to see her, and she...well, she wasn't *un*happy to see him. "Imagine that. I expected Cutter."

"Cutter went to Denver." It had been a surprise for everyone, but she was thankful—it opened up space for her here at Danny's, which, hour for hour, ended up being much more lucrative than her shifts at Turner's or Dr. Fields' office, though she still hung onto the latter for the few benefits it offered.

"I just missed him, then."

"What can I get you?" she asked, turning over a rock glass on the bar top.

"Just a beer. And I'll buy you an Old Fashioned." He nodded to the glass.

She pulled a bottle of beer from the front cooler and shook her head as she slid it across the bar to him. "I'm afraid I can't accept. I know you can't buy me just *one* drink, and I'm right at the beginning of an eight hour shift."

He raised a brow at her under the flop of hair nearly covering his eyes as he hunkered down around the bottle she'd given him. Eighteen-months-ago-Layla would have said sure, and been properly flattered. But today-Layla knew the Old Fashioned tasted like the heady adventure she'd begun, and the brief moment she'd felt desired by one Nate Montgomery, local celebrity bull-rider. And today-Layla was somebody's mama and didn't want to turn out like her own. Finally, she shifted and pulled a second beer out of the cooler, cracking it open and raising it to him.

"This one's on you."

He offered her a full smile this time, and lifted his bottle in response. "That's more like it."

~

There was a little part of Nate that had hoped to see Layla sitting on one of the barstools just the same way she'd been the last time he'd been in town. He was pleasantly surprised to find her behind the bar, in those blue jeans and that t-shirt that hugged her curves, a little softer and fuller than last time, in all the right ways. She'd been a blonde the last time he'd seen her—had been all her life—but she'd dyed her hair this rich mahogany color that shone under the lights of the bar. She'd been great as a blonde, but this sexy, self-assured brunette he watched move down the bar to tend to another patron was something else entirely. He couldn't take his eyes off her.

Since junior high, he'd had a soft spot for Layla Sullivan, Three Rivers' proverbial girl-from-the-wrong-side-of-the-tracks. She was a good girl who tried hard, but kept getting crushed down by life. He and his brother could have easily ended up the exact same way had it not been for Nan taking them in and raising them right.

Layla finished looking after the other patrons at the bar about the same time he finished his bottle and when she glanced back to check on him, he lifted it to indicate he wanted another.

"So what brings you back to town?" she asked, conveniently zeroing in on the exact thing he *wasn't* interested in talking about. It was the small-talk bartenders were *supposed* to make, so he couldn't blame her. She leaned one hip against the bar while she wiped down glasses from the dishwasher installed under the counter. Her question was casual. His answer wasn't. The real one, anyway; injured in the finals, followed by recovery, bankruptcy, and homelessness. So many words that would have killed an easy flirtation dead. He'd been beyond sure everyone in Three Rivers knew his business, but apparently he was wrong, or she was just too polite to let on. There was a good chance it was the latter, but the former wasn't impossible either.

He wet his lips and took a mouthful of his beer, stalling for time as he worked out his response.

"Been too long since I've been home. Nan wouldn't quit calling." That wasn't a lie. She *had* called him every day through his hospital stay and rehab. She'd even driven up when the doctors told him to quit riding bulls if he wanted to live a day past thirty, but only because Shorty Mac had called her when he'd gone off the rails, ripping up his house when the foreclosure notice came on the same day.

"You know she comes by every Wednesday afternoon and brings me flowers from her garden?" Layla's lips tipped up in a sweet smile when she spoke of Nate's grandmother, encompassing exactly the way every person in Three Rivers felt about the

7

woman. She somehow managed to keep tabs on just about everyone—what was ailing them, who was celebrating, who needed an ear or a shoulder or a secret keeper—and he was pretty sure the fundraisers she spear-headed kept the local high school's rodeo and football teams afloat.

He *was* a little surprised to hear she was visiting Layla regularly, though, especially from Layla instead of Nan. While she was kind to everyone, Layla's parents weren't notoriously easy to get along with. Even sweet-natured, long-suffering Nan steered clear of Rhonda and Gary Sullivan when given the opportunity, she just did it with a smile instead of a scowl.

"No shit. You still living out there past Lee's Creek with your mama and daddy?"

She shook her head—another surprise. The Sullivans had always kept a tight rein on Layla; their greatest resource, with her good work ethic and sweet nature, unlike her ne'er-do-good-brother he'd noticed sulking in the shadows tonight. Turned out more had changed in Three Rivers than him.

"No, I have the old Jenkins place on a rent-to-own. It's not perfect, but it's mine. Well, sort of. In a few years." She smiled and shook her head, and he could see a proud blush blooming across her high cheekbones. It looked as good on her as that t-shirt did.

"Yessir." He shook his head and took another pull from his bottle. It seemed while he'd been working his way down the ranks—from successful bull rider to unemployed, broken down, and coming home with his tail between his legs— she'd been working her way up. "Hey that place is older than Nan. Is it in decent condition?"

She shrugged, smiling. "It needs a little love...but everything is mostly functional. When I have a little more time on my hands, I'll get at the wish list, like the ugly wallpaper."

"Flamingos in the bathroom, right?"

"I feel like somebody's watching me when I'm taking a shower."

Laughing, he shook his head. He loved the ease between them; a lifetime of growing up in the same small town would do that to you. He wasn't some hotshot bull rider she was trying to impress, he was just Nate Montgomery, the kid who'd brought chicken pox to their first grade class. Maybe she remembered him as the boy who asked her to dance at the prom when her date from the next town over had abandoned her to smoke weed in the parking lot. He hoped she remembered him as that, and not the sonofabitch who'd had a one night stand with her eighteen months ago and then stayed away until now.

"Well, I'll be around for a while, maybe I'll help you get some of that wish list looked after."

Her mouth straightened and she took a little step back, crossing her arms over her chest. The warm, comfortable air between them suddenly turned frosty. *What'd I say?*

"I'm fine, I'll get to it." She smiled, one that didn't touch her eyes like the last few had, and moved down the bar, mixing a drink for another patron. She spent another thirty minutes preoccupied at the other end of the bar which looked a hell of a lot like unnecessary make-work projects, and purposely kept her shoulders angled away from him so he couldn't catch her eye. *What the hell?*

Finally, convinced she wasn't coming back, he slapped a twenty—twice what his beers had been worth—down on the bar, climbed off the stool carefully, and slipped out the door.

TWO

THE KNOCK ON Layla's screen door could only be one person. She'd told Nan a million times to just holler and come on in, but she insisted.

"It's open!" she shouted from her spot on the floor, sitting cross-legged, and reading to Mason.

Nan breezed into the house like a breath of fresh air, setting the fresh cut flowers and casserole dish she'd brought on the countertop. Mason lifted his arms, laughing at the sight of Nan and she crossed the floor and swung him up onto her hip like a natural. Nan *said* she came to bring the flowers and lunch, but Layla was pretty sure it was an excuse to play with the baby. Nan told her he was a 'trick baby'; a child who was so happy and good about sleeping and everything else, it would convince you to have another right away. Layla wasn't counting on *that* happening anytime.

"Hello, hello!"

"You're in a good mood." Layla chuckled, prying herself up off the floor with some effort. She watched as the pair settled at the kitchen table together, Mason's chubby fingers creeping to Nan's cheeks.

"It's my lucky day. I get to see all my favorite men. Banks came by for breakfast, now Mason, and Nate's all settled into the basement apartment," Nan said to the baby, then turned her eyes to Layla. "I'm just so glad to see him."

"I bet. He was by the bar last night." Layla started unpacking the casserole the older woman had brought and rummaged in the fridge for the ingredients for a little tossed salad to go with it. She left out the bit about how her stomach fluttered with excitement, even now, thinking about Nate coming into Danny's the night before, and also, the part where she did her best to crush those butterflies. And just for good measure, she didn't make eye contact, because the older woman was the most perceptive person she knew and just a sniff of Layla's feelings would set things into motion she wasn't ready to deal with.

Nate Montgomery had been the first boy in the history of boys to take a second look at her in high school. Nothing ever happened, but he had been *kind* to her, and that meant more than anything. Most of the other boys treated her like she had the plague. Justifiably so; Jimmy had been a year behind her but an absolute shithead—and that was *on top* of the reputation their parents had around town. Nobody wanted to mess with Layla knowing Jimmy came with the package. With time, and a variety of jobs working with the public of Three Rivers, things had come around. But nobody ever looked at her the way Nate did the night she'd seen him across the bar eighteen months ago.

This was why it absolutely killed her to have to shutter up her nervous excitement. Oh, she could be cordial to him in public, but his offer to come to the house and help out was laughable. The minute he saw Mason, he'd know. She saw parts of Nate in him every single day. And she was perfectly content to keep that to herself. Or she had to be, at least. She'd made the decision to do this on her own, so she was going to do just that. The last thing she needed was for someone to think she was looking for handouts, so she made Nan eat whatever she brought for them when she turned up with food.

Nan held Mason at arm's length, then brought him in to give him loud, exaggerated kisses on each round cheek until the child was squealing with laughter. Then she cuddled him close, pressing her cheek against his. Half the time, Layla was more or less convinced Nan knew her connection to the baby, but Nan would never ask...and Layla would never tell—anyone...including her parents.

Single motherhood wasn't easy, but she couldn't imagine any better life, really. A little person to love and love her back, to try to raise without all the mistakes made in her own childhood. That hadn't settled well with mama and daddy. They'd pushed, and pushed, and *pushed*, until they'd pushed Layla and Mason clear out of the house. They'd stayed in Nan's basement for a couple weeks until the deal with the Jenkins' place came up. Nan had helped with that, too.

"Oh he was, was he?"

"Oh you know when he comes and goes, don't pretend you don't." Layla teased as she tore lettuce and sliced cucumbers and tomatoes into a bowl. She arranged two plates on the kitchen island and dished out the casserole with the salad on the side.

"Well, as long as he keeps coming back," Nan said, settling Mason into the high chair at the table and retrieving a pair of glasses from the cupboard by the sink. When Kerri was unavailable, Nan happily cleared her schedule for the baby, and she was comfortable in the home. Layla liked it. Like family was *supposed* to be, or at least what she imagined it should. "I'd like to see him settle down back here in Three Rivers."

"I know, but it's hard to make a real living on the rodeo circuit when you're two hours away from it." Layla brought the plates to the table, then went back for silverware and salad dressing.

The three of them tucked in around the small, round, battered kitchen table. Nothing in the house was fancy; the payments and household bills were a big enough burden, but it all belonged to her. She got up early every Saturday morning since she'd moved in and hit every yard sale she could find to assemble her little ragtag group of possessions, but she was proud of what she'd accomplished. There were still a few small things on her wish list, but she anticipated being able to save enough pennies to buy them new by the end of the summer if she couldn't find them secondhand before then.

"That's true, if you were making a living on the rodeo circuit...but I feel like Nate won't be doing much of that, anymore. I'm hoping the basement apartment is a more...permanent...arrangement."

Layla's fork full of casserole stopped halfway to her mouth as she tipped her head and narrowed her eyes at the woman who was innocently tucking into the food she'd brought. Everybody knew about Nate's accident. There had been cards and well-wishes and even, apparently, a video of the wreck on the Internet Layla had never been able to bring herself to watch. But there had never been any talk that he wouldn't rodeo anymore. And Nan's implication that that might be the case gnawed at her insides. She'd arranged her entire life plan around the idea that Nate Montgomery would never settle back down in Three Rivers. She knew he'd never come back for her, but she hadn't banked on a career-ending injury re-settling him here.

Letting out a breath she hoped didn't betray her nerves, Layla straightened, pressing her lips together. Nan was about the only person who didn't fuel the rampant rumor mill in Three Rivers; not intentionally, anyway. Taking the older woman's example, Layla didn't probe further, because Nan had never probed about Mason's father. Oh, the rumors were busy, even now, and especially as the boy's blond hair was coming in darker and his cheeks got chubbier. She supposed those rumors and speculations would probably never die—it was something she'd have to get used to, just the same as doing this all on her own.

"Well, whatever he does will be exactly what he does," Layla reminded her.

"That's true. That boy has always had a stubborn streak, ever since he was *your* age," she stopped halfway through her words and patted Mason's chubby cheek lightly. He paused partway through his selection of cut up pasta and veggies Nan had given him in a separate bowl and offered her a smile that showed his two grown in bottom teeth and the top middle teeth starting to poke through. "Oh, are those new? My goodness, he's growing up fast."

"You can say that again. After lunch, he'll show you how quickly he can worm out of your line of vision on his belly."

"Already?"

"Already. Can't wait to get on his feet and running." She swallowed and smiled at her son. All at once, it was amazing and terrifying the way he'd grown and developed in the eight short months of his life. There were times she wished there was someone there with her to see, but most of the time, sharing like this once a week with Nan, and sharing the highlights with Kerri was almost as good as the real thing.

"Oh he will be, before you know it," Nan said, shaking her head. "Boys. They grow right up from under you before you even realize it."

THREE

"JUST FOR THE record, you have exactly two more weeks to feel sorry for yourself," Nan huffed, throwing a couch pillow at Nate, who was stretched out with his feet on her coffee table. The apartment downstairs was comfortable enough, but he liked the companionship of Nan buzzing around, so he found himself in her living room ninety percent of the time he had the choice and nothing better to do. Eventually, it would get old, but for now it was just right. "I didn't raise you boys to wallow in self-pity."

"Oh, you like having me around," he said with a laugh as he tossed the decorative pillow back at her, hitting her retreating backside. The look she gave him when she swung around reminded him all too much of his middle school days—in particular, the day Jack Anderson dragged him home by the ear when he'd found Nate clinging to the back of one of his good steers while Cutter and the Baylor boys had watched, whooping in delight. His brother, Banks, of course, had headed home at the first sniff of trouble, so Nan had been waiting on the doorstep with the flyswatter in hand. It didn't take much thought to remember how sore his backside had been.

After a second, his grandmother's face softened. "Of course. I *love* having my boys both in one place. Shame what caused it. But a woman can still take joy in having family around."

Nate got to his feet to follow her into the kitchen where Nan was in full Sunday dinner mode. She'd peeled a whole ten pound bag of potatoes, and the biggest chicken he'd ever seen had been roasting in the oven since before lunch. He flicked on the oven light and looked at the bird, his stomach growling. Nan had taught both he and Banks how to cook—'the most valuable skill a man can know', she'd insisted—but she'd have been disappointed if she knew how many microwave dinners he'd eaten when he lived on his own. Her homemade meals ranked high on his relatively small list of things he looked forward to when he'd faced down the fact that he had to come back to Three Rivers. The other had been waiting behind the bar at Danny's, all soft curves and new, sexy confidence.

"Did you adopt two more families while I was gone?"

"No," Nan retorted, swinging her gaze to him again. "Why?"

"Cause it sure looks like you're feeding two more families."

She took that opportunity to retaliate, snapping a dishtowel against the back of his thigh.

"As a matter of fact, I am. The leftovers will make a couple casseroles. One for the Andersons, and one for Layla."

"Do you feed the whole town now?" He laughed, skirting away from another threatened slap of the dish towel. He knew the Andersons had been having a tough time and he suspected Nan used the food as an excuse to make sure that old house Layla had told him about hadn't eaten her up. She was a braver man than he was, living at the Jenkin's place all by herself. If it wasn't falling apart, it was definitely haunted at the very least.

"Just the ones I like." A broad grin swept her face.

"That's everyone," Banks interjected with a laugh from the doorway. Nate's older brother had been by for dinner three times this week, but this was the first time he wasn't wearing his sheriff uniform. With such a small law-enforcement team, his brother was rarely not on call, but the deputy, Carter Collins covered the slow Sundays.

"You're one to talk," Nate quipped. Banks made a face.

"It's my *job* to be fair to everyone in town. That doesn't mean I have to like them."

The bigger man settled at the end of the table so he could observe the goings-on in the kitchen. He *was* good at his job—at least there weren't many complaints. He'd served with his predecessor as a deputy for enough years that when Sheriff Watling retired, he was the natural choice for election. Nan had been so proud. The youngest sheriff in the county's recorded history, Banks had a knack for resolving conflict with his quiet, even temper in check. There was no way in hell Nate could have done it; all the extra fuse Banks got had been cut out of Nate's.

"Same here," Nan added, poking into her pot of potatoes with a fork to test them.

His family had bigger hearts and stronger constitutions than he did, that was for sure.

"The last time I checked, grandmothering the entire community was not an *actual* job," Nate chided.

"It *is* my job. Somebody's gotta do it. And besides, I like it."

He recalled how Layla's face lit up telling him about his grandmother's frequent visits. Nan clearly wasn't the only one who liked it.

"Fair enough." He turned to Banks, leaning back against the counter, more in his grandmother's way than close by to help if she needed it. He'd been on his ass in front of the TV for most of the day so he felt like he needed to at least *look* like he could be helpful. "What about you? You still liking your *job*?"

"Wouldn't still be doing it if I didn't."

Three Rivers was the quiet sort of town where the most trouble the sheriff ever had to attend to was a drunken brawl. The majority of Banks' work was officiating marriages, with the occasional speeding ticket or domestic dispute. His brother readily admitted how unsuitable the job would have been if he had to deal with homicides and drug rings. But as it stood, the job suited him just fine, and gave him lots of time for his real passion—raising cutting horses. He had a small but superb herd and a hundred acres to devote to it. Nate had never been more jealous.

"Anything exciting?"

"Jonas Pierce had a loose cow on the highway last week." Banks shook his head, chuckling. "Everybody ran around like chickens with their heads cut off until Lily came riding up out of the woods on that little cutting horse Finn gave her and took him home. We were just lucky she happened to be in the area."

"That *does* sound exciting," Nate said, rolling his eyes. Everything moved slower in Three Rivers except the gossip. He peeked over Nan's shoulder as she mashed potatoes with one hand and stirred gravy on the stove top with the other.

"Can I do anything to help?"

He *was* living there rent-free, the least he could do was help with dinner. Except she wouldn't let him. He knew that much. But he *did* have to ask. And he and Banks would look after the dishes once they were done—because house rule said she who cooked didn't do dishes.

She shot him a signature Nan look. "No, go sit down."

He knew enough to do as he was told, and pulled up a chair perpendicular to his brother. No matter why, it *was* good to be home.

FOUR

"I'M TELLIN' YA, I have a spare bedroom. You're more than welcome to it," Banks insisted.

"And *I'm* telling *you*...I'm perfectly fine bunking with Nan for the time being," Nate returned, nodding out the open window in greeting to Stephanie Turner as his brother's patrol car trawled slowly down the main drag of Three Rivers. He knew all too well about Banks' property, recently renovated ranch house, and handful of quarter horse broodmares—things he thought Banks probably acquired to keep up with him in the first place. And now that Nate had lost everything he had, right down to the horses, he might have been a *tiny* smidge jealous of what Banks still had. It wasn't his brother's fault Banks had chosen the line of work with insurance and a pension. It might have, technically, been as dangerous as bull riding, but there was a safety net. Nate, on the other hand...*If I'd had a safety net, I wouldn't be here right now.*

"Hey, you know I think the Reichers might be looking for someone to work the cattle...since Chase is on the road, they're a little shorthanded."

"Uh huh," Nate said absently as they idled past Danny's Bar. Banks had asked him to ride along to try to stave off potential cabin fever, but Nate had accepted in hopes he might see Layla somewhere. He wasn't sure what she was driving, but it was worth a shot. "Hey, pull over."

When he didn't, Nate glanced across the seat to his brother who was giving him a dubious look.

"Sheriff in uniform in the bar, eh?"

"You don't have to come in." *It's probably better if you don't.* "Just pull over."

His brother's expression didn't change as he hit the blinker and pulled up to the sidewalk. Nate climbed out, shutting the door behind him, and then leaned back in the open window. "I'll find a way home."

If Layla wasn't there, he could at the very least forget his troubles for a couple hours, then hitch a ride back out of town toward Nan's. He straightened, then heard Banks' voice.

"Hey." His brother leaned across the seat to make eye contact through the window. "I better not be hauling you out of here later on."

Nate blew out a dismissive breath and rolled his eyes. His days of scrapping were well behind him—he didn't get drunk and unruly very often anymore...well, unless it involved a recently-won buckle. Yeah, his brother's sleep schedule was safe tonight.

"All right, Sheriff." He raised two fingers to his forehead in a half-hearted salute, and Banks gunned the engine only long enough for him to jump back before he peeled away from the curb.

Two long strides put Nate inside the door of the Danny's, tugging off his ball cap as he surveyed the interior. It was only just past supper time, so while the dark bar had a few patrons pulled up at the long bar, it was mostly quiet, save for Danny in the corner, cursing while he tried to set up a sound system. And behind the bar, looking pretty as a picture, Layla stood with one luscious hip cocked while she dried a beer glass and chatted with Rusty McLain. She wore the same dark jeans and white t-shirt that hugged every soft curve and line of her body, and her dark hair gleamed under the lights. He might have been imagining it, but he was pretty sure his heart skipped a couple of beats.

Since he'd seen her that first night, he hadn't been able to get her off his mind. The ability to turn his thoughts to her sweet smile or the soft sway of her hips was a bright spot in the otherwise bleak terrain of his return to Three Rivers. And she flashed that smile at him; the pretty, welcoming, fresh face of Danny's...until it died on her lips when her eyes met his. He almost checked to make sure he'd put on deodorant; he knew from personal experience crushed dreams occasionally led to poor personal hygiene, but...no, he was good today.

He bellied up to the bar, sliding onto the stool he'd occupied the last time he'd been in, and, because she was good at her job, she crossed the space between them and put a paper coaster down in front of him.

"Nate," she said, with another smile that didn't quite reach her eyes. "What can I get you?"

You... "Just a beer."

With practiced fluidity, she grabbed the beer from the cooler and popped the top off, setting it in front of him. She made the briefest of eye contact with him to make sure he was satisfied, then made to leave but he tipped his head toward her and then toward Danny in the corner. She stopped because she'd always been polite and he was playing on that because he was a desperate asshole.

"What's going on?"

"Karaoke Sunday never died."

He shook his head with a laugh. "So we'll be treated to the vocal stylings of Emma Pierce and Stephanie Turner tonight, eh?"

"Emma *Baylor*," Layla replied with an unreadable expression, then pressed her lips together. "And yes. You good?"

"Actually, one more thing."

She tipped her chin up, indicating he should continue. God, she was different. Cool, calm, and collected. Sexy in her confidence. The fact she had no time for him made him want her time that much more. It was usually the other way around, but he couldn't help himself. Yeah, desperate was the right word. And he'd never felt desperate when it came to women...except *this* woman.

"You should let me take you on a date."

She inhaled a slow breath, her chest rising, like she was preparing a long list of reasons why she couldn't, which were probably also the same reasons she shut him down when he offered to help her out with her house, but he held up a finger, interrupting the process.

"Wait. Don't tell me no."

"Then...probably not?" Her shoulders lifted in a shrug with her voice.

"I can work with that." A small victory...maybe even a challenge issued. A hard 'no' was a lot harder to change. He smiled and took a swig of his beer.

~

Layla moved through her Sunday evening routine like she'd done it a million times. There was a pretty specific group of regulars on karaoke Sundays; those who came specifically to perform, those who came specifically to watch, and those who came specifically to drink and didn't give a damn about karaoke night. Nate Montgomery didn't seem to fit into any of those categories, and it was unsettling.

She steered clear, but she felt his eyes following her as he nursed the beer she'd given him. He wanted to take her on a date. A real date. Not a hot-and-heavy-limited-time-offer like they'd had before, but a real date. Suddenly, she was extra self-conscious as she stretched to get a fresh bottle of Johnny Walker off the back shelf, aware of just how long she let Dell Ray flirt with her when she delivered his third drink of the night, and hyper-aware of her body language as Noah Baylor cut through the crowd to Nate's seat.

Three or four years ago, she had a brief fling with Noah that ended with him in a drunken stupor and his brother driving her to the emergency room while she miscarried a baby Noah hadn't wanted, but she had. They'd made peace, but that didn't stop her from drawing in a tight breath. He was in here at least once a week with his now-wife, and she wasn't jealous or upset, but Layla still hadn't figured out exactly how she was supposed to behave around someone she had that sort of history with. Especially since word around town was Noah and Emma had been trying for a baby going on a year now with no success, and Layla had managed to do it twice now by accident.

And now Noah stood next to the man whose baby she *hadn't* lost, the one who *didn't* know. The stuff of nightmares. When he caught her looking, Noah tipped his head up, indicating he was looking for service so she steeled herself with a deep breath, pasted on a smile she hoped looked convincing, and crossed the floor.

"'Evening, Layla."

"Noah," she said, willing the smile not to slide. Nate watched her with keen eyes. "What can I get for you?"

"Two tequila sunrises and a beer," Noah said, his nose wrinkling as he ordered the drinks of choice for the two women he was wrangling; his wife and her best friend. They ordered the same thing every week, and every week, he made a comment or pulled a face about their choice in what he'd once called 'frou-frou' drinks, but still he traipsed to the bar and ordered it for them, ever the dutiful husband. Noah Baylor had turned into a fine man, just not the man for her.

"Coming right up."

"Take your time." Noah nodded, settling onto the empty barstool beside Nate.

Layla moved efficiently around the bar, picking up a couple of refills for other patrons. Never much of a drinker, it had taken her some time to memorize the mixes, but she'd become an expert at pouring beer early on. Because he'd told her to take her time, she got a refill for Rusty and a new pan of ice from the ice machine in the back. She kept herself half tuned in to Nate and Noah, because she could still feel eyes on her from time to time, but she couldn't hear any of their conversation because a crowd favorite had taken the stage and was ramping up into a growling first chorus of 'Fancy'.

Noah being there put her on edge. The two were close friends, and that was yet another reason she couldn't say yes to Nate. It would just get complicated and muddled, like every other damn thing in this tiny town. Most of the time, she was happy to be here, but the rampant rumors that stirred up as easily as dust in the wind occasionally had her wishing she could pack up and run.

She stayed, though, because this was where she had roots, weak as they were. And as few friends as she found in Three Rivers, new places would have even fewer. She wasn't naive enough to think she could raise Mason entirely on her own, and even if half the people who helped raise him now weren't 'real' family, they were what she considered *her* family. This was where she belonged. But she would still do what she could to keep her name off the lips of others. And going on a date with Nate Montgomery, Three Rivers' favorite rodeo star, would be a sure way to do the opposite.

When Stephanie Turner took the stage, Layla put Noah's drinks together quickly, and brought them down the length of the bar.

"I was just trying to talk Layla here into letting me take her out," Nate started, once she was in ear shot. *Oh no.* Her stomach sank while she scrambled to paste on the kind of gently patronizing smile she used when Dell Ray had one too many and started hitting on her. So much for keeping things under wraps.

Noah's eyebrows lifted as his unreadable gaze passed from her to Nate.

"That so?"

Nate nodded, a stupid shit-eating grin gracing his features. He'd always had a great smile and she hated her body for reacting to the lines that framed his mouth and the way his eyes crinkled in the corners, because he was betraying her. Putting her in a shitty position now, whether she said yes or no. Of course, he didn't know what he was doing. When people in town talked about him, it was about his accomplishments, what a shame his wreck was, how great his Nan was for raising those two boys. When people in town talked about Layla, it was wondering who she was tramping around with, what shitty money grab her parents were up to now, or who the daddy of her baby was. *That* one she'd kept firmly under wraps by not telling anyone, ever. It didn't stop the speculation, but speculation really only hurt her, not anyone else. And least of all, the golden boy of Three Rivers.

Now they were both looking at her expectantly. She brightened her smile a little as she opened Noah's beer and set it on the bar next to the mixed drinks. Stephanie was belting out 'Before He Cheats' which was ironic because everyone in town knew Jamie Turner was the last man who would ever cheat on his wife.

"Harassing me, more like it."

"Eas-y," Nate teased, drawing the word out and holding a hand over his heart. He clearly found it amusing, and if she could forget about everything just under the surface of all of this, she could have gone along with it a little more willingly.

"I don't know how it was in Denver, with buckle bunnies falling into your lap, Nate Montgomery, but that's not how I work," Layla sassed. She had a particular role to play at this point, or else everything fell apart. And nobody wanted to see a bartender with running mascara.

His fingers clutched the front of his shirt and his eyebrows lowered as he tipped his head back. "You're wounding me, sweetheart."

"Maybe it's good for you," Noah piped up, clapping his friend on the shoulder with a chuckle. "I'm sure you'll recover."

"Maybe," Nate said with exaggerated doubt on his features. Layla shook her head with a little chuckle when she realized he kept an eye on her the entire time.

"Our table's over there if you wanna come on over in a bit." Noah tipped his chin up toward the stage area, where Emma and Stephanie had staked out their normal table.

"Yeah, I'll talk to you later, Noah."

They watched Noah weave his way through the other patrons back to his table with the drinks, then Layla turned back to Nate. It had taken him all this time, but his beer was finally empty.

"Can I get you anything else, Nate?"

He paused, his expression serious now that his friend was gone.

"I know that's not how you work."

She raised a brow.

"What?"

"I know you're not impressed by my wins or my rides. If I wanted to take one of the girls hanging around the bull chutes out on a date, that's what I would do."

His somber tone made her slam on her brakes. *No, no, no.* Playful Nate was dangerous, but this one was so much more. This was something else, entirely. It made her heart pound in her throat, blood rushing through her ears. She was so well accustomed to being the butt of a joke, even *that* would have been easier than whatever she was supposed to do about Nate wanting to take her out.

"I know."

She expected him to ask again, but he didn't. Instead, he pushed back his stool, peeled a ten dollar bill out of his wallet and put it on the bar top before he screwed his ball cap onto his head, tipped the brim at her, and headed out the door without looking back.

FIVE

NATE PAUSED OUTSIDE the door of Dr. Fields' office and drew in a big breath. *No better way to kick off the week than with an appointment full of disappointment.* He hadn't visited Three Rivers' resident physician yet, but he knew the files that had been transferred from the office in Denver would lead the kindly older MD to the same verbiage he'd heard for the last six months. Usually there was something in there about being lucky, and often something about his career being over. Same shit, different day. He figured he was doing well enough to accept it without having to be reminded every time he spoke to a medical professional.

He pulled the heavy glass door open and stepped inside the cool office. It was only early June but temperatures were climbing. He should have been standing ringside watching some of his buddies get their asses handed to them by Denver's finest bucking stock, but instead he was here.

And so was Layla. Suddenly being here wasn't that bad. He didn't expect to see her sitting behind the reception desk, and she didn't seem to expect him to be coming in, because what started as a warm, friendly smile froze on her features when he approached the desk, just like the other night at the bar. She recovered quickly, but he'd already seen it.

He thought they'd had a good time the last time he'd been in Three Rivers. He'd just dropped off Lily Jacobs-now-Baylor and her horse at the ranch and headed to Danny's for a drink. And there she'd been, a bit more brassy and confident than he'd ever known her to be. He'd checked all the right boxes; consent, expectations, protection. The definition of a no-strings-attached one night stand. It had been a lot of fun, but somehow, he'd left her...what was that? Angry? Scared? Bitter? Something that hadn't emerged right away, but had clearly been simmering under the surface since he'd gone back to Denver. Either way, he was looking down the barrel of a long summer in Three Rivers if she shut down like that every time he came around. Especially since she happened to work at the two places in town he was most likely to frequent.

"Nate. How can I help you?"

"I have a ten o'clock." He rubbed a hand through his hair and suddenly wished he had bothered to shave. It was easy to fall into the spiral of letting oneself go when you didn't have a job to get up for every morning anymore. A woman might have been sufficient motivation, but he hadn't been interested in *those* in months. Until last week, when he'd first watched Layla move around the bar and remembered just what that long-limbed, soft body looked like minus the jeans and t-shirt.

She was wearing a sundress and a cardigan today, with her long hair braided straight down her back. Conservative, but sexy as hell in little ways most of the patients who came in wouldn't notice. Her cardigan was halfway unbuttoned, joining together midway down and framing a good section of exposed bust and the creamy skin of her throat and chest. A couple strands of hair had worked their way out of her braid and framed her face in soft waves. She'd been overlooked all through high school because of where she came from, who her family was, but Nate knew she was a good girl underneath it all. A good girl who'd been handed a couple of shitty cards.

Layla tapped a few keys on the computer in front of her. She twisted the long braid hanging over her shoulder around her finger and bit her lower lip—God help him—and then finally nodded. "So you do. Dr. Fields will be with you in a few minutes."

"Hey," he said, leaning against the tall desk. A sign indicating a charge for canceled appointments clattered to the lower level of the desk in front of her. She'd turned him down once, but is inner Cowboy Casanova wasn't so dead he wouldn't try again. At least once more. "You should let me take you out sometime, Layla. I'm going to be here for a while."

She didn't lift her eyes from the computer screen. "Probably not a good idea."

"Probably not, but I've never been one to listen to logic."

She finally glanced up, amusement lighting up her blue eyes, and he felt like he'd scored a point. "That's probably right. You *are* a bull rider, after all. And I can't think of a less logical career choice."

Was a bull rider.

"Guilty as charged."

She paused, thoughtful.

"You aren't gonna give up 'til I give in, are you?" Narrowing her eyes, she leaned forward on her elbows. That sundress was not *quite* as conservative as his initial observation, especially for a woman as well-endowed as Layla. Despite his interest, basic decency made him glance away, shaking his head with a smile.

"You know it."

"I should warn you, I'm not the same woman you took home from Danny's last time."

He'd always liked a challenge.

"Fair play. I'm not the same man, either."

"Nate Montgomery?" Dr. Fields' voice sounded from the doorway of his exam room, and he didn't know whether to be grateful he didn't have to elaborate or disappointed their flirtation had been disrupted. He tipped his head at Layla and moved across the office to shake the doctor's hand, stepping into the exam room.

"Good to see you, Doc."

The older man closed the door behind him and gestured to a chair across from the heavy oak desk in one end of the room. This end of the room could almost trick him into believing this wasn't exactly like every other physician's exam room he'd haunted in the last year or so, but an exam table and a cabinet full of medical supplies inhabited the other end of the office, just behind him.

"Shame about the circumstances, Nate. That was some kind of wreck you had."

Most of the doctors he'd visited in the last year had everything on a computer, but Dr. Fields flipped through a thick stack of papers. His old file from childhood, maybe.

"Yeah, it was something all right." Nate sat back in the chair, resting his palms on his thighs. These appointments were all the same these days.

"How do you feel?"

That was a loaded question.

"Fine," he shrugged. "Everything's working the way it's supposed to."

The doctors all told him the same thing; everything had healed up as well as could be expected, and he could resume life as normal, with some stiffness and minor residual pain—but the bull-riding part of his 'normal' was out. He'd stopped hoping a doctor would give him a different answer a long time ago.

"Good. This is just a standard exam to touch base now that you're back under my care, Nate. Would you mind stepping over to the exam table?"

At the end of twenty minutes, the doctor looked over his glasses at him.

"You made the right choice to resign from the circuit, Nate."

As if he had any choice. He'd tried to show up for his buddies over the winter season, even flown to Nevada for a break, but the minute he got anywhere near the chute, his insides went to liquid, reducing him to a shitting, puking coward. Barely a man. A far cry from the fearless fan favorite he'd been for the last eight years. He knew he was lucky to have lasted that long; there were career-ending injuries every single season. Some of his best friends got that call from the doctor years ago. Nate was still dealing with the idea of being one of those busted up old cowboys who still hung around the bucking chutes just to feel the adrenaline, and he couldn't even be *that* right now.

But he didn't want to talk about it. And even though he'd known Dr. Fields his entire life and respected the man, he was over the whole doctor thing.

"So no more follow-ups?" he asked, jiggling his legs, anxious to leave.

"One more in six weeks, then not again unless something's bothering you." The physician closed his big paper file and pushed his chair back from the desk, offering his hand to Nate. "I'll see you soon, Nate."

"Don't take this the wrong way, Doc, but I hope not."

Layla's smile from behind the desk was a breath of fresh air when he left the exam room.

"Gonna live another day?"

"Guess so," he said, his mood lightening by leaps and bounds. He paused by the desk, tapping his fingers on the upper level. "Why don't I pick you up tonight at 7:30 and we'll go to Yvette's for burgers?"

A pretty blush washed over her cheeks as her eyes flickered down, and he thought maybe she'd say yes, but regret echoed in her eyes when she looked up. "I'm sorry, Nate. I really can't. I'd like to, but..."

He straightened, nodding. "Hey, I get it, Lay. It's okay."

She offered him a relieved smile, and he shifted back a step. She wouldn't say yes today, but she would, eventually. And that was enough for him.

SIX

THE REST OF the morning and into the afternoon were slow—a blessing and a curse. As busy as she was, Layla liked quiet time at the office to gather her thoughts, look at the week ahead, and reflect a little on the progress she was making with the house. But today, the quiet was filled with *Nate*. He was going to keep showing up at her place of work and she was going to have to figure out a way to minimize the effect. She was so immersed in distracting herself by penciling her shifts into her planner, she didn't realize someone was coming in until she heard the bell over the door tinkle. Nobody was scheduled, but in a small town where the hospital was a thirty minute drive away, it wasn't uncommon to have non-urgent walk-ins, and Dr. Fields always fit them in where he could. Her standard welcoming smile died on her lips when she lifted her eyes and saw her mother standing in the doorway.

"Layla." Rhonda Sullivan smiled, which immediately put Layla on edge. She did her best to maintain a relationship with her family for Mason's sake, but the incessant questions about paternity had started when she'd barely had a baby bump. She'd spent a few weeks in Nan's basement, insisting to her parents she was doing fine and just needed her own space, as an adult—something she hadn't had in her entire life—but the relationship had never been the same since.

"Hey mom." She tried her best to be pleasant, but the only times Rhonda Sullivan made contact with her were to have conversations about 'being reasonable', and making Mason's father 'nut up and be a man'. The life she'd carved out wasn't easy, but it was her own, and she wouldn't have traded it for the alternative. "What can I do for you? Dr. Fields isn't busy."

"Can't a woman visit with her daughter?"

No. Not when the very secret she was trying to keep from her mother was strolling around, insisting on taking her out on a date, and making her heart race.

Kind, but firm. That was the mantra Nan had helped her develop the last time her mother had come sniffing around. Layla worked to keep her features smooth, but a grimace was lurking just under the surface. *Your secrets are yours to keep.* Because it was never just a visit. It was always needling, poking, pushing about how much easier her life would be if she demanded compensation for her trouble. Her mother saw her pregnancy, and the struggle of single-motherhood as a burden, and that was the hard sticking point when it came to getting along with her family these days. She wouldn't have traded her life with Mason for anything. And the more her mother insisted, the more it felt like she was making the same argument about having Layla and her siblings.

"Sure," Layla said on a long exhale, straightening and pushing back from the desk a little. "What's new?"

Rhonda pressed her lips together, a tell that she had something to say that might make Layla unhappy. *Not that she really cares if she makes me unhappy or not.* It was good enough to know her mother at least *knew* she was being indecent—having enough control to stop herself was another thing entirely.

She couldn't be angry, though. Her mother had acted out of need and desperation so many times it had become habit, taking advantage of the kindness of others. Easier to take a handout than to fix what she could in her own life. Layla was thankful she'd managed to get off *that* particular carousel.

"I'd like to see Mason more."

That *was* new. All of Rhonda's energy had been directed toward Mason's father for so long Layla had given up hoping her mother would take an interest in the child. It was new, and strange, but it did plant the tiniest seed of hope they could perhaps someday function like a normal family, and she desperately wanted 'normal'.

"Mom, you know you can come over anytime." It would be awkward, at first. Tough, because of all the things that had been said before she'd moved out of the family home. But if it meant Mason got to have a relationship with both grandmothers, then she was willing to at least try. "Well, anytime I'm actually home."

Her mother completely missed her apologetic smile, gripping tightly to her last line. "You work way too much, Layla."

A whole speech about doing what she had to do to take care of her family on her own terms stuck in the back of her throat. She didn't want to make a scene, and she was still trying to hold onto the warm buzz of happiness Nate's visit had produced. Instead, she forced another smile.

"I know." Leaning forward over her planner, she ran her fingers over the squares of the week, where she'd carefully penciled in all her shifts. "I have the evening off Thursday. Maybe you could come by then?"

The smile that crossed Rhonda Sullivan's face gave Layla more hope than any of her words and internal reasoning had. Ultimately, at the end of the day, she was a mother, a grandmother, and surely that part of her was talking over the part of her that was always looking for an angle to make the most money out of something. Her mother straightened, rapping her knuckles on the desk lightly.

"It's a date, then."

Layla would rather have accepted the first date offer she got today.

SEVEN

"NONONO, PLEASEPLEASEPLEASE!" Layla cursed under her breath, pounding her fist on the steering wheel of her Fiesta as she watched the temperature gauge climb and climb. She'd just dumped a gallon of water into the radiator and driven halfway to work with her windows down and the heat turned up full blast, but the steam billowing out from under the hood as she limped it to the side of the road told her the thermostat had finally died, once and for all. Turning off the ignition, she drew in a deep breath and then covered her mouth to try and hold in a couple of self-pitying sobs. She was *so* close to being able to pay off the parts, but her bank account was still a hundred dollars away and without a reliable method of transportation, coming up with that cash would be much more complicated.

Dropping her head back against the headrest, she took a couple more breaths to get her emotions under control and then pulled out her cell. She dialed Nan's number and the woman picked up within a couple rings.

"Hey Nan, it's Lay…"

"Everything okay, sweetie?"

The warmth in the older woman's voice dulled the ache to simply have a family she could count on at times like these.

"Yes. Well, sort of. I'm stuck on the side of the road by the Milton farm. The car finally gave up the ghost. And I'm supposed to be at Dr. Fields' office at ten. I was just wondering if you could come give me a lift."

"Of course," Nan said.

Layla breathed a sigh of relief. Nan's house wasn't far, so she still had a chance of making it to work on time. If Nan hurried.

"I'll be right there."

"Thank you, you're a lifesaver."

"Don't be silly. You're my family. I'm doing for you like I'd do for either of the boys." The reciprocation in words of the way Layla had felt about Nan for the last year warmed her heart and Layla smiled.

"See ya soon," she said, hanging up before quickly dialing the number to the office to give Dr. Fields a heads up that she could be late. When she disconnected that call, she climbed out of the car, unfolding her long-legged frame. She bent back into it to retrieve her purse and heard a diesel engine rumble in behind her. Straightening, she smoothed her hands down over the front of her sundress and came face to face with Nate.

"My knight in shining…pickup truck."

His laughter was a deep, pleasant rumble.

"I hear you're in a bind."

"You are…considerably younger than who I expected. And the wrong gender, too." Pleasure to see him was underwritten by the nagging idea that she didn't want Nate's help. It started with a date, then he was trying to help her with the house, then they got close, and then she had a big problem on her hands. A hot, muscular, six-foot-four problem she wouldn't *want* to get rid of, but a problem nonetheless.

"Yeah, well Nan was just putting some bread in the oven and I'm not much of a baker, so I offered to take her place. Hop in." He headed back toward the truck and she pushed the manual lock down and closed the driver's side door of her car.

It was a big heave, even for a tall girl like her, to get into the passenger side of Nate's truck. It was designed for pulling a big stock trailer before anything else, and it took a grip on the handle on the door frame and a couple bounces to get in. Nate watched, amusement written across his features, and she felt her cheeks redden. She turned her face to hide it, pulling the seatbelt toward the buckle, but it didn't stick. The metal tongue slid out of the buckle as easily as it slid in, without catching. Before she'd even appealed to him for help, Nate's fingers covered hers to slide it into place, his rough, warm palm covering the back of her hand and twisting just so. The touch made her mouth dry, her heart race, and a heavy breath blow out of her. Whatever he did worked, and he slipped his hand away from hers, a little smile quirking the corner of his lips. The tension had lifted, but he'd clearly felt it, too.

"Thanks."

"I'm gonna get that fixed," he said, turning his attention to the road as he pulled off the shoulder and guided the truck toward town.

"Don't go out of your way on my accord," she said with a laugh, watching fields pass by as they got closer to the small hub of Three Rivers. They were maybe five minutes out of town, but the early sprouting farmlands turned to residential properties and small businesses surprisingly quickly. Maybe too quickly, but maybe not quickly enough.

"Well, I'd like to see more of you in that seat, so it's the least I can do." She felt the smile on his words, and when she looked over at him, it was there. Warm, and inviting, it squeezed her heart. He was a good man. Being raised by Nan, he had no choice but to be the dying breed that still held doors open and pulled over when women were broken down on the side of the road. He'd be the kind of man who would want to do right by his child, too.

"We'll see," she teased as he pulled up to the curb in front of Dr. Field's office, putting the truck in park. She climbed out, then turned back to thank him.

"Nate, you're a lifesaver. How can I repay you?" It was a standard line when someone got you out of hot water, but she realized she'd walked right into it before the words had even finished crossing her lips. Nate's broad grin told her he realized, too.

"Don't say no this time."

A long breath huffed out of her; she couldn't turn him down this time. Did she even want to anymore?

"Okay."

"Whaddaya know?" He laughed. "Third time's a charm. When are you off work?"

"Five."

"I'll pick you up. And give me your keys. I'll see about getting something done with your car."

"You don't have to..."

"I know I don't." He cut her off, and Layla shut her mouth. She could argue, but there probably wouldn't be any use. He *was* raised by Nan, after all. "And I wouldn't, if I didn't want to. Besides, what kind of man would I be to leave a lady stranded?"

She grinned big, handing her keys across the seat to him. "The average one?"

"Ridiculous. Now get going before you're late."

She glanced at the dash clock—somehow, despite the hiccup, she was running on time; five minutes early, even. And she felt like she was walking on sunshine.

"Thank you," she said, pausing to take him in one more time, one arm thrown over the steering wheel, watching her with interest. He wasn't doing much to calm the butterflies in her stomach; no, he was riling them up—and he might have been doing it on purpose. "See you at five."

EIGHT

LILY BAYLOR WAS standing on the front step of the cabin with her hands on her hips when Nate rolled into the Baylor ranch after dropping off Layla. He was in big trouble. He'd shot her a text after he'd towed Layla's car to Nan's, just to make sure she wasn't off in the woods on Tank before he showed up, and the only response he got had been a line of exclamation marks.

"Where the hell have you been, Nate Montgomery?"

He was barely out of his truck and she was giving him an earful. Typical Lily.

"Cool your jets, I've been around," he said, holding his hands out to show he came in peace...and also to ward off any flying attacks. She'd become nearly as cantankerous as her husband in married life. "Busy."

Truth was, these days Lily was as big a reminder as any about the life he'd lost. That was where they'd first met, around the chutes in Denver. She was an amazing photographer and she followed the circuit and got a contract for the National Stock Show just about every year. He'd initially set his sights on taking her out, but after a half dozen rejections, they'd settled into a solid friendship. The kind of friendship that didn't get left behind with everything else in Denver. Especially since she'd married one of his best friends and settled down in Three Rivers.

"Too busy to come see me? Seriously? You might be the lamest person I know."

"I know, I know," he sighed, dropping his hands. She took that opportunity to launch herself at him, and where he was expecting spitfire and possible scratching, he instead got a warm, tight hug. Maybe she *wasn't* as cantankerous as he thought.

"I missed you," she said into his shirt. He squeezed her tight. They'd each been through hell and back—with the other by their side. First, her accident with her horse, Encore, and then his wreck. Though he had no romantic interest in her these days, those traumas bound people together in ways normal friendships just didn't.

"I missed you, too. I just..."

"I know, it's tough." She released him and patted his shoulder. She might have been the only person who *did* know. But she was back at what she loved, now. Just in different circumstances than what she'd originally intended. "We're glad to see you, no matter *when* you turned up. But word is you've been in town for *at least* a week, so I am bound by contract to give you a hard time."

"Where're the boys?"

"Dane's got Gracie at swimming lessons, if you can believe that, and Finn and Noah are trading some horses with Reicher. They'll be sorry they missed you."

"Yeah, well I'll be around, so this visit isn't a limited time offer."

She cut a glare at him and he shrugged.

"And I promise it won't be a week next time."

"Good. Now, I want to know everything."

She settled onto the porch steps and patted the spot beside her. He settled into the offered place and she slipped her arm into his. After supporting one another through their accidents, the casual physical touch was second nature. They'd had moments of vulnerability much more intimate than this.

"It's been a week, not a year."

"Well, it's been at least two months since I last saw you."

Lily made an effort to visit every time she came to Denver for work, but the visits had become less frequent. She insisted it was because they were focused on trying to make little Lilys and Finns, not because she didn't want to see the sad mess he'd spiraled into.

"That's not *my* fault," he tried.

"Bullshit. It's been almost two years since you've come in this direction."

"Well, I *was* in traction for part of that. And rehab."

She smiled. "Fair point. So what's new then?"

"Saw the doc yesterday."

Lily brightened for a half-second, then registered his expression and slumped.

"Same story. No bull riding."

"We'll find you something else, then."

It was his turn to give her the cutting glare.

"Riding bulls is who I am, Lilypad. You know that. If I can't do that, there *is* nothing else for me to do."

She pressed her lips together, her dark eyes scrutinizing as she searched his face. After a moment of silence, she started.

"*Who* you are is a kind, compassionate, funny man, who just happens to have been stupid enough to make a living climbing onto the back of the baddest bulls in the country. You're honest, and upstanding, and a hell of a friend. I don't know anybody else who drops everything the way you do to help. So no, Nate Montgomery, riding bulls is not *who you are*, riding bulls is *what you did*. And you can always do other things. You're in your twenties, for God's sake, not your eighties."

"Almost thirty." He blew out a breath, feeling his cheeks warm. "Fine, okay. Bull riding isn't who I am, it's what I did. Happy?"

Nate tipped his head down, narrowing her in his gaze.

"Yes. Now. How about a ride into the woods? You're not too much of a 'failure' for that, are you?"

He hadn't been on a horse since the accident. When he'd finally been physically capable, it hurt too much knowing they, like the rest of the things he owned, would be sold off to the highest bidder to repay his hospital debts. It didn't scare him, not the way the bulls did, he just didn't have the heart for it like he used to. But Lily was looking at him with such hopeful expectation he wasn't going to have any choice in the matter.

"All right," he said, drawing out the word out with reluctance.

"Good." She smiled, pushing herself up off the step. "I was going to go myself anyways, but it's nice to have company. Sometimes Kerri comes with me but mostly she's busy working, and Finn usually has too much going on here. I foresee a lot of trail riding in your future, Mr. Montgomery."

"Oh Lord," he replied, drawing himself to his feet. Most of the time these days, he had no pain, except for when there was rain. Like Lily, he had half a hardware store bolted to his skeleton. "Go easy on me, though. It's been a long time."

"We'll get you back in riding shape in no time."

~

A short fifteen minutes later, Nate had managed to get astride Jet, Dane Baylor's semi-retired cutting horse. He wasn't an aged horse by any stretch of the imagination, but Dane and his wife were in the process of birthing a baseball team and that ate up most of the ranch owner's free time. It was strange, but less painful—emotionally, and physically—than he had imagined it would be. He did a couple of small circles, bending the horse around his leg to loosen him up, remembering the motion and the way his body needed to move to go with the horse.

"Hey, not bad." Lily smiled from atop Tank, the gelding she'd been gifted by Finn when he hadn't been able to rehab her endurance horse. That visit, bringing Lily and Encore to Finn, had been the same visit during which he'd had his tryst with Layla. Typical of a small town, everything was entangled. "Way better than I did my first time back on."

"Took you a couple of tries to actually agree to get on the horse in the first place, if I recall."

"Not true. Took a couple of tries for me to be able to get into the saddle without Finn's old heave-ho."

"Imagine if he hadn't taken that upon himself, you might be back in Denver."

His friend chuckled and shook her head. They had been at odds in the beginning; so badly, in fact, Nate had offered to take her back to Denver when he left. To her credit, Lily had stuck it out, and so had Finn, and now here they were, in love and crazy happy. Nate had never imagined himself as the settling-down type, but it was second nature to the pair of them, like breathing. He couldn't help but be happy for his friends.

"Ready to go?" Lily asked, nodding to him.

She'd had to fight through a lot of fear to get back in the saddle. For Nate, it was a lot simpler. Jet was easier to ride because he had no investment in him...and he didn't have a set of horns and moo. He reached down to pet the gelding's neck and then nodded back to his friend.

"Ready as I'll ever be."

She led him out past the heifer barn and onto a path that looked a little more worn than the last time he'd been on it. Finn had mentioned once she rode every day, putting in lots of miles, and the well-worn trail showed it. The property was hundreds of acres of mixed terrain, and Nate lost track of time until the alarm he'd set on his phone chirped, reminding him he'd have to go pick up Layla sooner rather than later.

"We gotta head back."

Lily reined in.

"Is this that 'busy' thing?"

He raised a brow at her. Lily might have been his best friend, but he wasn't about to lay out *everything* for her. She could be as perceptive as

Nan and there was no way he could handle *two* nosy women sniffing in his business.

"Maybe."

"Date with Layla Sullivan?"

Well how the hell had she come up with that? He glanced at her with a brow raised.

"Noah told me you were hassling her at the bar Sunday night."

"Christ, does nothing stay a secret around here?"

"Well it definitely doesn't when you're trotting it out at Danny's. But..." She tipped her head down, narrowing her eyes. There it was, that laser-like gaze, boring right into his soul and finding all his secrets. "It stops here."

"Promise?"

"Well, you know how little control I have over my brother in law..."

"I know."

"But you don't have to worry about me."

"Thanks, Lilypad."

She hadn't been raised in the same rumor mill as people who had been life-long residents of Three Rivers and she'd been appreciative when people in the know had kept their mouths shut about her and Finn in their early days, so he knew he could count on her.

They turned their horses and started back toward the ranch.

"Hey, did she ever say yes?"

NINE

TRUE TO HIS word, Layla saw Nate's truck pull up outside the office through the big front window ten minutes before her shift ended. Her heart skipped a beat as she tried to drag her attention back to the last patient file of the day that needed updating. There was one last client with Dr. Fields and then she'd be free to go. She'd told herself it had nothing to do with him, but she'd been floating on air all day. Not even a mid-day vomit cleanup from a sick kid in the waiting room could sink her good mood, and the day had sped by.

Finally, she heard the doctor's voice as he approached his exam room door and held it open for Sarah Murphy. She was already halfway into her cardigan when the elderly physician stepped out and bid farewell to his patient and let Layla go for the day.

Nate got out of the truck and was leaning against the side, all long legs, dusty jeans, and a cool smile; it was all she could do to stop herself from skipping out the door and across the sidewalk to him like a schoolgirl. Saying yes to the date had inexplicably lifted a weight off her shoulders. Every time she tried to consider the potentially tricky situation she was about to put herself in, excited butterflies batted any negative thought away. She'd never had a proper date.

"Hey."

"Hey," he said, pushing off the side of the truck and pulling open the passenger side door. "How was your day?"

She slid into the space between him and the door and lifted herself into the truck. "Good. Better than I expected."

"Good," he said with a smile, motioning for her to fold arms and legs safely away so he could close the door. He moved around the hood of the truck and slid in beside her, wasting no time to help her with the seatbelt. The prickling static when their skin touched was still there; maybe it was stronger than before. "I didn't have any luck with your car today, but I did get it towed over to Nan's. Rusty McLean is going to come take a look at it tomorrow afternoon. In the meantime, Nate's Taxi, at your service."

"Oh you don't..."

"There you go again," he said with a laugh, pulling away from the curb. "You need to make any stops?"

"No." She wouldn't have asked him even if she did. What he was doing was already too much, it made her feel guilty. "Look, before Rusty does the work, can you call me and tell me how much he thinks it's going to cost?"

He raised a brow at her.

"Don't worry..."

It was her turn to cut him off.

"No, I'm gonna draw the line on this one, Nate. You've already been beyond helpful. Get me a quote and we'll go from there."

She knew when to ask for and accept help when it came to just about anybody, but she wouldn't accept *this* kind of help. Not from Nate, especially. Her family had a long history of being known as the people who 'took advantage' and she wouldn't risk the rumor mill, already rampant with speculation about who her child's father was, latching onto Layla Sullivan working the sugar daddy angle. She figured she had just about enough to cover it and she might be able to convince Rusty to write off the rest for an extended tab at Danny's that could be taken out of her check.

"Yes ma'am." He turned his attention back to the road, and that was when she noticed the wrapped casserole pan on the floorboard behind the shifter. On top of it sat a loaf of bread so fresh there was a little condensation inside the bag.

"What's this?" she asked, feeling prickly.

"Nan sent supper." She narrowed her eyes at him across the cab of the truck and he glanced back at her. "Seriously, it was Nan."

She pressed her lips together and settled back into her seat. Nan sent food all the time. The fact that Nate was delivering it meant nothing more than he had already been on his way to get her. And she would invite him in, because it was the polite thing to do. Because that would be Nan's expectation. And that meant Nate would come face to face with Mason.

Anxiety prickled in her bloodstream. It was too soon. Even if she omitted the truth about who the child's father was, the potential for suspicion was there, and if he asked her point blank, she couldn't lie to him. He wasn't an idiot, he could do the math. Even the butterflies couldn't blow this thought process out. She swallowed, her mouth feeling like it was full of cotton, as they pulled into the yard. She closed her eyes and let out a breath through her nose to try to calm herself.

Okay, you've got this.

~

Nate guided his truck into the driveway of the old Jenkins place. It was an aging, square farm house with a wrap-around covered veranda. Almost before he had the truck in park, Layla had unbuckled herself and opened the door. She'd just accepted a date with him this morning, and here she was again, running off like he smelled roadkill.

"Hey," he said. She whirled around like she'd been caught doing something bad. Nate unbuckled and reached to grab the casserole and bread Nan had sent and unbuckled himself. A look of sheer terror crossed her face. "You forgot the dinner Nan sent."

He climbed out and she shot around the front of the truck like her ass was on fire.

"Great, thanks again." She reached for the dishes but he didn't hand them to her, turning instead toward the house. "What are you doing?"

I didn't invite you in. He could almost hear it on the end of her question. Smiling to himself, he started toward the house. She followed, but he wouldn't have called her willing, *or* enthusiastic, dragging her feet to the porch of her own house. From a distance, the house looked as it always had, but once he got closer, he saw the paint on the wide wood siding was peeling and the roof over the porch needed a few new shingles. Minor things, but as busy as she seemed to be, probably overwhelming.

She got ahead of him then, climbing the two steps to the porch and wedging herself between him and the door. With surprising strength, she wrestled the food dishes from his hands. This was the part where he expected she'd invite him in to share the dinner, but instead, she followed his eyes to the flaking paint.

"I know, it needs..." She let out a sigh, shrugging. "A lot of work."

And then she seemed to gather herself up, shaking off her defeated demeanor and lifting her chin. She was making a conscious decision not to feel bad about it. He could admire that. He wished he could figure out how to flip that switch in himself.

"Not so much that it can't be done."

The windows looked relatively new, and apart from the roof, the porch was in good shape. His eyes slid along the floorboards until they landed on something out of place. A brightly colored kid's toy, the kind a baby sat and bounced in, with a tray and little toys on springs to play with. There were a couple soggy pieces of cracker on the tray, so it was clearly something in recent use.

Layla, as a mother. Lots of things started to make sense, from the extra softness of her curves to the fact that she was guarding the door of the house like a mama bear at the door of the den after a hard winter. When he glanced back up at her, she was staring at the toy in horror. She finally ripped her gaze from it, and swung it to him.

"Okay, thanks for the drive. See you later." She turned for the house but he stopped her with a hand on the old screen door. Her body was close to his, not quite touching, but close enough he could smell the fragrant honeysuckle shampoo she used, her dark, glossy hair near enough to stroke. She didn't turn right away, her body stiffening at the proximity. He hadn't meant for this to be anything but a means to stop her before she scampered off, but he couldn't deny the closeness reminded him he was a man, with needs, and Layla had once fulfilled that need. He hadn't felt that way in a long time. It was a beat before he could speak.

"Same time tomorrow?"

"No, uh...what?" Finally she shifted, turning in the small space he'd trapped her in, and lifting her eyes to his.

Something deep in his chest twisted. This was a girl who had never asked for a handout in her life. Pride was clearly the big barrier between her and getting a bit of extra help that would have made her life easier.

"Well, you don't have your car, so should I pick you up the same time tomorrow?"

She blew a breath out; like she felt the electricity crackling in the air between them too. She'd told him she wasn't the same woman he'd first slept with, but in many ways she was. Soft, giving, trusting, and undeniably attractive. Better, even, than she'd been two years ago.

"Okay, yes." He didn't move right away, and she shifted, her voice turning tremulous. "I'm not inviting you in, Nate."

Taking a step back, he grinned, wiping a hand over his chin. "You're not, but you want to."

"Not tonight," she said.

"That sounds like a someday, so I can live with that. Besides, we still have a date to look forward to."

A little grin twisted her lips, and he was relieved he wasn't the only one looking forward to it.

"Good night, Nate."

He tipped the brim of his imaginary hat and headed back to his truck like he was walking on air.

TEN

"DID YOU SLEEP at *all*?" Kerri asked when she stepped inside the door the next morning and found Layla dressed and ready for work.

"No, what?" Layla frowned, shifting from foot to foot at the kitchen island where she was hurriedly chewing a bagel and balancing Mason on one hip. She didn't get to spend nearly enough time with him with her work schedule so she took every opportunity she could find to hold him and talk to him, even if it meant multitasking.

"How did you even shower?" Normally, Kerri showed up to keep an eye on Mason while she got ready, and she was short enough on time by that point she usually ran into Hinkley's for a coffee and a muffin for breakfast.

"Oh. Mason slept late." She shrugged, but she could tell the astute teen wasn't going to give up her interrogation yet by the slow way she put her laptop bag down on the kitchen table and narrowed her eyes at Layla.

"What's going on?"

"Well, my car is busted."

"Right. And Nate Montgomery brought you home last night."

"How did you know that?"

"Come on, Layla." Kerri shook her head, folding her arms over her chest. "I heard him. And saw his truck. And you were school-girl-flustered when you came in."

Right. She'd forgotten Nate was practically an honorary Baylor, and Kerri's brother-in-law ran that whole ranch. This could go in one of two ways. She decided to err on the side of confidence because Kerri was the closest thing to a girlfriend she had besides Nan.

"Well, Nate Montgomery is picking me up this morning. Because the car. And...he doesn't know I have a kid, so..." She gestured with her free hand to her sun dress and braid—standard uniform for Dr. Fields' office.

"Oh, I get it. You think if you keep it a secret from him, he'll never find out." Kerri nodded exaggeratedly as she took Mason from Layla's arms, hitching him up on the hip in a mirror image of the way his mother had been holding him. "Yes, excellent plan. People have babies, Layla. *You* have a baby. He'll have to get over it. Besides, he's great with Gracie and Jacob."

"Right. It doesn't matter. I don't care."

"Except you do, because you like him."

Layla's gaze cut to Kerri.

"And you care what he thinks of you."

In the grand scheme of things, she *didn't* care what Nate thought of her. He'd seen her pretty damn vulnerable...at her worst, so to speak; naked. But this one thing. The single mother stigma, the 'can't-keep-a-man' thing that was actually a 'don't-want-a-man-because-that's-the-definition-of-being-vulnerable' thing, the big secret thing...yeah, he would judge her. And rightly so. And it scared the hell out of her.

"I do."

"If he thinks anything besides that you are a great, hard working mom and a good person, then he's not worth your time."

"Ker..."

"Nate's like a big brother to me, but I don't even care. He doesn't deserve your time if he's going to be..." Kerri paused, pressing Mason's head to her chest with her hand over his other ear. "A shithead."

Layla laughed.

"But, I'm pretty sure he's not going to be a shithead," Kerri continued, remembering a moment too late to cover Mason's ears.

Still laughing, Layla gathered her house keys and phone from the countertop, much of her anxiety dissipating with the lighthearted turn their conversation had taken. She passed around the end of the kitchen island to press a kiss to Mason's chubby cheek. And just in time, because the low rumble of Nate's old diesel truck sounded from the yard. She could maybe explain away the exersaucer on the porch as babysitting in her spare time, but once he came inside the house, there'd be no mistaking it was a baby's domain. *Her* baby's domain. She wished she could just throw caution into the wind and ditch him if he turned out to be a shithead, but the truth was the little warm buzz in the pit of her stomach when she thought about him was addictive and she liked it.

"Be good," she said as she pushed open the door, where Nate was just mounting the stairs. The smile that brightened his features made her heart skip a beat.

"Good morning."

"Morning."

"Your chariot awaits," he began, gesturing behind him to his truck, which he'd pulled in next to Kerri's SUV. "Though I see you *have* wheels. Which were here last night."

"Oh, that's Kerri," she said dismissively as she started down the stairs, realizing a beat too late she'd stepped in it.

"Kerri, eh?"

"Yeah, she, uh...helps me with the house."

Nate paused at the front bumper of his truck and cocked his head at her. "Is that so?"

"Yeah...with...renovations."

"Didn't you say you didn't need any help?"

She scrambled for a second, then flashed a smile at him as she rounded the fender of the truck and pulled the passenger door open, hoping she portrayed the confidence she didn't feel. "I don't. Kerri helps."

"Ah ha."

She felt his eyes on her when she climbed into the truck. He didn't buy her story. He was a tough customer and she was fooling herself to think he'd buy the idea she *babysat* in her spare time, too. She couldn't have been happier when he helped her buckle herself in without a word, and spent the rest of the ride in silence.

When they pulled up in front of the doctor's office, she could feel his hesitation before she even moved for the door handle.

"Layla."

Oh, his voice wrapped around her name sounded about as good as she remembered his body feeling wrapped around hers. She swung her gaze to him, convinced she was about to be called out for her flimsy lies.

"Yeah, Nate?"

"Tonight?"

She shifted, clearing her throat, her fingers curling around the strap of her purse.

"What about tonight?"

"Dinner. I'd like to cash in on our date."

Of course her calendar was clear. She couldn't put it off any longer, and when he decided he wasn't interested in a woman with the kind of baggage that required late night feedings and diaper changes, she'd at least have the memory of a date with Nate Montgomery to hang onto. The linchpin to this plan was Kerri. Or Nan, failing everything else.

"Um, I'll let you know."

"You'll let me know."

"Yeah, uh...I just need to check if I have a shift scheduled at Danny's."

Nate shrugged. "All right, then. Just send me a text."

She nodded, letting herself out of the truck and hitching her purse over her shoulder.

"Hey Lay," his voice sounded behind her. She swung around, and saw him leaning toward her door, one arm folded over the top of his steering wheel.

"Yeah?"

"Don't let me down."

ELEVEN

RUSTY MCLAIN GRABBED the rag hanging from his back pocket and began meticulously wiping grease and car fluid off his hands. He made a face that made Nate worry. The key here was the work required had to be inexpensive enough that Layla could afford it, or if it was more, sound simple enough she wouldn't know the difference when he figured out how to float the extra money for it.

"I gotta order the part." In typical Rusty fashion, everything came slow, but the older man was kind. He'd always been good to Nan, and Nate knew he didn't charge nearly enough for the innovative jerry-rigged solutions he came up with when time or money were in a pinch. "A few days to come in, maybe a week..." Rusty did some mental figuring, his fingers and lips moving as he calculated. "I'll clear my schedule for that day and give you a call. Couple hundred bucks. But then it should last her until this thing dies."

Judging by the look of the aging Fiesta, and the numbers on the odometer when he got in to put it in neutral to tow, Nate figured she had maybe a year, with a bit more money sunk into it. Two, if she was really lucky and twisted her mouth the right way.

"Anything else?"

Rusty's brow rose, thinking. "She's way overdue for an oil change."

"Do that too."

"That's another...twenty?"

"That's fine," Nate said, stepping forward to shake the man's hand. "I really appreciate this, Rusty. She needs this vehicle to be as reliable as possible."

"No problem, buddy."

Nate left Rusty to gather up his tools and climbed into his truck, pulling his cell phone out of his pocket to let Layla know the prognosis. For the fifth time, he read back over the text she'd sent him an hour ago to tell him their date was a go; Kerri would pick her up after work so she could get ready and he could pick her up at six at the house. Despite the mediocre news about the car, nothing could deflate his excitement. It had been quite some time since he'd had something he looked forward to as much as seeing Layla Sullivan. Framing his day with her pretty smile and quiet presence gave him a distraction from the shambles his life was in. Her phone rang to voice mail, so he left a message and turned the key in the ignition.

The drive to the Baylor ranch was short and familiar and felt almost as much like coming home as rolling into Nan's. He honked as he passed Emma and Noah's little spot at the end of the driveway and kept going, pulling his truck up beside Finn Baylor's brand new pickup in front of his newly-expanded cabin. Things had been moving and shaking with the newlyweds.

He'd expected Lily on the front step, but instead, she found Lily in the arena across the driveway, with a fully tacked up Jet standing nearby.

"What's this?"

"We're just waiting for a cowboy to come along." Lily shrugged innocently, reaching out to stroke the horse's neck. He checked for another mount for her—he'd been sore after their ride, but the good kind of sore, not the body-torn-apart-by-a-bull-sore, so he wouldn't have declined another jaunt into the woods. He'd kind of enjoyed it, in truth. It brought him back to his roots; back before the bulls and the buckles, tooling around on horseback with his best friends, imagining the future.

He raised his brow when his search turned up empty. "And what about you?"

"Oh I've already been out today."

"And you're just humoring me."

She nodded toward the other end of the ring, where a plastic steer model was hooked up behind the ranch's work ATV. A pink helmet sat on the seat of the machine.

"Okay, what is this?"

"Well, if you can't ride bulls..."

"I'm gonna rope." He rubbed a hand over his mouth, looking at the plastic target, then back at Jet. "Lily, I don't think..."

"Just try it. Humor *me*."

"You know I haven't been on a horse in well over a year, and here I am, twice in one week?" He shook his head with an exaggerated sigh, and then climbed up the side of the gelding, pushing his foot into the opposing stirrup and gathering up the reins. He reached down to stroke the gelding's neck. "I never was much of a roper."

"But you were, once. I saw the pictures."

Early in his career, he'd thought the All Around Cowboy title was something he'd strive toward—until he realized how good he was on the bulls, and how much more quickly he could get into more money doing just the one thing. Ropers and bronc riders were tough, sure, but bull riders were the rock stars of the whole outfit. Those boys were badass and had followings that would make a headlining band jealous—who could resist that?

He'd shown pictures of his early rodeo days to Lily and now it was backfiring.

"I should have burned those."

"Should have, but didn't. Now pick up the rope."

As he was told, he picked up the lariat hanging off the horn of the saddle, looping the excess in his left hand that held Jet's reins, and shaking the loop out into his right hand, beside his thigh. Jet lifted his head, an ear twitching back as he paid mind to what his rider was doing. This was a finely tuned, well-trained horse; Dane wouldn't have had anything else for a personal mount, and Nate had discovered that on their trail ride.

"Easy," he said under his breath, and the gelding stilled.

It had been a good long time since he'd even *held* a rope, let alone tried to throw it over anything. Drawing in a deep breath, he flipped his wrist and twirled the loop once.

He glanced up at Lily, who was watching him with an expectant expression that just about broke his heart. He'd try. But he wasn't going to lay any money on being the Comeback Kid. Not in team roping, anyway.

Urging Jet forward, he approached the plastic steer, glancing over his shoulder at her.

"I don't think you'll be doing any driving today, Lil."

She shrugged, following him across the arena. A few feet out, he straightened his shoulders and started working the loop up. His first throw missed by about six inches. He heard Lily let out a breath. He reeled the rope back in and glanced back at her with a laughing shake of his head. He hadn't expected to do anything, really. Hell, it was only his second time back on a horse. All the parts of his body that were supposed to work together for this were still rusty.

"You sound like it's *your* career we're thinking about here."

"What the hell do you think you're doing?" Noah's voice sounded from behind them just as Nate released the rope for the second time. It landed haphazard around the horns of the target and Jet immediately took a couple steps back.

"Eas-y," he breathed to the gelding, dropping the rope and reining the gelding around to face Noah. "Your sister-in-law thinks I'll make a heeler."

"*Header,*" Lily scolded. "I didn't give you that much credit, and neither should you."

"What does a man have to do to get a break around here?" Nate laughed, shaking his head.

"I don't know," Noah replied, just as incredulous. "They make you think they need you and then just when you get feeling a little big, they knock you down a peg or two."

Nate held up a finger. "You know there isn't a Baylor woman on this property that *needs* any one of you boys. They like having a choice."

"He's not lying," Lily quipped from behind.

Noah shot her a look.

"Don't listen to her harebrained ideas, Nate. *I've* got an idea."

"Good Lord. *There's* a scary thought."

"And you won't have to be a heeler *or* a header."

"Well that one was pretty obvious anyways."

"No listen. Rodeo school." The middle Baylor brother splayed his hands out in the air in front of him as if laying out a cityscape.

"Rodeo school," Nate repeated, avoiding eye contact with Noah to try and curb his desire to laugh out loud. "I don't think I'll be heading to *rodeo school* anytime soon."

"No, no, not learning. *Teaching*. You know what they say about 'those who can't do teach'."

"That's usually reserved for people who were real shitty at it in the first place," Nate said with a frown. But the seed was planted. He needed to start generating some income; he couldn't lick his wounds forever. And driving two hours each way to work cattle for Reicher's every day wasn't a viable option.

"Or people who literally *can't*. You can't ride bulls again. But I bet you could give some young, wet-behind-the-ears cowboy a tip or two on how to do it as good as you once did."

"Nobody's gonna pay me to stand behind the chute and give them pointers on their ride. I can't even get near a bull chute without shitting myself."

"Are you kidding me? How many times did you end up in Vegas?"

Nate reached down to stroke Jet's neck lightly, drawing a breath as he thought about the years he'd made it to the NFR in Vegas. Something pretty damn special for anyone, but amazing for a small-town boy like him. "Three times."

"And it would have been four if it hadn't been for Night Train. Trust me, brother, your skills will be in demand. Emma and I will do barrel racing. We can get one of the Reicher boys in for roping. Mine some of your Denver contacts for steer wrestling and broncs. Of course, the big draw will be the bulls, but it's nice to offer something else."

Noah seemed so convinced it was a good idea; Nate wished he could add his enthusiasm. But he wasn't even sure he'd be able to get into the arena and look at a bull, never mind give pointers and stand over the chute giving words of advice to the cowboy below him, about to put his life on the line for a few dollars.

"I don't know, Noah."

"Just think about it, Nate. You got time."

He didn't, really. Nan had already mentioned the job at Grant Reicher's a couple of times—they were short-handed since Chase had hit the road with his growing country music career—but that meant leaving town, and leaving Layla behind. And call him selfish, but he'd done that once, and he wasn't ready to skip town again without exploring this thing with her a little more. Beggars couldn't really be choosers, but if this was something that could generate some cash...

"I don't have anything to invest."

"Don't worry about that. Finn and Dane want to invest. We'll use the ranch. You get to just show up and collect a paycheck, let us worry about everything else."

"I couldn't..."

"You *could*, Nate," Noah said, pulling the gate of the arena open for his friend. "You were more than kind to me when *I* was down and out, kept me and Black Jack while I was working things out with Emma in Denver, and you didn't charge me a damn cent. So when you're down and out, we want to give you a hand."

He turned to Lily.

"Did you know about this?"

She responded with a shrug, slipping out the gate and heading for their cabin across the yard. "I gotta get ready for a stock shoot. I'm not responsible for *anything* he says. Later, Nater."

Nate watched her back for a moment, then swung down off of Jet. He was pleased that, despite all the time away from riding, he could still get on and off okay. That was one thing Lily had really struggled with, and he couldn't imagine enjoying Finn's hands on *his* ass, either.

"You've already talked with your brothers about this?" he asked, turning back to Noah.

"Sure have. And they're all in. But we're not going to do it without you. No sense. We couldn't muster the talent on our own. You're the heart of the whole idea."

The thought crossed his mind the Baylor family might have been creating something out of nothing specifically for the purpose of giving him a leg up. He probably wouldn't have let that slide from anybody else. But these men were as close to him as Banks; they'd grown up together on this ranch, and while he could be a proud man, if anybody was going to help him, it would be Dane, Finn, and Noah.

"No pressure or anything," he said with a laugh, rubbing the back of his neck as they made their way into the barn. He clipped Jet into the crossties in the barn and started stripping his tack.

"No, no pressure. But what we'd do is start putting it together through this fall and winter and start taking students in the spring. So you can think

73

about it for a few weeks. We'd hire you on as a consultant until we actually set up the school. You'll be busy—we'd need to collect more instructors, and the stock. We have the land and we'd build what we need for extra facilities. But you know more about any of this than we do. So it would be your baby. Lily would look after the books. Everybody here would be a little bit involved. You just tell us what you need and we'll make it happen."

Nate considered all of this while he ran his hands over Jet's legs, doing an overall check to make sure the horse was in the same condition he'd started in. He'd never imagined being in this kind of a position. It hadn't been his dream, but Noah's excitement was starting to become infectious. They'd never get rich, but it would be a chance to give back. To provide the kind of resource he'd always wished he'd had to young cowboys looking for a competitive edge going into the rodeo circuit.

"Noah, this is...a lot. It's a big deal. You guys would be putting a lot on the line for me."

His friend shrugged, crossing his arms over his chest as he leaned back against one of the stall doors.

"It's been a good year for beef."

Nate laughed out loud, unclipping Jet and turning him toward the door at the end of the barn that opened up to the yard for the working horses. The big gelding lazily sauntered past him and out the door to join his friends, and Nate closed it behind him, turning back to Noah.

"It's always a good year for beef."

Baylor beef, anyway. The family had great connections with most of the locals, from Yvette's burger stand to the grocery store, and that didn't include the major buyers they dealt with on a regular basis.

"And it would be good for the rest of the economy in Three Rivers. Think about that, too. Good chance to give back to the little town that gave you so much growing up."

That was a big point. This would be the kind of work Nan would be proud of. The ability to give something back to the community she loved so much. They had embraced him and Banks like they were the town's own when his folks had skipped the county line and never looked back. There had been fundraising and support and a big homecoming party after his first NFR appearance.

Sure, there would be lots of out-of-towners; that was the whole point. But he wanted to make sure young people in the community got in on it, too. Kids like Layla had been—born on the wrong side of the track or folks too poor to support their dreams of rodeo.

Thinking of her, he smiled at Noah.

"I'm in."

TWELVE

"I'M HEADING OUT for lunch," Layla said, poking her head into Dr. Fields' exam room where he sat with a stack of files. She was quite sure the kindly doctor never took a break during the day, and at first she'd wanted to be in the office whenever he was. Eventually, with his daily prodding, she let go of the guilt.

The physician looked up, pushing his glasses up his nose. "See you in an hour."

When her car was working well, she'd sneak home for a few spare minutes with Mason, but today she'd have to settle for a phone call. She flipped the door sign to 'back at 1', and stepped out into the sunshine of the day.

Mid-day during the week in downtown Three Rivers was not as busy as one might anticipate. There were several cars parked in the lot at Hinkley's just across the street, and a couple pickups in front of the sidewalk of the Baylor's general store. Danny's wasn't open yet, but otherwise the street was quiet. She tugged out her cell, punched in the home number, and looked both ways before crossing the street.

This was the part where she couldn't let Nate down. She'd said yes, so now she had to follow through, whether it was a good idea or not. She was nothing if not a woman of her word. Kerri picked up on the second ring.

"Hey, how's my rugrat?"

"Trying *hard* to crawl. Time for some more babyproofing, mama."

Having made it safely to the other sidewalk, Layla let out a breath and closed her eyes. Sometimes things went too quickly. Sometimes she felt like she missed too much. She should just go home tonight and stay in, and catch up on everything she was missing. But she couldn't let Nate down.

"On it. Hey, can you do me a favor?" she asked, pushing open the door of Hinkley's and nodding a greeting to Tina, the friendly regular waitress. Tina noted the phone at Layla's ear and pointed to an empty booth silently.

"Of course, but you owe me."

Kerri said it every single time, but also refused to collect every single time.

"Can you pick me up from work tonight?" She slid into the booth and took the menu and coffee Tina set in front of her.

"Nate out of commission?"

"Actually, there's a second part to this favor. Can you stay a couple extra hours?"

"You know you don't have to ask twice. Extra shift at Danny's?"

Layla smiled.

"Not quite. A date."

Kerri's squeal on the other end of the line made Layla pull the phone from her ear until she was finished.

"With Nate, right? I know it's with Nate."

Aware of those around her that could take this kind of information and run, Layla simply replied. "Yes."

"Oh my God. I knew it!"

Layla sometimes forgot, as mature as she was, Kerri was barely not a teenager anymore. Moments like this reminded her. Truth was, Kerri's excitement was contagious, and now she felt far more excited than cautious about the date. She flagged Tina while Kerri continued to babble on the other end of the line.

"The regular. The turkey soup and a BLT, please."

Tina didn't even bother scribbling on her pad, but went to the kitchen. Layla only came in a couple of times a week—a little indulgence to treat herself—but the order was always the same. It was the cheapest thing on the menu, but it was also delicious.

"So if you two can swing by around 4:30, that'd be great. Now put my baby on the phone."

Mason would just chew the receiver but she figured the next best thing to actually being there to see him was him hearing her voice. She babbled on to him for a few minutes before Kerri came back on the line, right about the same time her meal was ready. She said goodbye and hung up, turning her phone face down on the table as the steaming bowl of soup was slid in front of her.

"Looks good as ever," Layla said, offering Tina a warm smile. The waitress probably didn't know it, but Layla considered them kindred spirits. Both of them single mothers, both of them busting their humps to make things good for their children. She wouldn't consider them friends and they never saw each other outside of their respective workplaces, but they had a friendly rapport.

"You bet. Say, did I hear you say you had a date?"

Layla took pause. It was pretty well known the majority of gossip in the town came out of Hinkley's, and she always tried to keep her head down when she came in. But she couldn't exactly lie to Tina, after she'd overheard her phone conversation. So she smiled and crossed her fingers that there was something more interesting going on in Three Rivers this week.

"Sure did."

"Anybody I know?" the waitress asked slyly.

"Probably not. Nobody real special." *That* was a blatant lie if she'd ever heard one, but Tina didn't know that.

The redhead's brow raised and she smiled as she seemed to catch on that Layla wasn't going to spill. "Ah, gotcha. Well, you enjoy. The soup *and* the date. Holler if you need anything."

Layla smiled, thanking the waitress and set to work on her lunch, willing the rest of the afternoon to go quickly.

THIRTEEN

NATE COULD HAVE sworn Nan had a sixth sense for when he came and went, because he was pretty sure she was supposed to be manning the popcorn stand at the high school football game tonight, but instead she was sitting on her porch when he closed the walk-out basement door behind him. She was clearly dressed for the game, so maybe his timing was off an hour or two. Or maybe she had called in late specifically so she could be nosy.

"And where are you off to?"

"You haven't asked me that since I was seventeen, Nan."

"Well, I'm just glad to see you going out."

"I leave the house every day. I didn't think I had a choice." He stopped, narrowing his eyes at his grandmother. She'd always had a keen sense for what was *really* going on underneath everything. It was what made her so invaluable to those who were down on their luck in the community. She noticed and remembered every progressive sniffle or cough and showed up on your doorstep with a pot of chicken soup and a little extra attention when the cold was the worst.

"Don't think *that* went unnoticed, either. You specifically told me you were coming home to wallow."

"You told me I had two weeks to feel sorry for myself. You should be happy I've already snapped out of it."

"Doesn't have anything to do with who you're chauffeuring around lately, does it?"

He tipped his head down, giving her a teasingly warning look. Nan didn't dance around any subject for long when it came to her grandsons. She was much gentler to those she wasn't related to by blood.

"And if I said it did?" There was no sense lying to Nan, but he could dance around any topic for at least twice as long as she did. Maybe he'd get out of here without having to detail *all* of his plans.

Nan sat back with a look of satisfaction that told him he wouldn't.

"I'd say that's good."

"You had nothing to do with this, you know. She turned me down twice. And she only gave in this time because she figured she owed me for playing taxi. So don't sit there like the cat that ate the canary, like you put any of this into play."

His grandmother's eyes crinkled at the corners with the smile she pursed her lips to try to hide.

"Unless you broke that thermostat on *purpose*..." He shook his head, then laughed. "No, you're devious but not *that* devious. But did you *really* have bread going in the oven when her car broke down?"

"I did." Nan nodded fervently. "It just might have still had thirty minutes of rising time left."

He narrowed his eyes briefly at her and turned toward his truck.

"Well, I haven't actually taken her out yet, so don't start congratulating yourself. She was reluctant enough that this could still fail."

"If she said yes, she'll go. So you have a good time, sweetheart." His grandmother rose, pausing. "And take the girl flowers. She deserves flowers at the door."

Right. Flowers. He glanced at his truck—if he didn't get moving soon he'd be running late, and he didn't want to give her any excuse to turn the tables on him and back down.

"I'll stop at Turner's on my way."

"Don't be silly, that's not on the way," Nan fussed, taking a large bouquet from where it had been waiting in a vase on her little round bistro table. He hadn't noticed it immediately, because Nan had an enormous garden she took great pride in, and the house had always been filled with fresh flowers. Something to keep her busy in her retirement, she'd said, as if she wasn't busy enough. This one was tied with a broad purple ribbon. She extended it over the railing of her porch toward him.

"Is this why you're late for the popcorn stand? So you could give me flowers to give to Layla, because you knew I wouldn't think that far ahead?"

"Betsy has it under control. It doesn't get busy until the end of the first quarter anyway. This is the first time I've had a chance to see you off on a date in ten years."

He frowned at her, taking the flowers. It was a beautiful selection of the fullest summer blossoms, and the broad ribbon under his fingers was silky with a fancy bow. Clearly not something she'd just had together for decoration.

"How did you even know I was going out tonight, anyway?"

"I'll never reveal my sources."

He narrowed his eyes. "You are absolutely impossible."

"To live without," Nan filled in, laughing. "You've had your share of being impossible. It's my turn. Besides, you're gonna wanna put up with me—I have an in with that girl."

"So you've been plying her with casseroles and loaves of bread because you knew this moment was coming?"

Nan's eyes twinkled with mischief.

"Impossible." Nate shook his head with a laugh as he walked toward his truck, raising his voice so she'd hear. "I'm leaving. Because if I spend too much more time with my *impossible* grandmother, I'm going to be late for my date."

Nan didn't respond, but she stood at the edge of her porch and he could see her waving until she was a tiny pinprick in his rearview mirror.

FOURTEEN

"UGH, WHAT ARE you even thinking?" Layla asked her reflection as she tugged at the hem of her shirt. She'd changed three times and she couldn't stop fiddling. The soft lavender tank top she'd settled on was probably the newest item in her wardrobe, and even *it* had come from Goodwill. And only because the hot summer sun had forced her to pick up some new wardrobe items. It wasn't often she did things for herself, least of all go out. She had no business going out on a date with Nate Montgomery. Not only was it an unnecessary and somewhat dangerous luxury, he was *way* out of her league. She barely had two cents to rub together and she was pretty sure people who posed on winner's podiums with giant checks made out to them had a lot more than that. They'd spent a couple nights together, but that was a long time ago, and it had never been intended to be anything more than what it was. Filling a passing need.

"What?" Kerri asked from the hallway, where she was heading toward the tub with Mason.

This way there was no chance of Nate coming in and seeing the baby. And she'd grabbed the exersaucer off the porch on her way in after Kerri picked her up from work.

"Nothing." Layla glanced over her shoulder, then back to the mirror with a sigh. It wasn't going to get any better than this. Not in ten minutes. Maybe...ten years.

"You look nice, Lay." Kerri stopped in the doorway with a still spaghetti-sauce-stained Mason on her hip. "You're gonna knock his socks off."

Her stomach flip-flopped, and she reminded herself this was *just* a date. A date with a cute guy. It was for fun, and it would only happen once, so she was just going to let herself enjoy it. She hadn't done that in a good long time. Putting on a smile, she turned to the pair in the doorway. Mason babbled happily and reached for her, and she started toward him, never faltering, even when she saw the red handprints on Kerri's shirt. She took him in her arms, all the bits of her that were strung out on nerves coming back where they belonged for a brief moment as she held him against her chest. She drew in a calming breath and exhaled slowly, stirring the downy blond hairs on his head.

"I could cancel."

Kerri's brow shot up and she held her hands out for the baby again.

"Not a chance."

"It's reasonable, right?"

"No." Kerri pried the baby out of Layla's arms and shook her head. "You haven't gone out in at *least* eight months. You're going out if I have to push you out the door with my bare hands. Have fun. Relax."

Layla did a quick inspection of her shirt—no spaghetti sauce stains; a sign *and* a miracle, because the rumble of Nate's diesel engine rolled into the yard and she didn't have any more time for dilly-dallying, unless she wanted him on the porch looking into her house. Which she didn't.

"Be good, love you," she said, planting a quick kiss on Mason's cheek. She jetted for the door, grabbing her purse off the island on the way through the kitchen, and darted out the door, running head long into the broadest, warmest chest. Her hands shot out to catch herself at the same time Nate's fingers found her waist, steadying her, and a jolt of electricity ran through her. The firm muscles of his pecs under her fingers were covered only by the thinnest t-shirt, and the memory of what they felt like bare, with a faint slick of sweat on them was just as close as they were. This was bad. This was real bad.

"Whoa, easy. What's the rush?" His voice was quiet in the space between them.

She brightened up her smile and looked up to him. There weren't many men in the town of Three Rivers that outranked her height, but Nate was a big man, and in a weird way, the size he had on her made her feel much more feminine. It was nice, for a change, not to be towering over a man.

"Just excited."

"Good," he said, a smile stretching across his face. He hadn't released her and his mouth was so close all she'd have to do was rise up on her tiptoes to have a taste. The memory of his taste would come back just as quickly as the memory of his skin under her fingertips; fingertips that were still splayed across his chest because he still had a firm hold on her waist. This was why she'd said no initially. Because she couldn't be this close and not want him. Wanting something when you were in her position was dangerous. It lead to irrational behavior and someone almost always got hurt—almost always her. "I'm excited, too."

He lifted a huge bouquet of fresh cut flowers; she'd been so wrapped up in the feel and smell of him she hadn't noticed he'd had them. The only person who brought her flowers was Nan—when she'd been in the hospital after having Mason, and now when she visited she brought them. She suspected these were sourced from Nan too, but she was still touched. Her heart twisted a little. So far, she was losing the battle of 'just for fun' and 'not wanting'.

She swallowed back tears and let out a breath.

"These are beautiful, Nate. Thank you."

He held her gaze for a long moment and she was sucked in, so much she only saw the crinkling around his eyes and realized he was smiling. He clearly liked getting the reaction out of her almost as much as she had enjoyed what had produced it.

"You're welcome. Now you wanna get out of here?"

She nodded, cradling the flowers in the crook of her arm—going inside to put them in water would put her in an awkward position and besides, she wanted to look at them for a minute longer. He touched the small of her back, his warm fingers sending a shiver up her spine as they turned and headed for his truck, and she did what she could about   the   butterflies.

FIFTEEN

THE DRIVE TO Yvette's was second nature for Nate. Or at least it had been when he was younger. It had been a few years, but Finn assured him it still existed and the food was still as good as ever. It had been a popular spot to hang out when they were in high school, and the go-to date destination within thirty miles. The food at Hinkley's was good, but if you wanted a chance to spend some face time without every other person who walked in the door stopping for small talk, Yvette's was the spot.

Layla had never joined them there. Now that he thought about it, she'd never spent a Friday night at Yvette's with them, or the swimming hole, or in the barns at the fair rodeo. Those were some of the best memories of his life in Three Rivers, cementing his bond with people he could still count on ten years later. And she'd missed it. So he was going to cover a lot of ground quickly.

He signaled and turned off the highway, watching Layla sit up straighter in his peripheral vision.

"Are we...?"

He couldn't help but smile at the childlike eagerness in her voice.

"Yep." She'd leaned forward a bit, but when she caught him glancing over at her, she settled back into the seat, trying to downplay how excited she was. "I haven't had one of these burgers in a dog's age. 'Sides, I thought it would be nice for you to get out of town for a bit."

"Nate, that's..." She paused, and he considered how much he enjoyed doing things that made her lose her words like that—like bringing her those flowers from Nan, but how heartbreaking it was they were the smallest things. Like nobody had ever given her the time of day. "That's really nice of you to think of that."

He hit his blinker and pulled into the little dirt lot where Yvette's, a refurbished travel trailer, was parked. It had been outfitted with fryers, a big neon sign, and old Christmas lights; the most unassuming roadside canteen, it served the best burgers in Colorado as far as he was concerned. Yvette had been a school teacher before retiring, so it had always run seasonal and was usually pretty busy on weekends in the summer, but weeknights were quiet. There were a couple of cars in the lot and a handful of the scattered covered picnic tables were occupied, but it was what he had hoped for. Some one-on-one time, with almost no risk of running into anyone who might try to redirect his attention from her.

"When's the last time you left Three Rivers?" he asked, killing the engine and unbuckling.

"I can't even remember," she said all too quickly, but her deer-in-the-headlights eyes told him she remembered, she just wasn't willing to spill. He bet it had to do with the thing he'd seen on her front porch; the nearest hospital was outside of town limits, and while she had proven to be about as independent as they come, he was pretty sure she hadn't done *that* on her own.

"Ah well, I intend for you to remember *this* excursion."

His words made her blush, and the reaction made him feel like a million bucks. He'd spent a good year feeling about as useful as a piece of shit wedged in the heel of a cowboy boot, but if he could still make a woman smile, maybe he was doing all right after all.

He opened his door and climbed out, glancing back at her, still buckled in and wiping her palms on the thighs of her jeans

"You're not chickening out on me, are you?" he asked, feeling her nerves in the small space of the cab between them.

She let out a whoosh of a breath and brightened almost immediately. He'd seen it before, the automatic smile when anyone tried to get under her skin and figure out what made her tick.

"Never."

"That's my girl."

She blushed more, but she got out of the truck—without hesitation, this time, so he counted that as a point for him.

Once they got their food, they sat down one of the picnic tables with nobody nearby. After the appropriate comments about how amazing the burgers and shakes were, they settled into quiet, but not for long.

"So, I noticed Kerri was helping you again tonight."

"What?" Layla looked up, wetting her lips.

"Her car. It was in your yard tonight when I showed up. She peeling wallpaper or laying tiles?"

"Uh..." She let out a huff of a breath, and he felt bad for having cornered her. But he wanted her to know he knew and didn't care if she had a kid. He'd discovered a few things worse than a woman with a child during the period of his life he sometimes referred to as the 'buckle bunny buffet'.

"She's babysitting, right?" He tipped his head down, doing his best to relay the rest of his message. *It's okay. I don't care. I still want you. God, do I ever want you.*

Her lower lip trembled and he regretted it immediately.

"Um, yes." Her voice shook the same way her lip had, and then she tipped her chin up, much the same way she had when he'd looked appraisingly at her house that first night when he dropped her off after work. In the blink of an eye, she'd gone from defeated to proud, and strong. He wished he could be as strong, as brave. More than anything, he wanted to reach out and slide his finger along that stubborn jaw and touch her lips.

"I saw the toy on your porch and I figured."

She pushed her burger basket away from her a little bit, like she was done with the date. "I'm sorry I didn't mention it, Nate. I understand if you..."

Bless her, she thought he was done with the date. He wasn't even close.

"If I what?"

"If you want to just call it a night and go home." She was offering him an out. The take it or leave it attitude was brave. And smart. And he would take it.

"Why would I want to call off a perfectly good date when you've got a babysitter hired for the night?" he teased, dropping an eyelid in a wink. "Now don't let that good Baylor beef go to waste."

~

It took a couple minutes and a few good appraising looks at Nate's face for the tension to drain out of her and her appetite to return. She'd been making plans to get back to Three Rivers on foot when he quietly tucked back into his burger like nothing had happened at all. Her heart had jack-hammered when she'd realized maybe this entire date thing was just some kind of ploy to get her hopes up and make her look like an idiot. A cruel ploy, yes; something well beyond anything she could ever imagine Nate Montgomery doing in a million years, but a small part of her was still the unpopular grade school girl that had been invited to a birthday party in the fifth grade and had turned up to nobody there except two girls, hiding, to see her reaction when she realized she'd been tricked. A part of her was still distrustful about kind gestures, and this could have easily fallen into that category.

Except it didn't. Because Nate was still sitting across from her, quietly working at his platter of fries, glancing up every now and again to steal a look at her, and his eyes hadn't changed at all. If he'd come to the conclusion she had a child the day he'd seen the exersaucer, he'd clearly had time to come to terms with it. But if it was that easy for this little secret to come out, would she be able to hide the fact Mason was his from him for any period of time?

"I don't know why I didn't think *somebody* in town would tell you about the baby eventually. It's not like *nobody* knows. It's just not how I wanted to lead when you were asking me out." She shrugged; she could give him this much honesty.

"I get that," Nate said, nodding. "But you don't have to keep any secrets from me, okay?"

Having just one person in this world who knew everything that went on inside her head—all her secrets and worries and fears—would have been a huge relief. Nate Montgomery wasn't that person—couldn't be—despite his offer.

She tried a smile.

"A girl's got to have *some* secrets."

"Of course. But the heavy ones, the important ones...I can take them." He leaned forward, leveling with her across the wood table, so serious she stopped chewing her fries.

If you only knew what you were asking for.

"First date's a little *heavy* for those sorts of promises, isn't it?" she teased, trying to turn the conversation the best she could.

He sat back, his intensity decreasing to a more comfortable level. Nate Montgomery was a good old boy, a sexy cowboy you could have fun with—she knew that much. But he was also the type of man you could get lost in, and that...that was dangerous.

A sexy little smirk deepened the smile lines around his mouth. "This is hardly our..."

"*First* date. It is." She interrupted him, nodding. The feel of his hands on her skin was burned into her memory, but that didn't mean they'd ever been on a first date.

He shrugged, conceding. "So it is."

"So lay off on the deep stuff, Montgomery."

"All right, all right. I'll save it for date number two."

She laughed. "What makes you think there's going to be a date number two?"

"Oh I just have a feeling," he teased with a wink. He wasn't wrong.

SIXTEEN

LATER, ON THE drive home, their bellies full and the cab lit by the green glow of the old radio in the truck, Layla felt Nate's hand creep across the seat toward her fingers. He didn't hold her hand, per se, but looped their pinkies together. It was an innocent gesture that made her giddy, like she imagined having a middle school boyfriend would have felt like.

Dinner at Yvette's wasn't as bad as she'd thought it might be. She didn't know what she'd expected—jerked up eyebrows of people incredulous that she was out in public with Nate Montgomery, small-town rodeo hero? She should have known better. People in town were friendly enough. Working with the public, she'd started to get a reputation that exceeded what people thought of her family. And nobody had ever truly aired their feelings about her parents and their shady income practices to her face. But she knew people talked. And she knew people would talk about this.

"I don't wanna be 'that person', but I'm real proud you've got your own place, Layla. You seem to be doing well for yourself."

Layla chuckled, shaking her head.

"If you count working nonstop and a car that's begging to die on me as doing well, I guess that's what it is."

"Your parents must be proud, too. How are they doing anyway?"

"You didn't ask me out so you could ask about my parents, Nate Montgomery." She was still a little itchy when it came to talking about her folks. They'd never done her any favors. As far as she was concerned, Nan and Kerri were her family now, and that was all she needed. But telling Nate about the discord in the Sullivan family was just a segue into talking about Mason and she figured the less she shared, the less likely he was to ask the right questions to get the answer she didn't want to give.

He chuckled. "Yeah, you're right."

"How about you? How long you planning on sticking around?"

The way he shifted, swallowing, without turning his eyes to her told her she'd hit her mark when it came to making him feel just as itchy as she had when he'd cornered her about having a kid.

"A while, probably."

"A while?"

"The foreseeable future."

"Right. So..." She pressed her lips together, trying to figure out how to put her thoughts to words. It could have been exhaustion or her new role in life, but she'd become a lot more forthright in the last year, more aware of her truths, and more willing to speak them. "Remember how I said I'm not the same girl as eighteen months ago?"

He glanced at her and suddenly, she felt uncomfortable bringing it up. What would it hurt to have a little fling? The problem was little flings turned into bigger things in such a small town; drama, or trouble, or *babies*. And she didn't have the time or energy to beat around the bush anymore. Every minute of her free time was measured, and precious. And giving any of it to him meant taking it away from Mason, and her son was the one who would still be around in twenty years, and he'd remember.

"Yeah."

"I had a really good time tonight...but I don't know if I gave you the wrong idea by accepting this date..." She blew out a long breath. Might as well nip it in the bud. "I'm not really interested in the type of thing we had going on last time."

Nate's brow furrowed and he glanced at her again, then flicked on his blinker and pulled the truck over, shoving the shifter into park.

"Neither am I."

She'd wanted him to say oh, okay, and drive her home and drop her off. To be cordial to her when he saw her at the bar or the doctor's office, friendly, even. Instead, he turned his gaze on her, too intense, and reached between them, undoing that silly seatbelt buckle that had given her so much trouble this week. The moment stilled, and her mouth went dry as she watched him lift his hand and touch the back of her neck. Then the moment quickened again, catching up with itself all of a sudden and she was being tugged across the bench seat and Nate's lips were crashing into hers like she was water and he was a man who had been in the desert for too long.

Layla didn't remember making the decision to slide across the bench seat and press her body into his, but there she was, with her fingers curled around his bicep. His tongue slid into her mouth and she let out an involuntary, soft noise as she let him in. His free hand glided over her shoulder, back up to her neck, slid down her arm, and then found her waist, his palm covering territory as if he was remembering her body the same way she had remembered his earlier. She didn't even have the presence of mind to think to suck in her stomach.

This sure as hell didn't *feel* like he didn't want the same type of thing they'd had before. And right now, she wasn't sure she cared.

The last time he'd been in town, whiskey had fueled the initial encounter. The next night, she'd been stone sober and a little self-conscious, but completely perplexed by the way their bodies fit together so perfectly, and encouraged by Nate's enthusiasm. Every touch was a combination of worship and awe and it wasn't like anything she'd experienced before or after. Until now.

When he left town, she hadn't deluded herself into thinking he'd come back for her. Oh, he'd be back—his entire family was here—but she wasn't the kind of girl men came back for, and she was okay with that.

Now, her body betrayed her brain, pressing against him, her hips lifting when his fingers worked in under her shirt. Her skin remembered his touch all too well. His mouth traced over her jaw, into the crook of her neck, and he let out a heated breath, his fingers curling into her flesh as he drew her impossibly closer.

~

What she'd said didn't matter; he'd been wondering all night what she might taste like—promised himself just a sample—and now he couldn't stop. It had been that way since he'd seen her at Danny's, working behind the bar. Whether it was thinking about her, or tasting her, or fantasizing about what life in Three Rivers might be like with Layla at his side, he had no self-control. It wasn't that he had pined for her while he was in Denver, either. She crossed his mind from time to time—occasionally when he'd just had a lackluster physical encounter, he'd think of the way their bodies fit together like they were made for one another; her soft, lush curves, and the way she gave and gave. But once he came back to Three Rivers and saw her again, it had been almost non-stop. So bad he was convinced maybe Nan didn't even *need* an informant.

He pulled away for just a second, brushing her hair off her forehead and letting his fingers wander back to the back of her neck. The wanting in her eyes made his stomach churn. *I feel it too, babygirl.* Funny how there'd been no shortage of women in Denver—before the accident, anyways—but nobody permanent, nobody who made him feel the way she was making him feel right now, with just a couple of sweet kisses in the front seat of his pickup. It took every bit of his willpower and then some not to take her mouth again. He pressed his forehead against hers, holding them there for a moment, nothing but their heavy breaths filling the space between them. It might not be easy, but he'd prove she was more than just a body—no matter *how* badly he wanted that body—and he'd be around for more than a couple nights. Because he wanted to be, not because he had no choice.

"I gotta get you home."

Her throat bobbed when she swallowed—God, even that was sexy—and she gave a tiny nod, letting out a soft, short breath through her nose. He'd pulled her into the girlfriend seat, and when he shifted the truck into gear, he slid his arm over her shoulder to keep her there, content with her warm body curled against his side.

Nate was almost disappointed when his headlights swept over the front porch of her house; over the now empty spot where he'd seen that baby seat before. It struck him funny she hadn't opened up when she'd confirmed she had a child, but then again, he hadn't exactly spilled everything when she'd asked how long he would be in town. He had all the time in the world.

Putting the truck in park, he helped her slide across the seat and out of the pickup.

She took a couple steps toward the house, and cocked her head back at him when he caught stride beside her.

"What are you doing?"

"Walking you to your door. What else?" He couldn't resist a little chuckle.

"Okay," she said quietly, and it occurred to him maybe nobody had ever taken her on a proper date, talked to her daddy while he waited for her to be ready, walked her to the door and kissed her goodnight. He would have liked to think it had more to do with the fact that her father was an ornery old sonofabitch nobody could tolerate, and her brother was well on the way to being the same, but he knew it was because she'd been painted with the very same brush of distaste, even though she'd never been anything but sweet and quiet. If he thought about it, he'd never seen her with anyone in high school, and he remembered someone saying the guy from two towns over who had accompanied her to prom was a friend of a friend.

Well, that just wouldn't do.

Walking side by side toward her house, the backs of their hands brushed, electricity crackling through the off-and-on space between them. Two strides later, he wrapped her slender fingers in his own. At the bottom of the stairs she stopped, turned toward him and smiled, their joined hands hanging in the space between them. She bit her lower lip for a second before a smile spread over her pretty features, right up to her eyes.

"Thank you for a wonderful night, Nate."

"You weren't the only one who enjoyed it." It was the first time in months...no, almost a year, that the reminder of his failure wasn't pressing at the back of his mind, dictating his actions. Her company had put that all out of his mind. For tonight, he was just a man spending time with a beautiful woman he was attracted to.

She looked up at him; she was a tall woman, Amazonian, but he still had a few inches on her, and her lips parted just so slightly. Like an open invitation. One he wanted to take, badly. Instead, he reached out to cup her jaw, his thumb rubbing lightly over the rise of her cheekbone, taking in those sweet, trusting eyes, and the little smatter of freckles on the bridge of her nose she'd never grown out of.

Her eyes were locked on his as he got closer, sliding his fingers around the back of her neck as he brought his lips to her ear, missing her mouth entirely.

"Goodnight, Layla."

A breathy sigh came out of her when he pulled back and dropped his hand. Clearly confused, her smile was a little weak.

"I'll see you in the morning."

She didn't say anything as he turned and headed back to his truck. She might have invited him in this time. And he wouldn't have been able to say no.

SEVENTEEN

LAYLA SUSPECTED KERRI had been watching out the window, because the girl was halfway across the kitchen with her back to the door, her arms crossed defensively around her midsection when Layla let herself into the house. Almost immediately, the younger girl flew across the floor to the door, peeking beyond Layla to watch Nate's headlights swing as he turned and pulled out of her driveway.

"So?" Anxious excitement made her voice high and loud.

"Shh, don't wake up my baby," Layla chided, closing the door behind her and making a slow show of crossing the floor and putting her purse on the end of the kitchen island.

Kerri rolled her eyes, positioning herself on the other side of the counter top from her employer. "You and I both know we could make enough noise to wake the dead and Mason would still be sleeping."

"That is true," she said, rooting in her bag for her phone.

"So?!" Kerri repeated.

"So what? Don't you have to go home or something?"

"I'm not leaving until you tell me about this date." The girl crossed her arms over her chest defiantly.

"Okay," Layla started. "We went to Yvette's. We ate hamburgers. I came home."

Kerri's eyes went wide with exasperation.

"And that's it? Did you talk about Mason? Did he *kiss* you?"

Pressing her lips together, Layla considered what she *could* tell Kerri, knowing how close the Baylor and Montgomery families were. She trusted Kerri with her son, but maybe not her secrets. Kerri had never probed into who Mason's father was, and for all the girl knew, Mason could have been her cousin if things had gone differently all those years ago with Noah Baylor.

"Sort of. And yes."

"You sort of kissed or sort of talked about Mason?"

"Well, he figured out I had a kid."

Nodding vigorously, Kerri uncrossed her arms and leaned forward with her palms on the counter top. "And he was a decent human being, wasn't he?"

She couldn't help the smile that crawled across her lips, thinking of how absolutely, unequivocally chill Nate had been upon confirming she had a kid. Maybe she could tell him. Maybe he would handle it in stride, the same way. Maybe not tomorrow, but soon, she could tell him. This hope was risky.

"Of course he was," Kerri answered herself. "He's Nate Montgomery. Now, about that kissing."

"Go *home*, Ker. You have to be back here in about ten hours."

Kerri gathered up her laptop bag and her purse, huffing exaggeratedly as she did. "I know he didn't kiss you."

"As a matter of fact, he *did*," Layla replied, moving toward the door and holding it open for her. "Just not in front of the steps where you were *watching*."

The guilty smile Kerri flashed when she paused in the doorway confirmed Layla's suspicions. "Now go home."

She watched out the window, as she always did, until Kerri's tail lights were out of sight, and then let out a long breath.

As she prepared for bed, Layla went back over the details of the night, from the gentle way he'd hooked his pinky in hers, to his hot hands on her skin. And the rest of the drive home, he'd made sure she sat in the 'girlfriend seat', the middle of the bench seat in a pickup—something she'd heard girls talk about in high school but had never experienced. But then he'd stopped short of kissing her goodnight. Had he changed his mind somewhere between wrapping his arm around her shoulders and getting out of the truck? No, the quiet, deliberate way he'd come so close, his hot breath tickling her earlobe and the rough scrape of his stubble against her jaw said otherwise.

She snuck into Mason's room and put her hand on his back gently to feel the rise and fall of his tiny, shallow breaths. The butterflies in her stomach quieted. This. This was important. Nate was being dangerously decent, though. Enough to give her silly notions about families and happily ever afters. Yes, this hope was risky.

EIGHTEEN

NATE SHIFTED HIS truck into park in front of Layla's house. She was already trying to shimmy out of the seatbelt and the truck, ready to bolt for the door like she often did; he wouldn't be invited in tonight. Little did she know he'd already made up his mind he'd be sharing the pan of lasagna on the floorboard Nan had sent. He unbuckled and grabbed the food she'd left behind, and saw the toy that had tipped him off to the baby in the first place was currently occupied by a round-cheeked, light-haired little boy. Nate's stomach did something funny. Layla as a mother in theory was different from real life. Not bad, just different. He climbed out of the truck and followed Layla, catching up in a few easy strides.

Kerri had been sitting on the bench next to the child, and she put her laptop aside and stood up, crossing an arm over her midsection as they approached. Her questioning gaze turned to Layla, who gave her a nod Nate only caught out of the corner of his eye.

"Hey Kerri."

She flashed him a big grin, erasing the uncertainty she'd showed. "Hey Nate."

The girl had only been a member of the Baylor clan for a few years, but she could have easily been blood, which made her practically his own kin. He hadn't been around much, but she'd made a couple trips to Denver with Emma and Noah to watch the rodeo, so they'd cemented a pretty good bond. She was like the kid sister he'd never had.

He finally turned his gaze to the child, getting a closer look. He was a cute little guy, with blond hair, almond-colored eyes, and the roundest, chubbiest cheeks he'd ever seen. He lifted his arms for Layla in the universal signal for 'up'. Nate had never considered a family—hell, he could barely remember his own father, so how was he supposed to be that for someone else? But he wanted Layla, and this surprisingly happy baby wasn't going to put a damper on that.

"So who's this?" he asked.

Layla set her purse on the bench Kerri had been occupying as the girl gathered up her laptop and books, then bent and swooped the boy out of his seat, up onto her hip like it was the most natural thing in the world. She looked *right* with a baby on her hip. And not in a way that seemed to be synonymous with her family. It was like the last time he'd been in town she'd been missing something, and now all the right pieces had fallen into all the right places.

"This," she said with a sigh that sounded like sheer happiness, then pressed a kiss to the boy's chubby cheek. "Is Mason."

"Hey Mason," Nate said, balancing the casserole dish in one arm as he reached out to touch the boy's hand. His heart warmed when he was rewarded with a toothy grin. So far, so good.

Kerri emerged from the house with a purse and laptop bag slung over her shoulder, stepping between them to press her own kiss to the baby's cheek. "See you tomorrow, buddy. Bye Layla. Nate."

"See you in the morning, hun."

"Later Ker." Nate watched Kerri's back as she descended the stairs light and easy, then looked back at Layla.

She wore a white sundress with a tiny flower print that offset dark skin that had clearly already seen a lot of summer sun. It hit just above the knee, exposing long, shapely calves. Her dark hair hung loose around her shoulders, not unlike that first night he'd seen her at Danny's. Mason grabbed a fistful of it and she gently extracted it from his fingers, then brushed his own hair off his forehead, swinging her gaze to meet Nate's.

"You wanna come in?"

It sounded like a challenge.

He never backed down from a challenge.

"Yes." Didn't matter the challenge was exactly what he'd wanted in the first place.

She pushed open the screen door and he followed her into the house. It was as he'd imagined—tidy, but dated. The furniture inside was relatively sparse, mismatched, and aged, but when he glanced again at Layla, he could see defensive pride. She'd pulled herself up by her bootstraps and she was providing not only for herself, but her son. It was the same reason she wouldn't let him look after her car repairs.

"It isn't fancy." It sounded like another challenge.

"Who you looking to impress anyway?" He dropped the lasagna and garlic bread off on the kitchen counter while she buckled Mason into a high chair next to the kitchen table. The unreadable look she gave him as she moved around him to turn on the oven prompted more words, a little more serious this time. "I meant what I said yesterday. You've done well for yourself. You should be proud."

"Do you wanna stay to eat?" she asked, turning from the cupboard with a couple of plates in hand, clearly more interested in changing the subject than asking him to stay. He smiled.

"Sure. Let me know what I can do to help."

NINETEEN

THE EVENING MOVED past faster than anticipated, and once she warmed up a little, and saw the easy, inclusive way Nate interacted with Mason, Layla was finally able to relax a little. She was so used to quiet evenings alone she hadn't even realized how much she would like company. The fact that it was Nate Montgomery's company made it even a little better. They chatted about anything and everything, carefully dancing around too much talk of Mason or her pregnancy, or the reason Nate was in town, which she attributed to his wreck. When the conversation lulled, Mason entertained them with his antics, and before she knew it, it was nearing the baby's bedtime.

She got a washcloth and did the best she could with his hands and face, and turned to Nate, at odds. She was surprised to find she wasn't quite ready for him to go home but knew it might be awkward to just sit in her kitchen waiting while she went through the nighttime routine, which included a bath, a nurse, and a little quiet time in the rocker.

He stood and gathered up the plates and cutlery from the table. "How about I make some coffee?"

She smiled. "I won't be long. He usually goes down easy."

"Take as much time as you need," Nate responded, moving back into the kitchen. There was no dishwasher, so, like he belonged there, he started filling the sink with water. She cradled the babbling baby against her heart for a minute, the ache there taking her by surprise. Blowing out a soft breath against the child's fine hair, she moved through the house toward the bathroom to get started.

She didn't want to rush through their nighttime routine, because it felt like she had so little time with Mason already, but he made things blissfully easy, dozing off almost immediately after he nursed. She stood over his crib for a few extra minutes, watching him sleep, and feeling guilty about the pull of the man she could hear still moving around in her kitchen.

The scent of fresh brewed coffee drew her down the hall, back into the kitchen where her dish drying rack was stacked with clean dishes, the coffee pot was full and waiting, her junk drawer stood open, and Nate Montgomery was tinkering with her dry goods cupboard door and a screwdriver. She took a second to drink him in, his t-shirt drawn tight over his shoulders, broad and expansive, tapering down to a narrow waist, a slice of which was exposed because of his lifted arms. The most perfectly fitted pair of jeans hung low on his hips, hugging every line of his back end and thighs in a way that left little to the imagination. The image of what that body looked like unclothed was all too close in her mind, a memory she hadn't been able to get rid of, that had only amplified since the scorching kiss in the front seat of his truck last night. The subtle muscle of his biceps, honed from years of hanging on tight to a bull rope, shifted under his tawny skin as he tightened the hinge she'd been meaning to get to for weeks.

She thought she'd been quiet, but he must have heard her because he turned, smiling, and twisted the screwdriver one more time. "Hey, I just noticed this was loose when I got the coffee." He opened and closed the door a couple times to show her he'd repaired it. It had been loose and squeaky but moved freely and noiselessly now. Something checked off her never-ending to-do list.

"You didn't have to."

He let her finish this time, but when she was done, he tipped his head down, raising a brow. "You fed me, it's the least I can do."

"Technically your *Nan* fed the both of us."

He waved his hand in the air to dismiss that point, then dropped the screwdriver back into the junk drawer and bumped it closed with his hip. "Little guy sleeping?"

She nodded, moving to the coffee maker where he'd set out two of her least chipped mugs, and pulled the carafe off the hot plate to pour them each a steaming cup. "He went down super easy. Big day, I guess. New friends."

When she looked up to smile at him, Nate was standing close, and it did something funny to her heartrate. She blew out another slow breath, and he slid the mug closest to him off the table and lifted it as if in a toast. "To new friends." He took a swig, then tipped his head toward the door. "Porch?"

Quickly stirring some sweetener from a crock jar on the counter into her coffee, she nodded. "Sure."

They moved through the house quietly, and Nate held the door for her, letting it close gently so as not to make too much noise. She settled onto the bench Kerri had been sitting on when they arrived—it felt like a long time ago—Nate felt like a normal part of her after-work schedule already. He sat next to her, and she cupped her hands around the steaming mug, looking out over the lawn toward the road, quiet. She often did this on her own after a long work day, but his company felt right. There was no need for words.

Eventually, he shifted beside her, sliding his arm along the back of the bench and over her shoulders, drawing her in close. She resisted at first, then let herself go. Because it was easy. Because it felt good. Right, even. She took in the clean, sharply masculine scent of him, felt the heat of his skin under the thin t-shirt he wore, and imagined she could even hear his heart beating at that proximity. He hadn't touched her this morning or tonight in the truck on the way home; not since the date, which meant he'd taken her proclamation about the type of thing she was looking for seriously, even if the wanting feeling growing deep in her belly hadn't.

"Little slice of paradise," he said quietly.

"Right now," she said with a laugh. "On any given day, it's not quite this peaceful. Or quiet. But I don't think I'd have it any other way."

"It looks good on ya, Lay. Motherhood, I mean."

Her heart thudded in her throat and she swallowed it down the best she could. She could feel the next question coming. Nate wouldn't ask '*who's the father?'* He'd ask if he was, because he'd have to be an idiot not to realize the timeline worked. Instead, he surprised her.

"And you're doing a hell of a job on your own. But you *should* let me help you out with the house."

She glanced up at him, curbing her initial response to decline, like she'd been trying to this whole time. Instead, she considered, took a sip of her coffee, and thought about how little spare time she had to devote to all the little fixes that didn't actually cost much, like that cupboard door. He wanted to be her friend, and she needed as many friends on her side as she could get. And maybe he needed a friend or two.

"Okay."

"I want to...wait...*okay*?"

She chuckled, and shook her head.

"Yes, okay. What's your going rate?"

She felt his body relax a little at the same time he lifted his shoulders in a shrug. "Dinner once in a while?

"That's hardly a fair wage."

"All right, let me take you on a couple more dates. How about that?"

His insistence was kind of endearing. And she was treading a dangerous line between being able to keep her secrets and falling clear off the ledge and right into love with him.

"Sounds good."

~

Nate had never felt his soul as quiet as sitting on her porch with Layla curled up under his arm. After all the time he'd spent trying to convince her to go on just one date in the first place, seeing her so at ease with him felt good. A comfortable silence settled over them just like the dark night blanketing her lawn. This was a quiet part of town; he hadn't seen a car go by in at least an hour. There was a time when he couldn't have quieted his mind like this. He'd always be thinking about the next ride, the next rodeo; 'keeping his head in the game' is what he'd called it. Compared to this, it was overrated.

He'd never imagined domesticity to be this comfortable. When Layla left to put Mason to bed and he found her loose cupboard door, fixing it gave him some purpose. And the way she looked at him when she'd come back out...well, that was worth a couple hundred hours of odd jobs for her. He'd always known her to be a nice girl, but tonight he'd seen her for what she'd become—a remarkable woman. He didn't have much to measure her against since he barely remembered his own, but by his estimation, Layla was one hell of a mother.

And so natural—the way she spoke to and interacted with the baby. She'd clearly done a great job so far. Mason was cute, funny, and social. Not a bit shy, he'd rewarded Nate's efforts to befriend him with toothy grins and belly laughs that made him consider, for the first time in his life, what settling down and having a family of his own might be like.

It had really never crossed his mind because he didn't have any fond memories that included a mother *and* father figure—just Nan. And she'd done a good job, but that didn't make him want for a family portrait of his own. Besides, it seemed impractical to make a living putting your life on the line every time you got into the chute when you had a wife and kids depending on you to come home in one piece. Now he was in a position where he wouldn't *have* to put his life on the line every day, but he didn't have the income to back up the idea of raising kids. *Damned if you do, damned if you don't.*

Either way, this little peek into Layla's life with Mason had been warm and comfortable. Something he hadn't expected.

She shifted a little, taking in a deep breath and letting out a soft little noise before her breathing evened out again. She'd fallen asleep.

He glanced down, and sure enough, her eyes were closed and her lips just slightly parted. Her fingers curled into the thin fabric of his t-shirt. There was something about a woman as strong, as determined as she was in the softness of sleep, her features slack, her breathing light. The opposite of the nose-to-the-grindstone, cautious woman she was when she was awake.

Nate hated to disturb her, but if he didn't go home tonight, Nan would give him some serious side eye. He *was* a grown man, but as far as he was concerned, so long as Nan was lending the use of the basement apartment to him free of charge, he owed her the respect of letting her know where he was, and he hadn't planned to stay out all night. Even though sitting here, holding Layla until sunrise sounded a hell of a lot more tempting than the sad double bed in his grandmother's basement.

She was so peaceful, and so close. He gently slid her coffee cup out of her clutched hands, dipped his head, held his breath, and brushed his lips over her hairline. Not with the intent to wake her, but because he couldn't help himself. Her hair smelled of honeysuckle and citrus, and she was so soft and warm.

He shifted a little, hoping that would rouse her, but she slept through it. Pressing his lips together, he slid his hand over her hair, onto her shoulder, and gave her a little squeeze.

"Hey Lay..."

She drew in a sharp breath and her eyes opened. She didn't lift her head right away, but as her eyes focused on his, she smiled. It went all the way to her eyes.

"Hey," she said, her voice rough with sleep. "I fell asleep. What time is it?"

"Late enough," he replied quietly. "Nan's gonna wonder where the hell I am."

Slowly stretching her body like a cat, she sat up. His body missed her warmth almost immediately. "Well thanks for staying for dinner."

He wasn't stupid enough to think it hadn't made her uncomfortable at first; she hadn't wanted him to stay—*he* should have been the one thanking her.

"I really enjoyed it. Thanks for feeding me. And for introducing me to Mason. You're raising a heck of a kid."

She smiled, a tiny yawn escaping as she straightened her clothes and smoothed her hands over her hair.

"I can't take all the credit. Or even most of it. Kerri does a good job with him. And Nan, when Kerri isn't around."

"What's that saying about it taking a village?"

"Yeah," she nodded, slowly drawing to her feet. "I'm lucky to have such a good village. I honestly don't know how I could do it without them."

He got up, too, the realization striking him that he wanted nothing more than to be a part of her village.

"Then I'm glad Nan and Kerri have got you." He smiled, reaching out to slide a hand down her arm again. She lingered in the space between his arm and his chest, looking for a kiss, no doubt. And how easy it would have been to step forward, close his arms around her, and taste her sweetness. But the timing wasn't right. Not yet. It didn't matter how badly he needed to kiss her—she needed this message of value and worthiness more than he needed to kiss her. "Goodnight, Layla."

TWENTY

LAYLA SAT BACK in the passenger seat of Nate's truck and glanced over at him as they turned in her driveway. She'd fully expected him to pick her up in her own car after work today, but the parts were delayed, he told her. She'd enjoyed dinner with him so much the night before that she wasn't bothered, and by the casual way he steered with one wrist over the steering wheel and the other slid along the seat behind her, neither was he. When she saw her mother's boxy gold sedan sitting in the yard next to Kerri's, she wished she had her own car and Nate was fifty miles away. *Right. Thursday.*

When she'd agreed to the visit, she hadn't known Nate would be around. That he'd be driving her to and from work all week. That she'd fall asleep with her head on his chest and his heart beating under her ear, feeling more comfortable and safe than she had in years. All things she wanted to hide from her mother. In truth, she hadn't even expected the visit to actually happen, based on her mother's track record.

The woman was sitting on the front porch with Mason on her knee. Kerri sat next to her and they both had tall glasses of what looked like lemonade. Damn those Baylors for instilling so much hospitality in her babysitter.

Nate put the truck in park and before she could raise an objection, he was unbuckling his seatbelt and pushing the driver side door open. Damn Nan Montgomery for raising the boy with manners.

Rhonda rose, swinging Mason onto her hip, and smiled as Nate approached the porch, Layla two steps behind with her heart in her throat. Despite a lifetime with her mother, it was hard to guess what she'd say or do at any given time. Kerri got up, grabbing her computer bag from the spot it had been resting beside the bench. No matter how much hospitality and kindness the Baylors had trained into her, she'd clearly had enough of Rhonda Sullivan. Layla didn't blame her. The younger girl gave Mason a quick kiss and started down the stairs. Layla reached out and squeezed Kerri's arm as she passed by.

"Later Ker."

"Bye Lay... Mrs. Sullivan. Nate." The girl ducked her head as she stepped of the porch and headed toward her car. Layla made a mental note to slip her a few extra bucks for the pain of having had to deal with her mother.

"Mrs. Sullivan, I haven't seen you in ages. How the heck are you?" Nate extended his hand and Rhonda shook it, while Layla could barely contain the dread rising up from the pit of her stomach. This wasn't how any of this was supposed to go. And why was he being so nice?

"Nate." Her mother smiled broadly, obviously pleased with the attention. "I'm doing fine. It's nice to see you but I sure didn't expect you *here*." Rhonda shot a look, a questioning look at Layla. They weren't, by any measure, close enough at this point, for Layla to tell her mother about the date, even if she *wasn't* trying to protect him from her prying and manipulating.

Layla forced a smile. "Nate's been running me back and forth as a favor to Nan. My car broke down this week and Nate's been hauling me around."

"Oh honey, you know you could call me." The older woman jiggled the baby a little, all but ignoring Nate as she narrowed Layla in her eyes. This helpfulness had been noticeably absent for too long for Layla to fall for it.

"I don't like to bother you." Her smile was so hard to maintain her cheeks ached. Nate shifted beside her. "I know you're busy."

"I'm glad to do it, Mrs. Sullivan," he insisted. "Not much else for me to do around here, anyway."

Rhonda's eyes snapped to him, scrutinizing—entirely too calculating for Layla's liking. She ached to reach out for Mason and hug him to her chest, protecting him, but instead, she twisted her fingers together. The baby, on the other hand, was perfectly happy to twist his fingers in his grandmother's hair, though the word better described Nan's relationship with the child than Rhonda's.

"That's right, you're fresh from Denver."

"I've been home a couple weeks," Nate said with a nod. "But seeing as I haven't lived here permanently in a decade, it still feels pretty fresh."

Layla shook her head in disbelief, watching Nate engage in small talk with her mother.

Handsome, handy, friendly with Mason *and* able to field her mother? She was in trouble now.

"I would have thought you'd have been home sooner after that wreck. I heard that bull sure messed you up good. And you haven't been to the rodeo since, have you? Buckle money must be drying up."

In one fell swoop, Rhonda had already talked more to Nate about his wreck than Layla had in the whole time they'd spent together. She glanced up only to see Nate's jaw tighten almost imperceptibly, and his shoulders shift. If she hadn't known that stance inside and out from her own use of it, she never would have guessed it as defensive. But good manners won out.

"Well, it sure wasn't pretty." He smiled, and Layla knew it was as forced as her own. "But I figured it was time to come home anyhow. And it put me in the right place at the right time to help your daughter." He paused, glancing at Layla and the smile softened a little.

"Well, I always said you Montgomery boys were raised good."

"Nan did an excellent job if I do say so myself," Nate agreed.

Any other time, she'd have wished he'd stay, but now she wished he'd leave. For his own safety as much as any other reason. Every second longer he spent standing on her porch was another second her mother had to detect familiarity, compare the shade of Mason's eyes to his; to figure out the secret she'd spent the last eighteen months hiding from her. But more, for her to hurt him with her seemingly-innocuous comments about his bull riding career.

"Well, I don't wanna keep you, Nate. Thanks again for seeing me home," she prompted. She was relieved when he nodded.

"I'll call you tomorrow, Layla."

She would have killed for a kiss or a hug—any kind of touch as a gentle reminder there was good to look forward to, but definitely not in front of her mother, and he must have sensed it, because he tucked his hands in his pockets and backed away. He paused at the bottom of the steps, glancing back at her and she offered him a reassuring smile, even though she didn't feel it. One-on-one with her mother in the lobby of Dr. Fields' office was one thing; alone on her porch with her mother was an entirely different thing. She wasted time watching him climb into his truck and pull out, and he honked his horn once as he drove away. She lifted her hand and waved, steeling herself for what was to come.

"Well, Nate Montgomery," her mother said behind her. Layla turned to see Mason reaching his arms out for his mother and Rhonda surrendered him almost immediately. Layla took him, cradling him against her chest as she often did when she was feeling stressed or lonely and his hot little body curled into her right away. "He's a nice catch, Lala."

Cringing at the nickname from her youth, Layla shook her head. "It's nothing like that, mom. He's just helping me out. You wanna come in for a minute?" She hoped her mother picked up the tiny extra inflection on the word 'minute', but imagined she'd be as obtuse about it as everything else in her life. Still, inviting her in was the polite thing to do, and there was still a deep-rooted part of Layla that wished for a normal relationship with her family—especially her mother.

"Oh, I've been here a while already." Rhonda glanced at her car, then back at her daughter with her lips pressed together, trying to hide a smile. "You know, men don't just help women out unless there's some motive, sweetie. What does he want?"

All the blood rushed to Layla's face as she considered her mother's question. She wanted to answer with outrage, but that had never been the most effective way to deal with Rhonda. She pushed another smile onto her face—*story of my life*—and let out a slow breath.

"Just what he said. To be nice. Those sorts of people still exist. Around here, anyway. People don't always have an ulterior motive, mom." *Unlike you*.

"All right, let me give that sweet face a little kiss. Bingo is tonight." Rhonda reached out for Mason and pressed a kiss to his forehead. "I'd like to do this again sometime."

"Sure, just let me know ahead of time," Layla said, relief rushing through her as her mother awkwardly slung an arm around her shoulder to give her a sideways half-hug, and then started down the steps, turning to wave at Mason.

"Bye sweetie."

"Bye mom."

She stood on the porch with her cooing child cradled against her chest for a long moment after her mother left, thankful to be alone again.

TWENTY-ONE

"ARE YOU SURE your brother doesn't mind?"

"It's a little late for that," Nate said with a chuckle and shook his head at Layla, who was standing across the aisle of Banks' barn, holding the reins of a tall bay mare. When her expression didn't change, he tipped his head down. "And yes, I'm sure he doesn't mind."

"Where is he, anyway?" she asked, glancing behind her.

"Patrol. Will you calm down? You're going to spook the horses."

"I just...you know, people talk enough..."

"Layla, my brother is the last person to fuel the rumor mill about you and me. You're not getting out of this. I promise you'll like it."

She made like she was going to protest, but she didn't produce any words, so he charged ahead, leading the gelding he'd saddled up outside. Similar to the setup at the Baylor ranch, Banks had a big rectangular uncovered riding pen for working cattle, and a smaller, more intimate round pen closer to the barn. It was useful for first rides, timid riders, and quarantined horses, and judging by the way she clutched the reins as she led her horse toward it, Layla fell into the second category pretty firmly.

"Are you afraid?" he finally asked when they reached the pen. Layla's throat bobbed as she swallowed, then she nodded. He hadn't realized it at first, but when he'd suggested they go for a ride and the color drained from her face, it became clear this was another one of those regular parts of his teenage life she hadn't taken part in. He reached out to touch her cheek lightly. "You'll be fine, sweetheart. Sassy and I will take care of you."

Sassy was one of Banks' most prolific broodmares, and she'd normally have a foal at side this time of year, but his brother had given her a season off, and instead she'd been used in Noah and Emma's lesson program. She was quiet and slow moving, and so wide it was almost impossible to fall off. Perfect for Layla.

"And if you're not comfortable in the round pen today, we won't go into the woods. Easy as that."

Her face changed, some of that stubborn pride that amused him so much lighting her eyes and tipping her chin up.

"Wanna give it a shot?" he prompted.

"Okay," she said, fixing Sassy in her sights with a determined expression. "Hard to believe I grew up in this town and don't really know how to ride, right?"

Nate shrugged, tied his horse to the round pen rail on the outside, and then held the gate open for Layla to lead Sassy in.

"Not that unbelievable." Not with the kind of selfish parents she had, but he kept those thoughts to himself. "Besides, never too old to start."

She shot him a rueful look.

"I'm not old."

She was rounding pretty close to thirty, same as he was. Most days he didn't feel old, but anytime his body didn't act the way he expected it to, he felt like he was a hundred.

"I didn't say you were old," he said with a laugh. "Get on the horse."

He crossed to the off-side and put his hand into the stirrup, pushing his weight down. Sassy was tall and it didn't matter how much a new rider weighed, they could often pull the saddle all the way down around a horse's belly on their first mounting attempt. It was about how you moved your weight around, not the number on the scale.

"Okay, so left foot in, hand on the horn and the cantle, right here." He paused to tap the back ridge of the saddle seat. "Give yourself a couple bounces and then just come straight up over the saddle, don't drag it down into you."

She made eye contact with him over the leather seat and then nodded, her mouth set in a firm line of determination. Her hands went where he directed, and then she bounced once and, with barely any drag on the saddle, she had swung into it, her thigh inches from his face. Wrapping his fingers around her calf lightly, he directed her right toe into the stirrup he'd been holding.

"Like a natural, I'm impressed."

She drew in a breath as he handed her the reins and showed her how to hold a loop in each hand, crossed over the horse's neck. "Yeah, we'll see."

"Let out that breath. Leave your feelings on the ground, 'cause otherwise the horse will pick it up and then you're in for a bad time." He slid his hand up to her thigh, just past her knee, and squeezed. He felt the muscles there relax, and heard her let out a breath, her body softening. "There you go."

~

When he phrased it like that, it was easy. How many times had she pushed her feelings down, or put them out of her mind in order to focus on the task at hand? And she trusted him. His warm hand on her thigh conveyed the same message as his earlier words. He'd take care of her. She wouldn't get hurt. It was just that suddenly, anything even remotely risky felt that much more so because if something were to happen to her and she couldn't work, her baby would go without. And that was something she was entirely unwilling to subject Mason to. She'd had enough of it growing up, she'd never let it happen to him. But she could still have fun. And, she thought, as Nate clucked to the horse and her long, easy gait started moving forward, this *could* be fun.

Before long, she was getting the hang of it, with the occasional pointer or reminder from Nate, who still led the horse.

"I'm gonna let you go now. But you got this, and Sassy will take care of you either way. Remember your steering and brakes?"

She nodded, very gently lifting on each rein in turn, the horse's nose tipping in either direction as she requested. Then she sat deep, as he'd instructed her, moved her feet forward a fraction of an inch and picked up the reins, saying "whoa" deep and clear and the horse stopped immediately.

"You got it, then. Let me see you."

He stepped backward into the middle of the pen and watched her make a couple of laps around the outside of the ring.

"Good, Layla. Total natural."

A happy warmth spread from the middle of her chest at his encouraging words. Hearing him praise her grew her confidence and was almost as pleasurable as a physical touch from him. At the end of the day, a tiny part of her still sought the approval of those she cared about, as much as she'd repeated to herself over the last two years all that mattered was surviving.

"Not bad for someone who's *never* done this before, eh?"

His sound of surprise made her turn her head to find his eyebrows raised and a big, crooked grin covering his face.

"No way."

"Not once."

"Not even pony rides at the fair?"

She shook her head.

"Shit. I'd never have known it."

When they'd started saddling up the horses, she'd had her doubts she'd be able to go on the trail ride he'd started out wanting. But now, with his watchful eye and a horse that was clearly accustomed to taking care of beginners, she thought she might be able to make it happen. She signaled for Sassy to halt and then turned her and crossed the sand to Nate in the middle.

"I think I'm ready."

He reached out to touch the mare's nose lightly, his smile mirroring the one she felt all over her face and in her heart.

"I think you are, too."

He stepped back and opened the gate to the round pen for her and she carefully steered the mare through, every little thing feeling like a big, silly accomplishment. She watched Nate untie his gelding and mount up—the thing that had seemed the *most* challenging to her was effortless for a man who had clearly pretty much been born on horseback. He settled into the saddle and gathered up his reins, giving her a nod.

"All right, we'll head up the back. Just a short ride or else nobody'll be able to walk tomorrow."

She shot him a look.

"Trust me on this one. I've been back in the saddle what, a week? I've already used my share of painkillers for that. And you've *never* been. So you might need me to come take care of you tomorrow."

"As tempting as that is...you know I have to work tomorrow."

"Then after work."

"Did you bring me riding just so you'd have an excuse to spend the evening with me tomorrow, too?"

Playful guilt was written all over his features. He shrugged, a rueful smile playing over his lips—she couldn't get enough of *that*, those smile lines around his mouth when he was even a little happy. And she'd been seeing it a lot lately.

"Maybe." He drew the word out long and slow.

She tried, but it was impossible to stop the smile that twitched at the corners of her mouth.

"All right."

Sassy followed the gelding Nate rode without much prompting from Layla, all the way toward the back of Banks' property. It was beautiful, all green and lush. The spring had seen lots of rain and the summer was still reveling in the glory of it. They cut out the back of a pasture, where a trail extended into the woods beyond the fence line, and Nate dismounted there. He stopped between the horses, reaching out to stroke Sassy's neck, then to touch Layla's knee lightly.

"How you making out? Good for a bit more?"

She nodded quickly because she'd hired Kerri for the afternoon, and because stealing a few minutes with him outside of the confines of her home was rare, exciting, and good for her soul. She watched him open the gate and she steered the mare through, then turned and waited for him to close the gate and remount.

They started out a trail that was dark and green, with a carpet of old pine needles and tall, mature evergreens converging over a path wide enough for them to ride side by side, knees almost touching, without speaking for a while. Though she'd grown up in a town full of them, she'd never *really* seen the appeal of a cowboy. Not until this one, anyway. He had an easy, quiet way around the horses that seemed to calm them, and it extended to her. She'd barely had a thought about not knowing what she was doing since they left the yard. When it came to the horse *and* when it came to Nate.

TWENTY-TWO

LAYLA SHOULDN'T HAVE been surprised to see her mother push the door of Dr. Fields' office open again later that week, but she still wasn't used to the idea of Rhonda sniffing around. This wasn't exactly fair, though. She was a captive audience; there was nobody to spell her off and she couldn't hide in the bathroom until her mother left. Luckily, there were a few afternoon appointments coming up, so she knew when things got uncomfortable, as they would, she could use that excuse.

"Mom, what brings you in?"

"Just visiting," her mother said with a sly smile—the one Layla knew meant she'd been thinking. 'Scheming', her mother had always called it, unapologetically. "I wanted to tell you how much I enjoyed my visit with Mason."

Layla returned her smile, because she wanted to take her mother's word on it, even though she'd fretted almost non-stop for the last 12 hours about Rhonda seeing Nate driving her home from work. "Good, maybe we should try to do it more. A Saturday, next time. You can come for lunch. And bring daddy."

She hated to give up the rare free Saturday afternoon when she would rather spend it with Nate, but if her mother's mind was working the way she thought it was, that would give her more fodder for suspicion. And she was cautiously doubtful the lunch would even happen.

"That sounds nice, Lala." Rhonda shifted, her fingers toying with the patient intake pen and clipboard on the desk. Layla resisted the urge to snatch it away from her—fidgeting was a huge pet peeve, and she knew what was coming next. A lifetime in the Sullivan home meant she knew exactly what to look for. "So that Nate Montgomery...he's a nice boy. How long has he been sniffing around?"

Layla chose her next words carefully. Too much protest would put her mother hot on Nate's trail. Not enough would suggest a lie.

"He came in to Danny's on one of my shifts a while back. He was a big help with the car down. And I hired him to do a couple of the odd jobs in the house that I haven't been able to get to myself."

"Isn't that fancy...a hired hand." Rhonda's eyebrows rose.

Layla almost laughed at the simple cover-up. Of course. Everyone in town knew Nate wasn't rodeoing anymore.

"Well, he needs work to do and I need some work done. So he'll be around a bit. No funny business. You know as well as I do...I don't have time for anything like that with the baby." The lies were easy to tell because they were still half-truths. She *didn't*, technically, have time for funny business with Nate. Oh, but she wanted it. She was beginning to question if *he* wanted it, though. He'd been close, casually intimate, and didn't hesitate to touch her in thoughtful and kind ways, but he hadn't even attempted to kiss her since their date. And that rubbed more than she cared to admit. She told herself again and again she was just happy to have another friend to add to the count, but as much as she hated herself for it, she wanted more.

"You know, I probably never said how proud I am of you for taking care of Mason the way he deserves." It was a roller coaster, talking to her mother, but Layla steeled herself for what was next. "And you do a great job, all alone. But wouldn't it be easier if you had some help?"

She didn't mean an extra body in the house—Layla had that with Kerri and with Nan. Layla knew, from previous conversations, her mother was talking explicitly about financial help. Manipulating social services to get money on top of her wages, or, more likely, pursuing Mason's father; a route she'd assured her mother multiple times during the pregnancy she wouldn't be taking.

"Of course. Everything's easier with help. But I've got plenty of help, mom. I don't need more than what I've got."

The self-satisfied look on her mother's face turned Layla's stomach. "You always need more than what you've got. You *deserve* it."

Layla clenched her jaw and worked hard to hold her smile, brushing off her mother's words with a motion of her hand. "We don't always get what we deserve. But anyways...Saturday works? I'm off tomorrow, so we could do it then."

Her countenance cooling significantly, Rhonda straightened and shrugged. "I'll talk to your father."

She couldn't help but watch the older woman's back with a feeling of foreboding nestled cold in the pit of her stomach.

TWENTY-THREE

"WELL YOU'RE NOT being helpful at all."

Layla laughed, leaning back against the porch railing, cross-legged and barefoot. Though she had the car back now, her cell phone had rung the minute she stepped out of Dr. Fields' office with Nate on the other end of the line, offering to replace a few rotten shingles and bring her ice cream. The view from this angle all but erased thoughts of her mother's visit to the office this afternoon. It afforded a pretty healthy display of Nate's backside and the bunch and stretch of his muscles as he tapped the last shingle into place. He was a fine specimen, in *or* out of that thin, faded t-shirt and jeans, and watching him work brought to mind other fantasies she let herself indulge for just a moment.

"I like to watch."

Nate's head whipped around, his brow raised. Though he hadn't made a move to touch her in a way that was even remotely like the things that had been running through her head for the last ten minutes, he was clearly on the right wavelength, because a sexy little grin tipped one corner of his lips up in a way that made her skin warm. He angled his body toward her and she drew her knees up toward her chest, crushing the pint carton of ice cream he'd brought her. There was only a spoonful or two left, anyway.

This is it, she thought, as he took a couple of steps toward her, stalking like a big cat, his eyes fixed on hers. *This is the part where I find out I'm not imagining this chemistry between us.*

He stopped a step or two away, peering into her ice cream carton.

"And you didn't even save me any ice cream. Disappointed." He shook his head and offered her his hand, helping her to her feet with such quick force the carton went flying out of her hand, spoon clattering across the porch, and she collided with him, their chests pressed flush. He caught her with a hand at the small of her back and she took in the delicious scent of him, the smoothness of his shower gel with a sharp undercurrent of pure maleness that came from working with his body. Not smelly, but *strong*, masculine, and as potent as a pheromone. She couldn't have stopped the breathy sigh that came out of her if she'd wanted to.

"You *did* bring me the carton and *tell* me to watch."

"I told you to watch because I didn't want you to get dirty."

"*I* don't mind getting dirty."

He growled then, a short warning noise as his arm tightened around her waist. It communicated his intent loud and clear, just as clear as the hand that slid down her waist, fingers curling into the flesh just above the curve of her hip. He'd touched her in more intimate ways, but this was different. Possessive. Proprietary.

He was close, so close. Her blood rushed in her ears, her heart pounding a million miles an hour. This was it. He was going to kiss her again. It felt like their heated exchange in the front seat of his truck was a hundred years ago, and she'd been wanting and wishing for this exact thing ever since. Turning her face up and into his gentle touch on her jaw, she let out a centering breath and waited...for a kiss that didn't come.

Nate held her chin in his hand for a long moment, his eyes tracking over her face like he was memorizing it. Her entire body, poised and waiting for his kiss, relaxed in one tingling, disappointed rush when she realized it wasn't coming. He had no intention to kiss her. She *was* imagining the chemistry between them.

"What?" he asked.

"You don't want to kiss me." Her brow furrowed as she opted for the truth, because she couldn't figure what his endgame was. They were close, closer than friends, that much was certain. They'd had quiet moments of intimacy that didn't require the touch of their lips, no matter how badly she wanted it; things that weren't shared between platonic friends. Things that told her this was more than that. But still, he hadn't kissed her. Somehow, he'd kept their physical interactions behind a line that both infuriated and aroused her. She'd never been so turned on from just *sitting beside* someone. At this point, though, she had to wonder what was wrong with her—he never crossed the line.

"I don't want to kiss you?" And then he laughed, a low, soft chuckle that produced the lines around his mouth she liked so much, and when he spoke again, his voice was rough. "Layla, I *want* to kiss you. I want to kiss you so often that I know what you taste like at any given time of day. I want to kiss you and feel the way you soften up under my hands, until you can't breathe, and then again. Layla Sullivan, I *definitely* want to kiss you."

That softness he talked about...she was *there*. In this particular moment, with her hands trapped between them on his chest, and his one arm banded around her waist, the other still touching her jaw lightly, Nate Montgomery could have asked her for anything and she would have given it to him. And she might have been imagining it, but he'd moved impossibly closer, flush against her body in a way that couldn't be described as platonic in any way, shape, or form. She swallowed hard, her eyes focused on his lips. The combination of his words and the way she was vised against his body stirred her arousal in a way she hadn't expected. Nobody had ever said anything so sexy to her in her life. But he still didn't kiss her.

It took a couple tries for her to find her voice.

"Why don't you then?"

"Because there's something I want way *more* than I want to kiss you."

She was almost afraid to ask. That creeping anxiety about being the butt of a mean joke twisted in her stomach, at odds with the close, intimate way he held her, the warmth radiating between their bodies, and the tingling heaviness of her limbs.

"What is it?"

"More than I want to kiss you, I want to show you I know you aren't that same girl you were before. And that it doesn't matter, because *you're* the woman I want. *This* woman. Trust me, I want you. I want to kiss you. I want to make love to you until you can't muster up the energy to get out of the bed. But I need you to know it's about more than just the sex, or your body. And if I'd kissed you sooner, I might not have been able to get that point across. Because there's something about you, Layla, that makes me want more and more of you. And it doesn't end with a kiss."

She lifted up on her tiptoes, then, his words giving her the courage she'd been lacking for the last two weeks, and touched her lips to his. Lightly, at first, and then more insistent, opening to him and inviting him in. If he wanted more, he'd get more. She'd give him everything, and then some.

And Nate took, his kiss taking her breath, her resistance, and any doubt she might have had about whether he wanted her *like that* or not. Pressing closer still, she wound her arms around his neck and drew him down to her.

~

She tasted like the perfect mix of want, longing, and desire with a damn strong undertone of forever. Now that he tasted her again, Nate didn't know how he had put it off this long. Layla was soft, and giving, and *delicious*, and if he wasn't mindful of the baby playing contentedly in the playpen just ten feet away, he might have jogged his memory about what the rest of her tasted like. She was different now, and so was he. She'd looked so hurt when she thought he didn't *want* to kiss her, but she'd never spoken up once. In the last few weeks, he'd seen her confident and decisive about just about every other part of her life but him. What was she so afraid of?

Her body bowed toward him, all of her softening up just the way he'd known she would, and he slipped his hands down her waist, to the lush swell of her hips, pressing her closer as he plundered her mouth. His rodeo buddies talked a big game about a warm, wanting woman making them feel like a man, but it was *this* woman alone that reminded Nate that he was still virile, young, and capable, despite everything the wreck had taken from him.

Finally, he pulled away. It was harder than a lot of things he'd done in the last year, including walking away from his little piece of paradise in Denver. Layla looked up at him, her lips parted, her cheeks flushed, and he smiled, tucking a strand of her hair back behind her ear. For a moment, only their heavy breaths hung in the air between them.

He wished they could stay this way— but he had plans and Layla had to get her evening routine started or they'd be foiled. The sound of his stomach growling replaced the sound of their breathing and she laughed, shaking her head.

"I suppose you *are* hungry, I worked you hard and didn't save you any ice cream. What did Nan send this time?"

He'd brought the covered dish not at his grandmother's insistence this time—Nan's participation was key to his plan, and when he'd told her what was up, she'd been more than happy to whip up the meatloaf.

"Meatloaf. Just needs a warmup. I'll slap a coat of paint on this while you do that?" He nodded to the new shingles he'd installed. It wasn't something he'd done before but a bit of snooping around on the internet had produced a couple of videos that made it seem simple enough, and fortunately, everything had gone exactly according to plan. There were a few other spots on the house that needed replacement shingles—technically, the whole house needed re-sided at this point, but he knew that was beyond her finances, so he'd patch what he could.

"Okay. You're okay if Mason stays out here? Just holler if he starts fussing." He nodded and she made a move to step out of his arms but he cinched her to him again and tipped his head to kiss her. Soft and quick, in the casual way that couples do in greeting or before parting. And then he let her go, swatting at her ass half-heartedly as she headed into the kitchen, leaving Mason in his playpen. He could get used to this domestic bliss.

TWENTY-FOUR

"HE WENT DOWN all right?" Nate asked as Layla emerged from the house and settled into the spot on the bench under his arm he'd left open. They'd fallen into such a comfortable companionship. When Rusty had called to say he was done with her car, she'd had a brief thought about how disappointing it would be not to frame her days with Nate anymore, but he'd made it pretty clear he wasn't going anywhere. Not for a while, anyway.

The sun had set but the light of day wasn't quite ready to give up the ghost yet. She could hear frogs singing in the pond further back on the property, and where the lack of sun had cooled the air, the warmth of Nate's body beside her and the mug of coffee cupped in her hands made a fine replacement.

"Yeah. He usually goes down well, but the last two nights have been *too* easy. Like, I'm waiting for the other shoe to drop."

He laughed and folded her in closer, sliding her legs over one of his knees, so she was *almost* sitting in his lap, but was more cradled against his chest. Like something fragile and important. It was the first time she'd ever felt like she was that something.

"It's just a testament to your excellent mothering skills."

"Okay, this isn't the first time you've told me what a good mom I am. Nate Montgomery, do you have a mom fetish?"

Another laugh rumbled through his chest and brought a smile to her face.

"I just feel like maybe you haven't been told enough that you're doing a good job. And you deserve the compliments. You're doing what you have to do to make a life for Mason, and that's admirable. Not everyone does that. *My* mother sure as hell didn't."

A complete turnaround, she could feel tears pressing at the back of her throat. Everybody knew Nate and Banks' parents had abandoned them with Nan, but she'd never actually heard either of them comment on it. Now, being a mother herself, she felt an entirely different kind of empathy for them. They'd been fortunate to have the amazing Aida Montgomery to fall back on, but not every kid was that lucky. She understood how overwhelming being responsible for a tiny human was, but she couldn't, in a million years, imagine taking the option of walking away.

He turned his torso into her, reaching over to touch her jaw lightly and tip her face up. "You make me feel quiet inside in a way I haven't felt...maybe ever. *That's* probably why Mason goes down so easy."

"Stop," she said, half-heartedly, but she couldn't suppress a smile.

He did, covering her mouth with his in a gentle, teasing kiss that made her blood rush. She'd never had the opportunity to enjoy the flutter of butterflies, the teasing flirtations of new love, and then she'd gotten so busy putting her nose to the grindstone. Nate made her feel like she was sixteen, not twenty-six, and giddy with the promises of something on the horizon. Something she could look forward to.

When he nipped her lower lip in a playful gesture, she slid her hand over his neck, drawing him closer, losing herself so completely to the kiss she almost didn't notice the sweep of headlights across the front porch. Almost.

She released him in a hurry, but there was no hiding the elicit embrace because Nan was already climbing out of her little sedan with a paperback under her arm. Layla sat back, carefully untangling her legs from Nate's, but he didn't take his arm off her shoulder or give her much space to get away. If Nan hadn't already caught on to what was going on, she would now. And Layla didn't know if that was more exciting or scary, being out in the open about their relationship.

As if she hadn't even noticed, Nan waved and started toward the porch stairs.

"What's this?" Layla asked quietly, glancing up at him, but he didn't meet her gaze, just smiled and shrugged innocently.

Nan mounted the stairs with a smile like the Cheshire Cat.

"Is this an intervention?" Layla asked with a laugh, rising to her feet and giving Nan a hug.

"No, but I was going to hold one if you didn't let Nate help you with the house, love."

"So you two were conspiring against me?"

Nate laughed behind her, rising from the bench.

"No, but you know nothing ever stays secret from Nan for very long."

"That's right, I see everything," the woman said, tipping her chin up.

The best part about Nan was even if she *did* see everything, she didn't run her mouth about it.

"Anyways...Nate asked me to come over and sit with Mason for a bit."

She glanced back at Nate and he confirmed with a nod.

"I don't..." Layla tried, working to figure out how to tell them she couldn't afford for Nan to stay; with the bill on the car she was already scrimping pennies. She didn't like to talk about her financial situation to anyone, even if it was plain as the nose on her face. And Nan probably knew it better than anyone else did. But she still didn't want to trot it out in front of Nate.

"My treat," Nate filled in the blank. Layla let out a shaky breath, grateful he'd heard the words she didn't want to say.

"Okay...he just went down like twenty minutes ago. There are a couple of bottles..."

"Layla." Nan used the stern-but-loving voice she used when Layla panicked. Instead of her mother, Nan was the one who got the late night 'is this normal' calls and worst-case-scenario brain bombs. "I *have* stayed with this child before."

And she was right, but Layla still felt ambushed. And guilty. She was already barely home as it was.

"Go," Nan insisted, edging in behind the pair of them and planting herself on the bench they'd just been occupying. "Have fun."

It was nine o'clock on a Thursday night. The time of night she'd normally be preparing to tuck into bed, but Nate clearly had other ideas. He started toward his truck, motioning for her to follow. She did, because she worried Nan would chase her off the porch if she didn't. And Mason was sleeping; it wasn't like she was missing out on quality time spent with him.

As they pulled out of the drive, she angled her body toward him, her eyes narrowed.

"So tell me what this is."

"Just a drive," he insisted with a grin that said it was not *just* a drive. "Relax."

She did her best to do just that, but it wasn't easy. He pulled off onto a dirt road and she almost immediately recognized the direction they were heading in.

"The swimming hole?"

She knew the road, but had never actually been there. In high school, once a couple of the boys got their licenses, they'd fill truck beds with bodies and head out there for the kinds of parties that got whispered about in the halls, sounding too crazy to be real. She'd never been able to discern the truth because she'd never been invited and never been brave enough to invite herself.

"I worked up a sweat working on your house."

"You could have just had a shower. I do have towels."

"This'll be more fun." He shrugged with a laugh, guiding the truck into the makeshift parking space. While they'd driven, dusk had fallen and the moon, heavy and full, had begun to rise, lighting the surface of the swimming hole which was simply a deep, low-current pool spurred off of one of Three River's namesake bodies of water. Nearby, she could hear water babbling over rocks, but the spot intended for swimming was quiet.

"I-I don't have a swimsuit," she stammered with a dry mouth. But you didn't come to the swimming hole with a swimsuit—not at night—even she knew that much. Nate turned to her once he'd killed the engine, and for the first time, she felt shy. Sure, Nate had seen her before, but her body had changed with motherhood. Soft spots were even softer, stretch marks more visible than they had been. She'd never been a small girl, but would he appreciate her rounder hips, her lower breasts, as much as he had appreciated her body during the weekend that had produced Mason?

"Neither do I," he said with a grin, sliding out of the truck. She watched him head toward the water, toeing out of his boots, and grasping the collar of his t-shirt between his shoulders to pull it over his head. He didn't even look back to see if she followed—he expected her to, and like a high-schooler feeling peer pressured, she found herself climbing out of the truck without even realizing what she was doing.

Without thinking how she'd retrieve them, Layla walked out of her flip-flops and into the soft sand of the beach, pulled by the sight of Nate's bare back, all the muscle she'd watched moving under his t-shirt the last couple of nights as he worked on her house illuminated by the silvery light of the moon. When he turned back to her, unbuttoning his jeans, she thought her knees might go weak. The broad expanse of his chest was practically a work of art—muscles honed to perfection from years with the rodeo and working the small spread he had in Denver—he clearly hadn't let his layup get in the way of it. Even in the dark, she could see the lines of scars and marks he bore from a variety of wrecks.

Many of them, she'd already traced with her fingers once. Some of them were new. With a sexy smirk, he tipped his head toward her and raised a brow.

The message was clear—*ball's in your court, Lay*—and she took a deep breath, her fingers scrabbling at the top button of the conservative sun dress she still wore from work that day. The neckline wasn't so high she couldn't have pulled it over her head, but she needed some time to work herself into the idea of undressing in front of him. Hadn't this been what she'd wanted that first night?

It had, but that had been different. She hadn't expected to be here, weeks later, feeling truly and properly courted by her child's father. She'd expected a quick tryst and nothing more. This was so much more.

Fixing her eyes on his, she willed his gaze to stay on hers and not her fingers as she worked the buttons down past the band of her bra, moving toward her belly button slowly, but not slowly enough. Nate stepped into her space then, close enough she knew he wasn't going to be able to see the spider webbing of stretchmarks around her navel, and tucked his thumbs under the straps of her dress, tugging them down over her shoulders. His rough fingertips, moving so gentle, made the backs of her arms prickle with goosebumps. His mouth found her collarbone, working its way upward until he nipped at the point of her shoulder. The dress slid down over her arms and fell away from her hips and she drew a tight breath. This was the part where his adoration of her motherhood ended, she was sure. Standing there in her bra and panties, she knew she wouldn't be enough. Or maybe she was too much.

When he drew back, there was nothing but adoration in his eyes. With a little wiggle, he stepped out of his jeans, grabbed her hand, and bolted for the swimming hole, pulling her along.

They hit the water splashing, until it got deep and impeded their progress. Then Nate wrapped his arms around her and fell into the water like a tree in the forest. They came up sputtering and laughing, and Layla splashed a wave of water at him with the palm of her hand before she swam out deeper.

He followed, matching her stroke for stroke, until they were deep enough her feet didn't reach the smooth rocked bottom, and she floated, weightless, her body buoyant even when she barely treaded water with her arms. She'd always loved the water and the best thing her mom had ever done was take advantage of an afterschool swimming program for less fortunate kids.

Nate narrowed the distance between them, and she slicked her wet hair back off her forehead just as he closed his arms around her, holding her afloat while she felt his feet churning at the water underneath.

"You're crazy," she laughed. "We're not sixteen."

"I *feel* sixteen right now," he said with a smirk, making a slow rotation in the water with her. She let out a breath, the cool water at her back making the heat of his skin against hers that much hotter. He dropped his face and pressed a kiss where her breast swelled over the cup of her bra, and she pushed her fingers into his hair, tightening them to tip his head back and kiss the corner of his mouth.

"I never did this when I was sixteen," she whispered. So she'd missed the wild parties, but this might have been better. It was quiet and beautiful, and the only person here to see her or judge her was him—and based on the obvious way his body responded to her, there was no judgment to be had.

"I know," he said quietly, his eyes tracking hers in the dim glow of the full moon. His arms tightened around her waist and she wondered what she'd ever been afraid of in the first place. "I can't rewind the last ten years but I can sure as hell still show you a good time if you want."

He shifted his hands lower, over her waist and then to her ass in such a way the most natural step for her was to hitch her thighs around his hips, putting them in an intimately compromising position. Her fingers came out of his hair, slipping down to the flexed muscles in his shoulders. It was barely believable a man this good looking was voluntarily naked with her, never mind that he held her so tight, something a shade darker in his eyes than she'd seen since that first night in the truck. She'd told him then she wasn't the same girl she'd been...so no one night stands...but this was technically their second date and he'd been sniffing around for two weeks now. She could break her own rules...a little, anyway.

~

Later, Nate sat on the tailgate of his truck next to Layla, with their feet swinging; as the warm night air dried their skin, he thought this was the happiest he'd been in a long time. Who knew that Denver, the one place he'd pined for as a youth, thinking things would somehow be miraculously different and better, didn't hold the secret to fulfillment? Oh, he'd had a good run—there was never any shortage of women lurking around the back end of the rodeo looking for a roll in the hay, and he'd had a nice setup—but those were things that could be taken away with one eight second ride. He was pretty sure nothing could steal *this* kind of happy.

"What time is it?" Layla asked, pulling her wet hair over her shoulder.

He leaned back far to read the digital clock on the dashboard of the truck. "Quarter to eleven."

"Crap, Nan..."

"She's fine."

"I know, but I hate to dump on her. I'm sure she's had a long day." Layla reached for her bundled up sundress and started trying to turn it right-side out.

Nate slid off the tailgate and retrieved her sandals from where she'd dropped them in the sand, then turned back to her. She was tugging the mostly-unbuttoned dress over her head, hiding the cute folds of her soft belly, much to his disappointment. He set the sandals down next to her and slid into the space between her open knees, his fingers going to the buttons near her belly button. He wanted to follow with his lips, but worked hard to be on his best behavior. On their date, she'd said she wasn't interested in the kind of hot, casual thing they'd had going before, and he wanted to prove to her that he was in agreement, despite the battle with his body when her soft, warm skin had been pressed to him in the water. It would have been so easy...but he still had work to do before he could totally lose himself in her physically.

"Look, I know Nan. If she didn't want to do something, she just wouldn't. Same as me. So trust that she *wants* to be with Mason, that she *wants* to help you out, and she *wants* to feed you every second night." He ended with a laugh.

"About that," she said, looping her fingers in the belt loops of the jeans he'd pulled on over wet legs and tugging him close enough their lips almost touched; a brazen move that both surprised and aroused him. "You gotta tell her to stop. I've got a fridge full of food that'll rot if she doesn't quit."

He laughed, kissed her, and finished buttoning her into her dress, leaving the last few at the top open. She slid down off the gate into his arms and he loaded her in the passenger side of the truck before climbing in and heading back toward her house.

Nan was exactly where they'd left her—reading on the porch with a light on, a cup of coffee beside her. God love her. When he'd asked if she'd come by tonight, she hadn't even hesitated. He didn't know if it had more to do with the relationship she'd built with Layla in his absence or her eagerness to encourage anything that gave him reason to settle his roots back in Three Rivers, but he'd go with the momentum for now.

"How was he?" Layla asked, her voice anxious, as they approached the porch and Nan rose.

"Oh he was fine. He fussed a bit about forty five minutes ago, but then he settled quick and easy. Nothing I've never handled." She winked at the pair of them and started down the stairs. Nate stopped her and pressed a kiss to her cheek.

"Thanks again, Nan. I'll be along. I'm just gonna get Layla settled in."

"All right, sweetheart. I'll be in bed. 'Night."

They stood on the porch and watched, waving, as Nan pulled out. When her headlights were out of sight, Layla turned to him.

"'Get me settled in', huh? What, exactly, does that entail?"

He smirked, tugging her toward him just as she reached behind her to shut off the porch light and leave them in darkness.

"I haven't decided yet."

TWENTY-FIVE

LAYLA USHERED NATE into the house behind her, stifling a yawn. It was late and she had to be up early for Dr. Fields' office in the morning, but she wasn't about to kick him out. Not after the magical night he'd produced for her.

"You look exhausted," he said apologetically.

She shrugged, covering another yawn with her hand.

"I just wasn't ready to say goodnight yet," Nate continued.

The feeling was mutual.

"You kept me up past my bedtime." Her smile was slowed down by her sleepiness, but she still couldn't help it.

"Good thing I'm here to remedy that." Nate took a step forward, pressing a hand on her shoulder as he turned her toward the inner corridors of the house. "Go on with you."

He guided her through the hall to the big bathroom across from her bedroom, then stepped past her to the big clawfoot tub in the end of the long room. She watched, amused, as he perched on the edge of the tub and turned on the water, taking great care to test the temperature until he seemed satisfied. He switched it to the shower, then stood and held out his hand to her.

When she approached, he grasped her dress at the waist, tugging it up and over her head in one smooth motion. She was hyperaware of the harsh lighting in the bathroom, and crossed one arm over her midsection. Yes, he'd seen this already tonight, but moonlight was different than artificial light, and she couldn't help feeling like the magic of the night was about to swirl down the drain with the water in the tub. Her cheeks warmed.

Nate watched her for a moment, his lips pressed together.

"All right," he said finally, turning his back. "I think your body is amazing and powerful, but if this is what you want, I can respect that."

"Thank you," she said quietly, then slipped out of her bra and panties and behind the shower curtain as quickly as she could. The water was warm enough to take any residual chill off but cool enough she wouldn't have any problem sleeping. Closing her eyes and bowing her head into the stream of water, she let it flow over her hair and her back, relaxing...until she heard the rustle of the curtain and realized she wasn't alone. Her back straightened and she let out a short breath. She couldn't *see* Nate but the warmth of his body behind her was undeniable.

Without any words, he touched her shoulder lightly. If he was going to be turned off by her body, he would have already been long gone, she reminded herself. And he'd put in way more time than any reasonable man would if he was just looking to hit it and quit it.

It took her a long minute to relax, and he waited, with no contact but his fingers light on her upper arm. Then he helped her wash her hair, strong fingers massaging her scalp, and soaped up her loofa, making a gentle, non-invasive exploration of her body that felt more intimate than sex. She turned and looped her arms around his neck while his fingers helped the strong pressure of the spray to rinse away the round of conditioner in her hair, their wet bodies sliding together like they belonged that way. His dark eyes met hers and a slow smile tipped one corner of his lips up.

A long sigh came out of her. The magic was still there. The kind of magic a busy, broke single mother couldn't have imagined finding. This was the sort of thing that happened in the movies, not in her own home. Not to Layla Sullivan.

When they were finished, he stepped out first, wrapping a towel around his waist, then finding one of her big bath towels—one of her few new splurges—and held it open for her. She stepped into it and he held her for a moment, pressing kisses to her cheeks and her forehead.

"You going to follow this all the way through?" she asked, tipping her head up. "Tuck me in and everything?"

He laughed, grabbed a smaller towel off the little shelf above the toilet, and started to rub the wetness out of her hair ever-so-gently. "Yeah, I'll tuck you in and everything."

From her hair, Nate moved down her shoulders, across her collarbone, paying special attention as he pressed the soft towel over every inch of her skin until she was completely dry. By the time he'd finished, she was flushed and aroused and all he did was hang the towel over the bar and usher her toward the hall.

Layla frowned when she caught sight of the clock in the kitchen through the doorway.

"It's getting late; you can take off without tucking me in..." He looked like he planned to protest, so she took a shot in the dark. *She* wasn't ready to say goodnight, now. "*Or* you could stay."

She held her breath and watched his expression change to one of hopeful joy.

"Is that what you want, Layla?"

She swallowed, and then nodded. Because despite whatever his intentions were, having him around made her feel good, and it might have been selfish, but she just wanted the comfort of him being there. "I wouldn't have offered if it wasn't."

"You don't have to ask me twice," he said as they moved toward the bedroom door.

"Just let me check on Mason." She paused and nodded toward the bedroom. "Go on in and make yourself comfortable."

She tiptoed down the hall, tightening the knot in her towel as she went, slid into Mason's room, and peered over the edge of the baby's crib. Snug as a bug in a rug, his chubby cheeks flushed with the warmth of sleep. She rested her hand in the middle of his back for a second, the way she always did, to feel the rise and fall of his breaths, and then let out a little sigh of relief. So maybe it was selfish to go to the swimming hole with Nate. Maybe wanting him wasn't something a good mother would do. But nothing bad had happened.

There wasn't anything in the world she wouldn't do or give up to give Mason everything she hadn't had from her parents in her lifetime, but today made her feel like maybe she *could* have something for herself, too. *Without* being a bad mother. Yawning, she checked that the monitor was on, and headed back down the hall to her room. Nate had done as she'd told him, stretched out on his back under the covers with the bedside lamp turned on. His broad chest was exposed, and a cursory glance around the room showed the towel he'd worn hanging over the back of a chair. He had turned back the blankets on her side of the bed and patted the exposed mattress, and she climbed in without thinking twice about their nudity. Because she was exhausted, and because she wanted to be close to him.

~

Nate drew her close, so she was curled into his chest with her head resting on his bicep, her warm softness flush against his hip, and pressed a kiss to her forehead. He curled one arm around her shoulders and stroked her hair, and though she had started tense, she relaxed with a long breath, settling against him.

"You know I'd never even actually *been* to the swimming hole," she said so quietly he wasn't sure he'd heard right.

"No way."

"I never got invited and I was too smart to go by myself. So...thank you." He felt her cheek swell with a smile against his chest. "I had fun, and it was better than I imagined it would be as a teenager."

He bent, kissing her forehead again, his heart swelling. There was a lot of stuff she'd missed out on, if town gossip was true. Silly, simple things that made great memories in his own childhood. Things he was now determined to help her experience. "It *was* better than it was as a teenager."

She was silent for a moment, and then she let out a little sigh, her soft fingertips tracing designs in the middle of his chest. He angled his hips away from her thigh so she wouldn't feel the evidence of his arousal. He hadn't in a million years anticipated the invitation to stay the night, so he definitely wasn't prepared. He could have easily turned over and fallen into her soft warmth for the rest of the night, but he knew they needed more time; and since it was the only thing he had to give her, he would.

"I'm glad Nan came to sit with Mason. It's not always that easy, you know."

"Hmm?" he inquired, closing his eyes and letting himself relax into her gentle touch.

"I can't just take off at the drop of a hat."

He cracked his eyes open and slanted his gaze down at her. Her eyes were wide open, her fingers paused. He frowned.

"I know that. I just thought this would be nice."

"And it was. But...I don't..." She blew out a breath and he felt tension stiffen her body again. She needed to sleep, because morning would come too early, but there was clearly something on her mind, so he didn't stop brushing his palm up and down her arm, encouraging her to get the words out when she was ready.

"What are you getting at, Lay?" he asked gently.

"This is how it *is* when you're a parent. Quiet nights at home. Can't go anywhere without the baby, or a babysitter, which I can't afford. It's just...probably not what you're used to." She didn't meet his gaze and he gave her shoulder a squeeze.

"You don't think?"

"I know what Denver's like. Or I hear, anyways."

"Denver hasn't been like that for me for a while now." He chuckled. "But I get it. And maybe it's a little different than I'm used to, but that doesn't make me want it any less. I can't think of a better place to be right now."

She remained quiet for a moment, her eyes trained on her fingers, still on his pecs.

"And if I didn't want to be here, I wouldn't be. Please trust me when I tell you these things."

Finally, she lifted her gaze and he smiled. "Okay."

"Now go to sleep, morning's gonna come early."

He reached over her to turn off the bedside lamp, pressed another kiss to her forehead and curled her in his arms.

TWENTY-SIX

LAYLA'S ALARM PLAYED an acoustic strum and she stretched to reach it, only to find herself trapped underneath Nate's blissfully warm, heavy...*naked* sleeping body. Further, she realized, as she willed her arm to be *just* a bit longer, pressing up from the foot of the bed with her toes and feeling the slide of skin on skin—she was naked, too. And nothing had happened.

He drew in a quick breath that was dangerously close to a snore, and shifted onto his back, freeing her to turn off the alarm. It wasn't nearly enough sleep, but it would have to do, and she wouldn't have traded last night's date for three extra days of sleep, no matter how badly she needed it. She slid out from under Nate's arm and observed him in the early morning light, his face slack with sleep, dark stubble peppering his jaw. She'd let him sleep a bit longer. Shouldering her robe from the hook on the back of her closet door, she walked along the cool wood floors into the hall.

Mason gurgled happily in his crib, keeping true to his 'trick baby' status, and smiled a huge toothy grin when she popped her head over the crib rails and reached down to draw him up into her arms.

They settled into the rocker in his room to nurse before breakfast. Mason was well started on solids but Layla still relished these quiet moments. It was just the two of them, and nothing else. She pumped bottles for Kerri to feed him but still nursed him when she was home; it was one of the ways she reconnected with the baby when it felt like she'd been away too long.

Mason was in his high chair while she mixed cereal for him when Nate finally wandered out into the kitchen and leaned against the doorframe. *Thank God he put on pants.*

She'd been too tired the night before to act on the fact that Nate Montgomery had been stretched out, naked and aroused, in her bed, but she could have eked out an extra ten minutes this morning, somehow, if he hadn't already dressed. Even with jeans on, that broad, muscled chest was a lot of temptation. And that slow, sexy smile he gave her as he watched her move about her standard morning routine was begging to be kissed.

"Morning." His voice rumbled with leftover sleep. "Anything I can do to help?"

She shook her head. "Not really...get your own coffee, I guess?"

He shuffled into the kitchen, entirely too close for comfort, and she found herself bumping him with her hip when she turned around. He dropped the spoon he was stirring his coffee with and grabbed her around the waist with his free arm, tugging her to him.

"And maybe put on a shirt," she squeaked, all the air gone out of her.

"What about breakfast?" he asked, ignoring her request as he released her and crossed the floor to peer into the fridge, perfectly at home. It hadn't bothered her before but now it unnerved her, and it might have had something to do with his state of undress. "You hungry?"

"Oh I usually just have a bagel or grab a muffin at Hinkley's."

"Because you don't have time, right?"

"You're not wrong." She picked up Mason's cereal bowl and crossed the floor, pulling a chair up in front of the baby to feed him. He was as good an eater as he was a sleeper, so things moved quickly, but not quickly enough for her to make a real breakfast for herself *and* feed him, especially when she was already moving slowly.

"Well, you're having breakfast this morning," he said as he turned from the fridge with a carton of eggs and the milk in hand. He caught her glancing at the clock on the wall and shook his head. "You have time, trust me."

"Careful now," she said with a laugh, spooning more cereal into Mason's waiting mouth. "I might get used to having you around in the mornings."

"That's the plan." Nate didn't look up as he started moving around the kitchen, finding a bowl and a frying pan, and assembling everything for what looked like scrambled eggs. She didn't have anything in the way of breakfast meat but a plateful of eggs would go a lot farther than a blueberry muffin from Hinkley's, and probably cost a lot less, too.

Not five minutes later, he brought two plates of eggs and toast to the table, and slid in across from her. "You wanna trade places so you have time to eat?"

She paused a moment, glancing across the table at him, then back to Mason, who had been eating well enough. Her stomach growled as she got a whiff of the eggs and her mind was made up. She pushed her chair back and got up, and they did a rotation without changing the untouched plates. Nate pulled up in front of Mason, who flashed him a big, soggy-cereal-mouthed smile, and if there was ever a time Layla wished she could tell him the truth, this was it. The two had struck up the cutest friendship she'd ever seen. Mason was always happy to see Nate and Nate seemed to reciprocate. He was so gentle and quiet and patient with their son it made her ache to share her secret.

One eye on the pair of them, she started into her plate of food; deliciously creamy and perfectly cooked. He was a natural, and the child seemed to kick into a second level of happiness as Nate fed him. It was heartwarming and heartbreaking all at once. It was easy to fall into this kind of family unit, but it couldn't last. Try as he might, Nate wasn't the settling down sort. Not with her, anyway.

A car rumbled in the driveway and she was almost out of her seat before she realized what she was doing. Kerri, early, as always.

"You *have* to go get dressed."

He raised a skeptical brow at her bath robe, and leisurely offered the baby another spoonful of cereal.

"I'm in a bath robe when Kerri gets here *every* day. *You* are not supposed to be here, never mind half-naked."

It was too late to hide his truck behind the house; he should at least *try* to pretend like he hadn't spent the night. For decency's sake, if nothing else. Kerri knew Nate was hanging around a lot, and she wasn't about to go spreading the word, but she'd be asking questions later. Questions Layla didn't have any answers to, anyway. What *had* happened last night?

She breathed a sigh of relief when he finally got up, handing her the bowl before he made his way back to the bedroom, not hurrying quite enough for her taste. He emerged, pulling his t-shirt down over his abs as she heard Kerri's feet on the porch.

"Morning..." The girl stopped up short when she saw Nate. "Good morning, *everybody*."

"Morning," Nate replied way more casually than Layla felt.

Awkward. Kerri always showed up early so Layla could grab a quick shower and get dressed, but since she'd showered the night before, she was farther ahead of the game than she would have been any other time. Besides, when she moved the right way, she could still smell the delicious scent of Nate on her skin and she wasn't about to go washing that off just yet, even if it was only from being held all night.

"I'm almost ready. We'll be out of your hair in no time." She shot to the bedroom to get dressed, leaving Nate to fend for himself with Kerri. She heard their voices, the words indistinct, but it sounded like small talk. Quickly, she braided her hair over her shoulder, smoothed on a pair of dark wash jeans and a sleeveless button-down blouse for 'casual Friday', and emerged from the bedroom just in time to see Nate scooping Mason up out of his chair. She had to wonder how he was so at ease. He was the younger of the Montgomery brothers, and there were no sisters. No close family to have babysat cousins. He was just a natural, evidently.

"All set." It must have been a joint effort to wash his face and hands because the baby was tidy and stretching his arms out for her.

Nate shuffled over and handed Mason off to her. "Here's your mama."

~

Layla folded Mason into her arms and Nate made himself take a step away, lest he make it a group hug. He didn't think there was much that could make him happier than the last eight hours had. He headed to the door and put on his boots while Layla said her goodbyes, giving the baby a kiss on the top of his head before she joined him at the door.

"See ya, Ker." He tipped his head and held the door open for Layla. She stepped out onto the porch. "Why don't you let me drive you?"

"Kind of defeats the purpose of fixing my car, doesn't it?" She glanced up at him, skepticism written all over her features.

"Humor me. I don't have anything else on my schedule for this morning. You're starting my day with purpose."

She smiled and shook her head, but when she stepped off the porch, she headed toward his truck.

"Besides, that means I'm guaranteed to see you again tonight."

"I swear, Nate Montgomery, you're going to get sick of my face eventually," she said as they climbed in.

"Not possible," he said with a grin as the engine of his truck roared to life.

They barely got out onto the road when he reached across the space between them and closed his fingers over her knee. She glanced over but made no move to deter him. Instead, she covered his hand with hers, brushing her thumb over the back of his knuckles. A simple, innocent gesture that heated his blood more than he cared to admit. He reminded himself of her proclamation on that first date—she wasn't looking for the same hot, casual thing they'd had before. His brain had a good hold on that one—his body...not so much. But he hadn't made it this far in life by not having any self-control.

"What's on the bill for today?" she asked absently as they navigated the streets of Three Rivers. Casual, comforting, like they were a couple.

"I thought I'd probably head over to the Baylors for a visit. The boys want to talk more about this plan for a rodeo school they've brewed up now that I think Lily's finally given up on a career in roping for me."

She glanced over and smiled. He waited for the other shoe to drop—eventually she'd ask about why he was staying, why he was planning a way to make a living in Three Rivers instead of going back to Denver, but the questions never came. They'd struck a balance, enjoying one another's company, but not prying too deep. He liked it that way—eventually, he'd have to tell her what was going on, but not yet.

He pulled up to the curb in front of Hinkley's and her look turned questioning. He shrugged, then tapped the digital clock on the truck's dash radio. "You're early. We'll grab coffee."

The diner was half a block from her work, and small town blocks didn't count the same as city blocks—there was time. They climbed out of the truck and he held the door to Hinkley's open for Layla. Tina was working and she blustered happily when he walked in. She'd always had a soft spot for him, and this was his first visit since he'd come home to Three Rivers.

"Oh Nate Montgomery, look at you!"

"Tina, my best girl!" Nate hugged the waitress—she acted like he was a celebrity come to town, which was laughable, now. There had been a time when he felt ten feet tall and bullet proof, but that had been before Night Train. Now, the friendliness meant more to him than the acclaim. He needed friends in his corner because he didn't have a whole hell of a lot besides that. And maybe that was why being with Layla quieted him so much. She had no expectations, no image in her mind of the man he ought to be. She let him see a slice of her authentic life, and he got to relax and be exactly who he was with her. "You gonna hook us up with some coffee?"

Layla had hung back; not quite the same girl who had been fearlessly manning the bar at Danny's when he'd first reconnected with her. Now she was a reflection of the girl she'd been in school. Quiet, reserved, and uncomfortable. Like she didn't belong, not a hundred percent. It had been her default when they were younger, but it surprised him now because she *had* said she stopped in for a muffin almost every morning. Her family had been an easy target—both of her parents unable to work, her brothers constantly getting into fights—the quintessential girl from the wrong side of the tracks. He was certain she heard the same whispers he had, and at some point, that had chipped away at her. Another change he resolved to make for her. She was as hardworking and fundamentally *good* as any other person sitting in this damn diner, she deserved to be treated that way, and act like it, too.

He reached for her hand, drawing her up to the counter with him, and Tina smiled broadly, never missing a beat. Layla pulled her hand out of his almost like he'd burnt her. He got that she was a private kind of girl but he thought they'd made a ton of progress in the last little bit, and people would have had to have been blind to miss how often his truck was parked outside of her work in the last week. So was he misreading everything by thinking they might be ready to take the relationship out in public?

"Morning, Layla."

"Morning, Tina." There—her voice didn't falter a bit. She was good at a brave face at least. He tucked the niggling away when the coffee arrived, dropped a five dollar bill on the counter, and bid the waitress farewell, ushering Layla out of the diner.

The walk to Dr. Fields' office door wasn't long enough. Pausing in front of the glass door to the office, she turned to him, looking as uncertain as a girl at the front door at the end of a first date.

He wanted to kiss her. Lean in and lay one on her like it was a normal part of their day—he'd spent the night last night, for crying out loud. But this was her place of work and the hesitance written on her face made him take pause too. He reached out and snagged her hand, giving it a gentle squeeze.

"I'll see you tonight."

Her smile was braver, and better.

TWENTY-SEVEN

LAYLA'S STOMACH GROWLED so loudly she was sure Dr. Fields' could hear it behind his closed exam room door. Frowning, she glanced at her watch and let out a sigh. She'd left the house without a lunch this morning and with plans to grab something at Hinkley's, but then she'd been in the diner already today, with Nate, with his hand on hers. Tongues would be wagging. Her heart wasn't ready to face up to that. Her stomach protested.

Finally, she pushed back from her desk and grabbed her purse, letting out a sigh as she did. Stepping out into the sunshine, she did a brief survey of the parking lot of Hinkley's—not too many repeats, but the most important one...the waitress...well, her little economy car was sitting in one of the employee spots, just like it did every week day from 7 to 3:30.

Layla paused with her hand on the door handle, lifted her chin, drew in a deep breath and let it out. It was just soup and a sandwich. She was under no obligation to be harassed by anyone about what she did with her person time and she had as much right as anyone else to grab lunch at the local diner, so long as she paid.

Tina greeted her with the same big smile she had this morning. "Hey hun. Just one?"

Layla nodded—she was always just one—and Tina pointed to the booth she typically took. Crossing the floor, Layla took a peek at today's patrons. Mostly regulars; just about anybody who worked in 'downtown' Three Rivers came here for lunch since it was the only option. Nobody she remembered seeing this morning. She slid into the booth and Tina brought her a coffee and a water.

She ordered her usual and pulled out her phone to touch base with Kerri at home, thinking she was nearly in the clear...until Tina paused after sliding her order onto the table in front of her.

"Say...you were in here this morning with Nate Montgomery, weren't you?"

The smile Layla pasted on was almost as forced as when she was visiting with her mother.

"Yes."

The waitress looked like she was waiting for more. Layla wouldn't be rude, but she wasn't going to volunteer anything, either. It just wasn't good sense. There *were* times when it paid to get out ahead of the rumor mill and set things straight before they started spreading, but she couldn't justify it in this case. Not when she felt like the next day could bring everything crashing down around her ears anyway.

"You know, the two of you make a sweet couple."

There it was, the other shoe. Layla drew in a slow breath and smiled up at Tina.

"Oh, it's not anything like that. He's been helping me out with the house."

"Well *I* wouldn't mind a little bit of Nate Montgomery on the side, Layla. He's a good guy. Maybe you should ask him to stay for dinner some night after he's done with the house stuff."

Doing her best not to laugh, Layla shook her head and took a mouthful of soup. If Tina only knew.

"He *is* a good guy. But you know as well as I do how hard it is to find time for a man when you've got to bust your hump feeding and clothing your kids."

Volleying the conversation back on the waitress helped, because she stepped back, her keen eyes losing their intensity. Layla had spoken right to the crux of the single mother's plight, and it seemed like it might work to curb the gossip. There were *some* things that couldn't be controlled, but this Layla felt confident about...as long as she could put her own spin on it.

"You're right, but if a girl had the time..." Tina grinned, shaking her head. "Did anybody think Nate Montgomery would ever come back to be Three Rivers' most eligible bachelor? Not a snowball's chance in hell."

Layla hid a little smile as her stomach fluttered. Someone was calling Nate a 'most eligible bachelor' and little did they know he'd spent the night in *her* bed. Layla Sullivan, of all people, had, for now, for all intents and purposes, snagged Three Rivers' most eligible bachelor. It was a small treasure she didn't want to let go of.

"It's like a stroke of pure luck that he had that accident and ended up back here. I mean, not that he *had* the accident—he was busted up *bad*, I wouldn't wish that on anybody. Or the part where he lost everything."

That fluttering was soon replaced by a couple of other things—a little bit of jealousy she couldn't explain, and then pain. He'd lost everything? He'd never mentioned it. She'd never asked. She knew he'd been laid up bad—she'd seen the medical file. But she hadn't ever thought about what that accident had truly *cost* Nate. What it meant for him to be back here for the 'foreseeable future'. She'd been so caught up in what their being together looked like for her, what it would cost her for the truth to come out, she'd never considered him as the second part to the equation.

"Anyway, I'll leave you to it."

With that, Tina turned and went back to her duties as if she hadn't just ripped a gash in Layla's world.

TWENTY-EIGHT

THAT NIGHT, AFTER Nate dropped her off to run errands for Nan, and Kerri left for the evening, Layla flipped open her laptop on the kitchen island. A small luxury, she'd bought it secondhand. Mostly to look up parenting advice online, but she used it once in a while to look up videos for the home repairs she didn't know anything about. Without it, she'd never have figured out how to clean the grease out of the pipes under the sink. And when she was feeling a little anxious, she watched cooking videos that she never actually tried to do—half out of fear of burning her house down and half because she couldn't afford the luxury ingredients.

One thing she hadn't done, not until now, was give in to the temptation to watch the video of Nate's wreck. Her brother, Jimmy, had mentioned it—mostly in a weirdly celebratory hateful kind of way, because he'd never been a fan of the Montgomerys...or the Baylors...or just about any ranch family in town—but it hadn't seemed right at a time when everyone was waiting for news that

Nate had come out of the woods. And then she hadn't thought about it again. Until Tina had talked about it today.

He *looked* perfectly fine—plus or minus a few scars she'd figured came with the territory. And the medical records indicated he was perfectly fine. But she knew from experience that, physically *or* emotionally, fine-on-the-outside didn't say anything about the inside.

It took a little digging around—as prolific as he'd been on the circuit, there were a lot of videos on the Internet of Nate Montgomery riding bulls. She could only remember that the accident had been sometime around her third trimester, so she tried a few different dates before she finally typed in 'Nate Montgomery Bull Riding Wreck'. There were a few results in the list, but she scrolled down to the one titled, in capital letters, 'NATE MONTGOMERY CAREER ENDING WRECK'.

She held her breath and pressed play, watching the coverage in the chute as Nate straddled the bull, wrapping the bull rope around his gloved hand. At least he had the good sense to wear a helmet with a faceguard and what she guessed was a Kevlar vest. All she knew about rodeo could probably fit in a thimble; her only experience had been locally, but as the camera panned back to get a wide angle of the arena into which they would release Nate on the back of this bull, named 'Night Train', according to the info banner along the bottom of the screen, the size and breadth of the grandstand told her this was nothing like the local stuff she'd seen. Ten times the population of Three Rivers filled the stands, and the noise was deafening.

A horn pierced through the chanting of the crowd—she could have sworn they were saying

'Nate! Nate! Nate!'—the gate flew open, and fifteen hundred pounds of pure, flea-bitten bovine fury erupted from the chute. Layla bit her lip, her eyes darting between the timer in the bottom corner of the screen and the bull and rider. She knew he needed eight seconds, but that timer seemed to move at an agonizing pace. 4...The giant animal's head rooted and his rear hooves flew into the air over and over and Nate stayed with him, tipping back when the bull vaulted his haunches upward and forward enough to stay with him when his head came up...7...Layla held her breath and watched the bull change direction, while Nate's body stayed perfectly centered over his tied-down hand, the other in the air. Finally, the buzzer sounded and the clock in the corner stopped and she let out a long breath, her stomach feeling like a bag of jelly. Until she focused again on Nate. He jerked his rope hand a couple of times, but it didn't come loose, and he seemed to be so focused on that that when the bull's head rose again, his body didn't rock back enough to avoid being struck, hard, by one of the bull's sawed-off horns. Hard enough that his body crumpled forward. As four mounted cowboys tried to close in on the pair, it was obvious something wasn't right.

All that wiggly feeling in Layla's stomach rose up into her throat and she thought she should turn the video off before it went any further, but she hesitated just long enough to see Nate's big body come unseated, dragging beside the bull by his caught-up hand. Two, three, four big bucks and close to the edge of the sand arena, the offside weight of his rider's lifeless body pulled the bull so far off balance that when he came down out of the air, he landed on his side, on top of Nate. The bull struggled for a moment, but was back up quickly, jerking away from the scene and leaving Nate Montgomery—a man she'd always known to be just a little larger than life—in a crumpled heap near the rail.

Layla sat back suddenly, slamming the laptop lid closed just a little too quickly. *Okay,* she said to herself, breathing through her nose to keep her stomach at bay. *Okay, he's still alive.*

She slid off her stool and looked around the kitchen, a little shell-shocked, but overwhelmed with the need to busy herself with something besides the image of Nate's body—which, today, appeared big, strong, and healthy—being crushed under the bull. She'd become a lot more emotional in the last few years, especially since Mason had come along, and tears pricked at the backs of her eyelids as she started filling the sink to wash the dinner dishes—something she might have normally left until tomorrow since they were so minimal.

It was times like these, alone in her house with tears in her eyes, she wished she had someone to consider a friend. Kerri was about as close as she came, but the Baylors and Montgomerys were so close, she was hesitant to really spill her guts. Her whole adult life felt like an intricate series of secrets woven together, and she barely kept the cover on everything, but only because she didn't have a large circle of friends who might accidentally leak something or be overheard talking about those bits of her life that she kept to herself, out of necessity.

Beside the laptop, her phone dinged with a text message. She dried her hands and crossed the floor. Wary of the closed laptop that had shown her so much gut-wrenching scariness, she picked up the phone, then turned her back to the counter and the computer on it, unlocking the screen.

Busy?

Despite herself, she smiled, because he should have known by now it wouldn't matter what she was doing, she'd drop it, because his visits were the best part of her day besides coming home to Mason.

Very. And important.

A couple seconds later, the phone buzzed in her hand.

Sounds terrible. I'll be there in five.

Which meant he wasn't coming from Nan's. When she heard his diesel engine rumbling in after about three minutes, she knew he'd been at the Baylors. She was still stationed at the island when she heard his boots on the porch steps. She'd told him early on he could—often, she'd be in the nursery with Mason and not hear the door, or not be able to get there quickly enough, so he let himself in.

It was silly, because she already knew he was fine—he'd been in this very kitchen a half dozen times—but she still felt her scalp tingle with relief when he opened the screen door and stepped inside. She held herself back from rushing to greet him, to take him in for just one second, and in that beat, his face twisted, a crease between his brows.

~

Layla looked like she'd just seen a ghost. Or been to a funeral. Or something. Awareness pricked at the edges of his consciousness as he took in the scene—her, with her back to the kitchen island, and her laptop closed on the countertop. Sadness written all over her face.

The house was quiet—Mason would have gone to bed a couple hours ago, and while he enjoyed spending time with the child, he just as much enjoyed the stillness and peace in her home when everything had wound down for the day and the only thing left to do was hold her on the porch and watch the stars. He'd tried to get away earlier to see Mason before bedtime, but the Baylor boys had been so excited about the funding they'd put together for the rodeo school—a sponsor, on top of the money they were fronting— he hadn't been able to get away until Emma and Lily were edging their respective husbands back toward their homes, with talk of morning chores. He couldn't help but feel like if he had managed to get here earlier, he could have helped Layla avoid the trouble that was furrowing a line across her forehead as she looked at him.

"What?" he asked. "Is everything okay?"

"Yes, yes, of course."

He watched her unsuccessfully try to smooth out the tells on her features—the lines around her mouth, her drawn brow. Crossing the floor in a couple of easy strides, he slipped one arm around her waist, and that was when a real smile touched at her eyes. Not a whole lot, but enough. He slid his free hand along her jaw, touching the corner of her mouth with the pad of his thumb.

"Tell me," he said quietly, the calm and serenity of the good day he'd had wrenched right out of him to see Layla so upset.

She pressed her lips together and let out a short breath through her nose, like she was making up her mind.

"I watched a video of..." she trailed off, but he didn't have to hear the rest to know. He'd taken for granted half of his circle in Denver had been there to see the wreck in person; the other half had caught it on the finals highlights. He didn't have to have this conversation with most of them. The rumor mill had taken care of most of Three Rivers, but the way Layla made her best attempt to skirt the edges of that small-town staple should have told him she hadn't seen the video.

He could barely stand the way she looked at him now, like he was some broken, fragile thing she needed to feel sorry for and handle with care. He'd seen that look before—it had been one of the reasons he wasn't that upset about leaving Denver, aside from the part where he lost his little spread and everything else he owned. At least here, people knew him as something besides 'superstar bull rider', but every buckle bunny who sashayed by after the accident gave him this very same look. It made him feel like less of a man.

And Layla had never looked at him like that yet. It was one of the things he liked about being with her. For a couple hours a day, he wasn't that guy in the video who lost everything; he was just the guy who felt like a million bucks when he was with her.

"I wish you hadn't," he said quietly, still cupping her jaw, his eyes fixed on hers. She was so pretty, and soft, and she did things to his insides he could barely admit to himself. And his body—well, his body appreciated her just fine.

"Why?" Her tone matched his, her voice low. He hadn't backed off, and still held her to him as a light flush began to creep up her cheeks.

"Because now you're looking at me like *that*."

"Like what?"

"Like I'm still that guy lying in the dirt in Denver." Putting words to it made him more vulnerable than he'd been when he woke up in the hospital after the wreck. "Like I'm half a man. Like I'll break."

She got a little closer then, her tongue darting out to wet her lips. Her fingers lifted to touch his jaw lightly. She'd touched him like this a dozen times since they'd started spending time together, but it felt different now, more charged.

"Are you?"

"What?"

"Are you still that guy lying in the dirt in Denver?"

In so many ways he was, but he'd never admit it. But in other ways, ways that had been cultivated over the last couple of weeks, being able to provide *something* for her, even if it *was* just hanging the kitchen cupboard door that had fallen off, he was shedding that man.

And the man who was emerging was one who wanted her so bad his knees were weak at this proximity. He'd respected her declaration from the first date. He'd spent the time and energy to show her just how valuable and worth it she was. But the desire to prove he was still all man pressed at the back of his mind, like a ringing phone that needed to be answered.

"No," he responded, shifting half a step forward, his hands sliding down her sides to grasp her hips and hike her up onto the counter behind her. She squealed, reaching behind herself to push the laptop aside. He settled into the spot her open legs made like it was designed specifically for him. "And I'm not the guy I was two years ago, either. But the one I am now, the one I am with you...well, he's a hell of a lot better."

"Yeah, I like him all right." A wicked grin bent her lips, and she tugged him closer, the mood lifting almost instantly as her fingertips slid along his scalp, her forehead pressed against his. She was so close, but not close enough. Her admission had been silly and playful, but it made his heart swell. He filled his hands with the swell of her ass and tugged her forward against him. When she sat back and raised an eyebrow at him, her light eyes clouded with desire, he knew she felt the same.

~

If she'd doubted for a second Nate didn't want her now like he had wanted her two years ago, he erased all of it when she sat back and he followed her, chasing her lips and covering them with his in a kiss that made her bare toes curl and her knees tighten against his hips. The weeks following their first date had been filled with so much intimacy but so little actual physical touch, she'd been almost sure they were devolving into something platonic. Comfortable, like a worn sweater—she couldn't say she didn't like that, but not headed back in the direction they'd come from. She was wrong. She'd never been so happy to be wrong in her life.

A shiver of delight ran up her spine when Nate's rough knuckles grazed against her collarbone as he drew back from the kiss and started to unbutton her shirt. His fingers moved sure, but slow, his dark eyes trained on the skin he was exposing, inch by inch. He'd even seen her—held her—naked in the last few weeks, but this felt different. Everything about this night felt different.

Wanted. That's how it felt. It tasted just like the weekend they'd spent together two years ago but with something just a bit sharper, just a bit heavier, with a little more meaning.

When he'd finally finished with the buttons, he slid her shirt carefully off her shoulders with a reverence she'd never been touched with before.

For the first time, she didn't feel like covering herself up or hiding herself from his eyes. No, it almost felt like an honor to offer herself up for his viewing pleasure. He took her in, all soft midsection and stretch marks around her belly button she hated, then his eyes lifted and met hers, and it was beyond clear *he* didn't hate them. His hands pressed to the back pockets of her blue jeans and he lifted her off the counter.

"Nate," she tried to reason. She was too heavy. He was a big man, as strong and robust as any she knew, but she'd seen the video, the crumpled heap. Nan had talked about the time spent in the hospital. Again, tears pricked behind her eyelids, but this time she was embarrassed. He'd drop her, or hurt himself. But he wasn't hearing any of it. He shook his head, shushing her, and she tightened her grip with her legs around his waist, her fingers twisted behind his neck.

"I told you I'm not that guy in the dirt," he murmured, laying kisses on the curve between her jaw and the strap of her bra as he crossed the floor into the back part of the house, heading toward the bedroom. "I can't stand for you to treat me like I am."

His voice was low and rough, laden with emotion, and she threaded her fingers through his hair and nodded, her heart pinching. All this time, he'd asked nothing of her—this was the least she could do.

"I won't."

"Besides," he said, lowering her onto her bed, and breaking their clinch just long enough to pull his t-shirt over his head. "*Your* doctor cleared me for 'all reasonable activity'. And I say making love to you right now is reasonable. *Beyond* reasonable, actually. And well overdue."

His words made her laugh, but they also tugged at something deep in her belly. Something that had been dormant far too long. Her eyes traced over the curves and lines of the muscles in his shoulders, across the little curls of dark hair on his pecs, down his midsection, right to the waistband of those jeans he still wore. Those needed to come off, too.

Before she had a chance to make that happen, he slid a hand behind her shoulders, and in one movement, she'd moved up the bed about a foot, and his belt buckle was out of reach. *Damn.* But then his mouth started at her collarbone, his teeth nipping, his tongue soothing with gentle flicks as he moved down, and all thoughts of his jeans disappeared as she focused on the top of his head moving lower. She felt his fingers at the button of her jeans. Soon, he'd come face to face with stretch marks—the ones she'd had since she was a teenager and grew too tall and too big too fast, and then new ones on top of those, from when her belly had swollen and grown with Mason inside. It felt silly now, but for a time, she'd thought of Nate anytime her fingers passed over those shallow marks on her body. Now it was *his* fingers touching them, and the urge to shrink away from his touch, to shield her body from his focused attentions, warred with the urge to push up into his touch, to beg for more. The latter won out as he slid a hand down to her hip, pressing his fingers into her flesh, and she turned her aching, needing body toward him.

With practiced agility, he undid the fly of her jeans, exposing the frumpy cotton panties she'd put on this morning because she'd never imagined this with the snail's pace they'd gone at for the last few weeks. For a second, she was self-conscious about that, until he reached between them, sliding his palm down over her belly until his fingers tucked into the waistband of the plain underwear. He moved slow enough, the callouses on his fingertips raising goosebumps on her sides, that her thoughts narrowed down to just where he was headed; how that would feel, arousing her to the point where she tipped her pelvis toward them. She felt his smile against her shoulder. *Just one touch.* So many times she'd nearly combusted just sitting next to him on the porch with those fingers playing over the skin of her upper arm, feather light and teasing, or stroking her hair—things that weren't *meant* to arouse her—now he was using them with that sort of intent, she wasn't sure how long much longer she could wait.

His fingers disappeared into her underwear, coming to rest just inches from the destination she needed most, and Nate lifted his head.

"What do you want, Layla?"

She held her breath, embarrassed to put words to the feelings inside her that moved her body toward him even when her brain told her it was a bad idea. She hadn't stopped reminding herself since Nate had come back on the scene how dangerous wanting something was. But right now, all she could think about was the press of his fingers and just how good it would feel if he just moved a bit lower. But she'd never been asked what she wanted, never felt like she'd deserved to have an opinion about it.

"Tell me," he insisted, his voice rasping when she didn't reply. She met his eyes, desperately trying to convey how uncomfortable voicing it would make her, but she didn't find sympathy. Instead, his intense gaze made it abundantly clear he would stop—would take away all the goodness—if she didn't give him what he wanted. Her words.

He wanted her desire; he wanted to know she wanted him. *That* would remind him he wasn't still that man in the dirt in Denver. But it would cost her, and she wasn't sure just how much yet. Still, he had given and given in the last few weeks, with almost nothing in return.

"You," she finally whispered, closing her eyes tight against the hotness of tears she couldn't explain.

He nipped at her cheek lightly, his voice close to her ear. He'd shifted back up the bed.

"Me to what?"

She let out a whoosh of breath, her heart burning.

"I want...I want you to touch me, Nate."

She was rewarded with the gentlest of touches, his fingers tracing over her most intimate parts.

"Like this?" he whispered.

"Yes...I need..." she whimpered, pressing up, and he gave, finding a light but steady rhythm of movement over her sensitive center.

"*Need*," he repeated back to her, and she felt like breaking apart. What she needed was *not* to need Nate Montgomery, but then he shifted, his movements speeding up, her hips pushing up into him, and she could feel an orgasm coming on her like a tsunami, swallowing up everything in its path, including any resistance she might have had left, until she was drowning in pleasure and need and the smell and sound of him.

She barely had time to gasp out about the condoms in her drawer—a precaution she'd picked up after his first sleepover. At the time, she'd felt like she was jinxing things but as much as she loved Mason, she wasn't ready to repeat that mistake again. He pulled away for just a moment to look after it, then moved over her quickly, working her out of her jeans and panties like magic, and covered her mouth with his as he pressed into her with no preamble, filling his hands with her fleshy hips and angling them for more contact while she was still spiraling to the surface of her orgasm. Dropping her head back against the pillow, Layla let out a sharp breath, her fingers scrabbling against his shoulders in an attempt to anchor herself to some semblance of sanity. The pace Nate set was quick, deep, and intense, and by the time she felt like she was catching up there was already another storm of pleasure brewing, threatening to drown her completely.

Nate's left hand moved from her hip to her thigh, drawing it up tight against his waist, touching on parts of her he hadn't yet. Too quickly, she felt like she was losing any kind of control she'd had over the situation. The last two years had been a careful balance of control and good judgment, and right now, Layla had neither. Her breaths measured out in time to the friction of Nate's body touching on the most sensitive parts of her and she couldn't stop herself from letting out a low moan as her eyes slid shut.

She felt his fingers at her hairline, and heard the smile on his voice.

"It's all right, Lay. Let me hear you."

She opened her eyes to find him watching her with an intensity and desire she'd never seen, never felt so keenly as she did then. This was their first encounter multiplied by all of the time and emotion they'd shared over the last few weeks. She swallowed hard, her breath coming out in short pants she couldn't regulate. Right now, he shifted and her world shattered. Her eyes went wide and she clung to his shoulders, sobbing his name like a prayer.

~

"You keep up like that and I won't let you go back to Denver *ever*."

Nothing made Nate feel more like a whole man than holding Layla, warm and soft, curled into his side, after they'd cleaned up. With her head resting on his bicep, and her front pressed against his side, her fingers drew circles over his chest, down his ribs, tracing over the big scar down his side. That was a new one, courtesy of Night Train. She slid her fingers down the length of it, then back up again, pausing at the top.

"The wreck?" she asked.

He'd been enjoying the quiet intimacy—something he hadn't had in a long time—and not thinking about Denver or his failed rodeo career at all. When he first came home, it was all he could think about; how the wreck had made him feel like less of a man. But the taste of her, the sound of her, the thought of her face soft and slack with pleasure; they'd erased any thoughts he'd had about the wreck.

He blew out a slow breath. He didn't *want* to talk about it, but they'd just crossed another line. One he couldn't cross back over. He had taken—maybe more than she could afford to give—and now he would give.

"Yeah."

She thought he'd go back to Denver. Maybe not right away—he *had* told her it was for the foreseeable future—but she believed he would someday go back.

She deserved truth. He filled the silence with it.

"I'm not going back to Denver, ever."

Her fingers stopped, he felt her head lift, her eyes on him. He didn't look down. Admitting to himself he'd never go back to the rodeo was one thing, hearing it from the doctor was another, but saying it out loud to the woman he wanted, that was entirely different. Bull riding had been his entire identity for the last ten years; it was hard to speak it into life. It was admitting he had nothing to offer her. No career meant no money, no security, and no future.

"But?"

"But the doc says not to ride bulls anymore. That's what I do, I ride bulls."

"There must be something else you can do," she said, her voice soft, tentative. She didn't know what rodeo was like, and she was trying to be positive. Sure, they were talking about this rodeo school thing, but who knew if that would even pan out. Was that something he could bank his future on? What if there was no demand?

"You trying to get rid of me?" He craned his neck to look down at her now, raising a brow. She caught him looking a second too late, pasting on the playful smile only *after* he'd seen her features shrouded in quiet thought. He sighed, lowering his head back down to the pillow, curling his fingers against the soft curve of her hip. Touching her comforted him. "That accident gave me a fractured spine and a lacerated liver, among other things. It was four days before I came to. Even if I wanted to, I couldn't get back on a bull. Not in this lifetime. And I don't want to. There's nothing for me in Denver, Layla. My ranch, my home—that's all gone. Three Rivers is my home. Noah and Finn are putting the wheels on the rodeo school. It might pan out—but if it doesn't, I'll find work somewhere else. Maybe I'll sell hammers. I saw the hardware store was looking for a clerk."

Her warm hand smoothed over his shoulder, down his side, pausing over that big scar she'd found earlier—they'd said it was from surgery, but he didn't remember it. He was being a big cry baby to have thought his whole life was over just because he couldn't ride bulls anymore. Layla did a lot more with a lot less, and she seemed happy. He wanted in on that.

"It will work out exactly the way it's meant to work out."

He lifted his head to look at her again. Her eyes were soft, and she put her fingers in his hair when their gazes met. "Do you believe that?"

"No," she said with a little laugh. "Not always. But it helps me sleep at night when things get hard. There are things in this life we can control and there are things we can't. You can't control your injuries, but you *can* control how you move forward from here. You can make yourself happy, whether it's teaching rodeo or selling wrenches."

"Hammers," he corrected her.

"Hammers at the hardware store. Or fixing my cupboards. Or harassing your Nan. I think you can be happy here in Three Rivers."

There had been a time he would never have imagined that. But being here with her made him believe he could.

TWENTY-NINE

NATE WOKE SEVERAL hours later, after the most restful sleep he'd had in ages, and carefully extracted himself from the tangle of Layla's limbs. She stirred, only slightly, and he pressed a kiss to her lips before he slid out of the bed and pulled on his jeans. He glanced at the baby monitor on the bedside, but he didn't hear anything. It wouldn't hurt to check. Being happy in Three Rivers meant Layla *and* Mason, and he'd missed the kid last night. He made his way quickly up the hall to the nursery and found the baby on his back with a big smile when he poked his head over the rail of the crib.

"Hey, buddy." He spoke quietly, worried the noise over the monitor might wake Layla. "You wanna get up?"

He'd seen Layla get him up and going for the day a half dozen times, he felt reasonably confident he could do this. Reaching down into the crib, he grasped the child under the arms and picked him up, immediately noticing the heavy diaper. He hadn't accounted for that.

"Okay...diaper first, then breakfast, right?"

Keeping up a steady stream of conversation half to himself and half to the baby, he located a fresh diaper and wipes, and carefully laid Mason on the change table, unsnapping his onesie.

"Score," he muttered to himself when he discovered the diaper was only wet. Careful to keep one hand on the baby at all times because he was pretty sure their natural instinct was to roll off of changing tables at any opportunity, he cleaned Mason up and secured the new diaper with minimal trouble, then found a fresh undershirt, t-shirt and pair of pants. None of it really matched, but it was on top of the basket of clean laundry in the corner, so it worked in a pinch. He was pretty sure Layla would be more appreciative of the chance to sleep than dismayed about the wardrobe choices.

He picked Mason up again, holding him upright against his chest and headed for the kitchen. Halfway there, he felt a warm, wet spot growing in the front of his t-shirt. When he held the baby out, the smell gave everything away. "What the heck, dude? Isn't that what diapers are for?"

He heard Layla's soft chuckle from the doorway of her bedroom. "Did you put his penis up or down?"

"What kind of a question is that?" he asked, as Layla crossed the floor and took the baby into her arms, cradling him on his back to avoid contact with his soaking wet outfit.

"You have to point it down or else he just pees all up the front of him," she said, eyeing Nate's wet t-shirt. "And you."

Just when he thought he might have had half a handle on taking care of babies, something he never dreamed he would have to think of. If he was on this team, he still had more to learn than he could anticipate.

"Huh...learn something new every day."

"Take off your shirt," she said, disappearing into Mason's room. He did as he was told, following her in. It took her a quarter of the time to clean the baby up, dress him in something he could wear in public, and turn around, trading the baby for his crumpled up t-shirt. He shook his head in awe and she flashed him a grin. "It was a good try, Nate."

"You do have a few months and some kind of preternatural instinct over me."

She held up his shirt. "Guess you're staying for breakfast."

With his free arm, he grabbed her around the waist, tugging her close. He brushed his lips over hers, and she squawked.

"Morning breath!"

"I don't even care," he said with a laugh, laying a firm kiss on her before releasing her. "You know what I think? I think I should probably keep a change of clothes here."

She raised a brow. "Isn't that a little serious?"

"Didn't I tell you last night I wasn't going anywhere?" He followed her into the kitchen, where she strapped Mason into his chair and started making cereal for him.

"Yes, but..." He could hear the hesitance in her voice a mile away. If she didn't trust when he said he wasn't going to be running back to Denver, that he was making a conscious choice to be here with her and Mason, he would just have to show her, over and over, with his actions, until she believed him.

"Shh," he hushed her. She didn't look happy about it, but she stopped, ducking back toward the laundry room down the hall. He went for the coffee maker, firing it up before he moved on to the fridge for eggs and bread.

While she fed the baby, he cut holes in the middle of the bread, toasting it in a pan before cracking an egg into it. It had been a while since he'd done much cooking, but if the only way he could contribute to the household was to cook meals and take care of the baby, that's what he'd do.

"What on earth is that?" Layla asked, peeking over his shoulder as she brought Mason's dish to the sink. He was assembling everything on plates, and had added cucumber and orange slices for garnish.

"Nan used to make it for us when we were kids. 'Egg in the hole', she called it. Silly...but still my favorite breakfast."

"That's sweet," she said. Nate smiled when he felt her fingers slide over his sides, coming to clasp together over his bare abs, her front pressed to his back, her warm body so close he couldn't help but think of last night. Craning his neck, his lips caught her forehead, but only because she was tall enough for it. So this was what they meant when they talked about 'domestic bliss'. "You know, I could get used to having a shirtless personal chef."

He laughed, picking up the plates. "Isn't that a little serious?"

She swatted at him, then let him go, picking up the coffee mugs and following him to the table. They were just getting seated when he heard a rumble in the yard.

~

Layla froze with a cucumber slice in her mouth. Nate looked confused.

"You weren't expecting anyone, were you?" he asked, leaning back in his chair to see who had pulled in.

"No. Kerri is coming at four to keep him while I go to Danny's, but..." Even as she said it out loud, she knew who it was. Her first instinct was to tell Nate to hide, but there was no use in that—they didn't have time, and then her mother was knocking on her door, and if she had even basic observation skills, she saw the giant, tanned, half naked cowboy sitting at her kitchen table with her. There was no way out of this one.

She got to her feet, icy dread slowing her steps, and pulled the door open. Immediately, Rhonda peeked around her, obviously taking in the sight of Nate sitting perpendicular to Mason. Too close for comfort. Maybe he was right; he *did* need to keep a change of clothes here.

"Hey sweetie," Rhonda drawled, in a sugary voice Layla had never heard before.

"Mom," Layla steeled herself with a deep breath and stepped out of the door. Not letting her mother in would have worse consequences than letting her in, so she made the only choice she felt like she had. "I wasn't expecting you."

"I was in the neighborhood today and thought I'd stop by."

No doubt she'd done a drive by and seen Nate's truck in the yard. *That* was the only reason she'd stopped in.

"Good morning, Mrs. Sullivan." She sensed Nate's body at her back and turned around to see he'd pulled Mason out of his seat and was holding him on his hip, as if it was the most natural thing in the world. As if he knew he was this kid's father and this was a totally normal, completely complete family.

A Cheshire cat-like smile twisted her mother's mouth, and she practically purred when she saw Nate.

"Good morning, Nate. I'm surprised to see you here so early, and..." she trailed off, one brow raised at his broad, bare chest.

"Nate just stopped by to help me peel the wallpaper in the bathroom...and then Mason had a little accident. So I'm washing his shirt for him."

"Is that so?" Rhonda asked.

"Yes, ma'am," Nate replied. He glanced down at Mason. "You wanna go see your grandma, kiddo?"

"Why don't you come in, mom?" Layla asked, since Nate had already crossed *that* particular line.

Rhonda started to protest, not stopping for long Layla was sure, but Nate had already foisted the baby off onto her and he was giggling and cooing and her mother hugged him close for a second as he appealed to what mothering instincts she still had. Layla ushered everyone into the living room. It was moments, brief as they were, just like this, that made Layla long for a conventional relationship with her mother again...but Rhonda reminded her all too quickly why she couldn't when she turned her shrewd gaze back to Nate.

"So, Nate," she began, settling on the edge of the loveseat with Mason on her lap, appearing to turn at least half her attention toward the child, though Layla knew better. "How long are you planning on hanging around?"

From the opposite end of the couch, Layla glanced back at Nate. The whole situation was absurd, his bare chest and feet distracting. He appeared completely unruffled. She supposed when you looked *that* good, you were probably comfortable half naked.

"Oh, the foreseeable future. I'll be settling in and looking for work." It was too much information, and Layla could almost see her mother's brain working. She pinned Layla with a brief, contemptuous look, before turning back to Nate.

"Riding bulls isn't paying the feed bill anymore?"

"No, ma'am. Doc Fields said I had to quit if I wanted to see thirty on my own two feet."

"Well that's a shame. That was a pretty good living, wasn't it?"

Nate shifted, clearly uncomfortable with the direction the conversation was going, and Layla bounced to her feet.

"Would you like a coffee, mom?"

Rhonda shifted, then got to her feet as well, handing Mason to her.

"Actually, like I said, I was just in the neighborhood, but I've got to be going."

"Well, it was nice of you to drop by. Just give me a ring next time and we'll have lunch ready."

A brief smile flitted across her mother's features, but died almost immediately—fleeting, like most of her mother's good moods; existing only until she started scheming again.

Nate rose and bid her mother goodbye and they both stood, a little shell-shocked, in the living room as Rhonda left the house and got into her car.

"Your mama…"

"Don't trust her. Whatever you do."

THIRTY

LAYLA PACED ACROSS her porch, worrying her lower lip. She still owed Rusty for the repairs on the car, and she couldn't afford to miss this shift at Danny's—right in the middle of Three Rivers' Community Pride day, when downtown would be busy as ever. Because of the timing, Nan was busy manning the Ladies' Auxiliary table, which left her exactly one option for Mason...that option was pulling into her driveway in his big diesel truck right now.

She'd even debated calling her mother, but that would have been worse. Nate had spent so much time with Mason by this point; she had no reason to worry. But she did, because it was her nature. And it wasn't even really about the level of care the baby would get—he was a pretty easy kid to get along with these days, and Nan was really only a phone call away. It just felt like if they spent time alone together, Nate would decipher her secrets. It wasn't like he was going to somehow convince Mason to tell him he was his father; the baby was miles away from speaking, though she did get the occasional 'mumumum' out of him—no, he just might have the chance to look a little longer at the shade of the baby's eyes, or the bridge of his nose, or the curls growing in his hair, all of which looked more and more like Nate's every day.

She watched him climb out of his truck and heard an excited squeal from Mason. Judging by the big smile on Nate's face, neither of them was going to be too sorry to be spending the day together, and that was enough to make Layla sigh with relief. *That* was one issue she *didn't* have to worry about leaving the two together.

"My knight in shining armor to the rescue...yet again."

Nate's smile slanted across his features in a way that still made her heart double beat as he climbed the porch steps. "Nobody's keeping count."

"I am. And you'll get fair remuneration for your trouble."

He crested the steps, and in two strides scooped her up with one arm around her waist. He pulled her close, pressing his forehead to hers.

"I think I'm getting 'fair remuneration'."

While they'd had casual intimacy for weeks now, they'd crossed into completely new and different territory since the night he'd found her watching the video of his wreck. It was intense—not in a bad way—but it felt like a floodgate had opened and now he couldn't get enough touching her, tasting her, sleeping in her bed. And she couldn't say the feeling wasn't mutual, she was just that much more intensely aware of the dangerous line she walked.

"Well, if *you* think it's fair, who am I to argue?"

He smiled, drawing her close to press a kiss to her lips.

"That's right, don't argue."

She kissed him quickly, then stepped away, because if she didn't she could have easily enjoyed being lost in an afternoon of quiet domestic bliss, and she couldn't afford that today.

"So there are bottles and a plate of dinner for Mason in the fridge and snacks in the cupboard. Help yourself to whatever."

"Where's the diaper bag?"

She quirked a brow.

"I was thinking I'd take him down to visit Nan."

Layla drew a breath—transferring the car seat out of her car was a pain—and if she was honest, she would have rather he *didn't* take his child out in public, a public that didn't *know* he was Mason's father, but would make fair guesses after they saw the pair out together. But she couldn't come out and tell him this, because she wasn't ready.

"All right, I'll get his seat out of my car," she said reluctantly.

Nate suddenly went full-watt smile. "Already covered."

She was pretty sure he hadn't managed to transfer the seat in a blink, so she followed him off the porch, glancing back to check on Mason one last time while he led her to his truck and opened the back door. Layla peered inside and saw what looked like a brand new car seat strapped in, in the rear facing position, just like it was supposed to be. The base had been tightened into the seat so well it had a one inch indent. When she turned back to Nate, he'd puffed up, proud as a peacock.

It made sense, really, but she hadn't expected him to take it upon himself. The rise of emotion at the thought that he'd done this on his own, without her asking, without any prompting, surprised her. Maybe he meant it when he said he wanted her and everything that came with it.

"You did this all on your own?"

Nate shrugged a little, rubbing the back of his neck with one hand. "Nan helped me figure it out. But yes."

While Layla stood there, shaking her head at the seat, he continued. "I just thought it would be easier for us to get out on some dates if we brought Mason with us once in a while. And we won't have to plan ahead, either. It gives us a little more option to be spontaneous."

Nodding, she turned, wordless, slipping her arms around his waist and pressing her cheek to his chest. He touched her hip and dropped his lips to the top of her head, helping her hold in her big emotions. After a time, he pulled away, cupping her cheek and kissing her forehead.

"All right, you gotta head out."

She let out an audible breath and he patted her hair.

"Get gone, or you're gonna be late. We'll be just fine. Don't worry."

He bent to press a quick kiss to her lips and then turned to open her car door. She paused in the open space before folding herself into the driver's seat.

"The diaper bag's by the couch. Just grab a couple extra diapers from the bedroom."

Nate nodded, kissed her again, closed the car door softly behind her, then hightailed it to the porch to scoop Mason up out of his exersaucer. The pair watched, waving, while she backed out of the driveway, blowing a kiss out her open window.

~

Nate ducked into the house to grab Mason's bottles and diaper bag and then headed back to his truck. If he was honest, being alone with Mason was scary. Sure, he'd spent tons of time with him with Layla there; he'd memorized every routine for bedtime and mealtime that he'd watched—he probably *could* have handled things at the house alone, but Nan's support would make him feel better.

And boy did he have her support. When he'd asked about the car seat, she'd zealously showed him how to install it and reminded him how to adjust the chest clips to the correct position to make sure Mason would be safe if they had to come to a quick stop. She'd practically been bouncing with excitement; even more so this morning when he'd told her his plan to bring Mason by her table.

He dropped the diaper bag into the front seat and opened the back door, settling Mason into his seat like he'd watched Layla do. When he slid in behind the steering wheel, it occurred to him he had precious cargo in a way he hadn't ever worried about before. He carefully guided the truck out of the yard and drove into town five miles under the speed limit...just in case.

Breathing a sigh of relief as he pulled into a parking spot in behind Hinkley's, Nate jumped out of the truck and opened the back door to a happily jabbering Mason. Thank God the child was so happy—he wouldn't have known what to do with him if he wasn't.

"What do you think, Bud? Boy's day?"

Mason responded with a hilariously deep chuckle as Nate unbuckled him from the seat, hoisting him out and onto his hip the way he'd seen the boy's mother lug him half a dozen times. It took him a minute to decide to bring the diaper bag along—it wasn't a long walk from the lot to where the main street of Three Rivers had been shut down to traffic and was dotted with tables and booths filled with games, handmade crafts, and delicious food, but who knew what could happen in that space? And he knew from seeing it before he didn't want to lug a baby with a poopy diaper for a minute longer than he absolutely had to.

As the pair made their way into the gathering of people—everybody in Three Rivers was there—Mason lifted his hands toward the pennant banners lining the street and waved and shouted to people manning tables. The kid was a social critter, he had to give him that much, and was making sure everybody knew he had arrived. Nate paused here and there to say hello, and by the time he found Nan behind the Ladies' Auxiliary table, he was pretty much finished socializing.

"There's my boy!" Nan exclaimed, reaching out to Mason who reacted in kind, stretching his chubby little fingers toward Nate's grandmother. Nate handed him off and watched the two interact. Mason liked him well enough but his face lit up like a Christmas tree when he saw Nan—there was no denying that was something an extra eight months with the baby would have changed.

"What am I, chopped liver?" Nate asked with a chuckle, sliding the diaper bag off his shoulder and tucking it under the edge of their table.

"You were cute once, too," Bernadette Hinkley supplied from where she was seated next to Nan. "It just wore off, that's all."

Nate shook his head with a chuckle.

"All right, all right. I'll take second string to the baby but you can't insult me."

"Well to be fair, the pair of you together is a pretty cute scene."

Nate glanced at Nan who nodded at him. "It *was* pretty cute to see you come traipsing down through here. You look like you don't have two clues."

"I *don't* have two clues, but Layla asked me to look after her baby so I did. By bringing him straight to you as soon as she left us."

Nan chuckled and shook her head, then blew a raspberry onto Mason's chubby cheek.

"I think your Uncle Nate has more clues than he thinks he does."

THIRTY-ONE

"WELL AREN'T YOU pretty as a picture?" Dell Ray sidled up to Layla's bar. The Saturday night rush was mostly gone at this point and there were still a few hangers-on. It had been a hell of a shift, so she looked like she'd just been through a mosh pit, and her feet were aching. On top of it all, Jimmy, who was never a welcome sight, had been camped out at the far end of her bar for the last couple hours. She could never tell if he was just being a shitty drunk or gathering intel for her mother, so she gave him a wide berth, and she'd been counting down the minutes until close for hours now. Nate was picking her up and all she wanted to do was go home and curl up in bed with him. The nature of the service industry didn't permit her to pull the face she wanted to when Dell laid it on.

"Well aren't you just full of shit?" She smiled sweetly, her tone teasing. She typically had an easy rapport with the man. He could be a little off-color, but she just turned her back and rolled her eyes three quarters of the time. He tipped well and the few times she couldn't manage him, Danny was at hand, ready to rein him in. Tonight, Danny had taken off and left her to count the till and close up. It wasn't uncommon once things slowed down.

Dell blustered a little at her quick retort as she headed down the bar to gather a couple of bottles and turn a few glasses over into the dishwasher under the counter.

The bell over the door jangled and she turned to see Nate shouldering his way inside. He nodded a greeting and she flashed him a smile as he found his way to the stool at the end of the bar he'd been frequenting since his return to Three Rivers.

"Last call, Dell," she said as she passed by him, one hand full of clean beer mugs for the display. "Then you gotta go home."

With her free hand, she tapped the bar in front of her regular to get his attention, and with lightning speed, he grabbed her wrist and stopped her so quickly she nearly dropped the glasses.

"Only if you're coming."

It was low and only meant for her to hear. She swung around, fully prepared to put Dell on blast. He could get a little handsy but he was always here. She could give him a little lip without worrying about the repercussions, and was fully prepared to do so, but as quickly as she could do that, Nate was out of his seat and had grabbed the man by his collar.

"You wanna say that again, Dell?"

The older man released her wrist and Layla took a step back. She'd never seen Nate look the way he did; almost feral, his features contorted with anger, his eyes slanted down intensely on Dell.

"What the hell's your problem, Montgomery? We're just having a little fun."

206

"Doesn't look like the lady's having fun to me."

She hadn't been, but watching her would-be-boyfriend put his hands on one of her regulars wasn't exactly a walk in the park either.

"Nate," she said, her voice low. He remained focused on the man.

"Why don't you apologize?"

Dell's red face was a testimony to one of two things; humiliation or anger. Despite the fact she'd served him every Friday and Saturday night since she'd started at Danny's, she couldn't tell which it was.

"Why don't you get your fucking hands off me?"

Anger, definitely anger.

"Okay, that's enough guys." Layla interjected, but it was clear neither man was paying her any mind. What had started as some strange bid to protect her virtue had clearly become a pissing match that had nothing to do with her.

"Why don't you apologize?" Nate repeated.

Dell tried to shrug off the fist Nate had balled in his collar, and turned back to his beer, muttering. "Fucking golden child think you can come back here after your epic failure and be cock of the walk." He looked up. "Too goddamn yellow-bellied to get on another bull so you came running home with your tail between your legs."

Before she could get around the end of the bar, Nate was on top of Dell and they were on the floor, fists flying, arms and legs flailing as each man did their best to flatten the other into the dirty tile beneath them.

"Hey! Hey! That's enough!" She reached into the fray and attempted to grab a sleeve or an arm or something, but when Dell's fist sailed past her face, missing her nose by a half an inch, she retreated, scowling. "I do *not* get paid enough for this bullshit. *Knock it off!*"

She thought to call Danny, but by the time he'd get there, it'd be all done but the crying. Moving quickly, she rounded the end of the bar, glaring at her brother. "You *could* be helpful." He shrugged, draining his drink as he watched the brawl with interest. Other patrons were intentionally diverting their eyes; it was one a.m. and nobody wanted to have to explain a shiner at church in the morning.

Danny kept a baseball bat behind the cooler for a little extra reinforcement but she wasn't particularly interested in maiming either man any more than they were already maiming one another so she grabbed the soda gun from its holster and climbed onto her knees on the bar top. The pressure wouldn't do much, but she hoped the icy sluice of water would do something, even if it was only to stop their fists long enough she could get between them without getting her own block knocked off.

Dell came up sputtering first, face full of blood as he scooted across the floor away from Nate, who was still intent on beating the ever-loving shit out of him.

"Everybody get the *hell* out of my bar!" she hollered in a voice that invited no nonsense. It stopped Nate in his tracks. Despite his previous inaction, Jimmy leapt off his stool. She was still on top of the bar with her soda gun gripped between two hands as if it might be as useful as a real one when all of the patrons finally pushed their chairs back and started to move toward the door. "*Everybody.*"

The bar cleared out quickly, until it was just Nate standing in front of her, a rip in his shirt, and the knees of his jeans filthy from the wet floor she would have to come in early to scrub. Complete with additional watery blood stains. He had blood on his knuckles and at the corner of his mouth, swelling already evident on his left eye and lower lip. All she could do was shake her head.

"*You* wait. Ten minutes. Until Dell pulls out. Just so I can be sure you two don't go at it again in the parking lot. And then *you* can get the hell out of my bar, too."

"Let me help you clean up," he said, gesturing to the mess on the floor.

"I think you've done enough, Nate."

He disappeared to the bathroom while she finished picking up empties from the tables and filled the dishwasher. She had her back turned to him, angrily sorting bills from her till, when he emerged.

"I'll wait in the truck."

"I don't care what the hell you do," she said to the money.

"Lay, he was out of line."

She didn't turn around, even though his voice had softened. She could hear him shift, the scrape of a stool. He thought he was going to sit at her bar after pulling a stunt like that? Pressing her lips together, she turned. If there was ever an image of a repentant man, Nate was it, sitting with his hands folded in front of him, his eyes lowered. She let out a breath.

"Do you know how many tongues are going to be wagging now? Why the hell is Nate Montgomery protecting Layla Sullivan's virtue?" She shoved the drawer of the register shut and gathered the bag of money for the safe in the back room. "If you cost me this job, so help me…"

"I *would* help you."

Layla stopped in her tracks, her mouth fell open, and then closed again. Most of the time she could forget what a dangerous line she was treading but this was one of those times she couldn't ignore it.

"That's ridiculous."

"Why? And why's it ridiculous for me to be protecting your virtue? Dell had no right to talk to you like that."

"Dell *always* talks to me like that." The look on his face made her glad he'd be staying at her place tonight, not chasing down Dell Ray and dragging him out of his wife's bed to finish the job he'd started on his face.

"Well maybe it's time for him to find a new bar."

"Would you stop? This is what happens to bartenders. Danny looks after Dell when he gets out of hand."

"And Danny wasn't here, so I looked after him."

"Yeah, Danny doesn't make him bleed."

He chuckled and rubbed the back of his neck in a gesture that was so 'aw shucks' she felt her anger begin to dissolve. A tiny bit.

"All right. I'm sorry. I just…I couldn't stand him talking to you like that, Layla. You don't have to put up with that bullshit. You deserve better."

She wanted to say something about Dell Ray deserving a bar where he didn't get the shit beat out of him but Nate's expression was so earnest when he said she deserved better, she almost believed him. If he only knew the truth of her deception.

"I'll come in with you tomorrow and help you clean up," he said, nodding toward the moneybag. "Now lock that up and let's go home."

~

"I'm still mad," Layla announced once they'd seen Kerri off, checked on Mason, and settled onto the couch. Nate held her and brushed her hair back from her face while she stretched her legs out over the worn floral fabric.

"I know." The almost tangible tension from the cab of his truck was starting to dissipate. There had been a minute there where he'd thought she might rescind her invitation to spend the night but he could thank his lucky stars she hadn't. She rested her head on his chest and her body softened a bit more. "Lily says bull riders are alpha assholes, so I guess I was just giving in to my inner beast."

"Are you about to talk about your feelings?" she asked quietly into the front of his shirt, her fingers curling into the fabric.

"Do alpha assholes do that?"

He felt her cheek swell against his chest; she was smiling. That was a start. He'd talk to Danny in the morning, apologize to Dell. He would fix things. For her.

"Probably not."

"Better not, then. But as a side note," he paused, shifting one hand down her waist to tuck his fingers against the warm skin under the hem of her shirt. She called that particular curve her love handle, and he loved its plush softness. "I can't stand to see someone mistreat you, Layla. I know you got a lot of it growing up and I was a boy; I didn't stand up for you. Nobody did. Now that I can...well, I don't care how many tongues wag. I know you want to keep this on the down-low, but I care about you, and I'm not going to let someone treat you like that. Not now that I'm with you."

She was quiet; she might have fallen asleep. His heart beat a million miles an hour, his head spun; he'd just laid out his feelings for her, and she was *asleep*. But then she stretched and yawned, shifting against him.

"You wanna go to bed?"

"You've got me hanging on a limb here, Lay."

She tipped her head back, raising an eyebrow. "Hmm?"

So maybe after a ten hour shift on her feet wasn't a good time to open up about how he felt about her. He spent at least half his nights here with her, she made his heart feel something it hadn't felt in a long time, and he couldn't envision another woman in her place. They hadn't put official words to it, and judging by the way she wanted to keep it out of the public eye, she wasn't going to want to, but this was what *he* wanted. *Her*, and this house, and that baby, and everything that came with it, whether that was her crazy family or Dell Ray's filthy mouth. He wasn't a young buck anymore, he was ready to settle down, and Layla Sullivan was who he wanted to do it with.

"I wanna be with you. Here, and in public. And I don't care who knows about it. Danny, Dell, your brother. I don't care."

"Nate," she said, her voice low.

"I've wasted a lot of time since the wreck, without any vision or direction. And being with you, for the first time, I feel like I want to plan for the future. So I gotta know, Layla. Do you wanna be with me as bad as I wanna be with you?"

She twisted, sitting up into his lap with a growl, but her smile gave her away.

"You're still here aren't you?"

A laugh rose out of him, his heavy mood suddenly lightened as he shifted, pushing her off his lap and onto her back on the couch, his fingers finding the spots he knew were ticklish.

"What kind of an answer is that, huh?"

Her laughter was high and light as she tried to wriggle out of his grasp.

THIRTY-TWO

A WHOLE LOT of tickling and teasing later found the two of them on the bed, Nate's fingers inching over her waist. When he paused, his fingers etching ticklish lines near her belly button, she knew he was tracing stretch marks, every one of them a testament to the time Mason had spent inside her.

"Nan says you labored for ten hours before you even called for anyone to be with you. And when you did, it was her, not your mama."

She could feel hot tears rising, but she swallowed them down. Talking about how Mason actually came into being with the man who didn't even know he was the baby's father felt too close to telling Nate he was a daddy.

"It was."

"Why?"

Rolling onto her side to face him, she lifted her hand to cup his jaw. She'd never get tired of this new, comfortable feeling; her body exposed, her emotions laid out. Almost as good as when Mason smiled at her, it was warm, satisfying, and even if it was temporary, it felt good to relax into, like a hot tub full of bubbles.

"Why are you asking?"

A line formed between his brows and he covered her hand with his own. Almost immediately, she missed the warmth of his touch on her body.

"Because I'm curious."

"You're nosy." She couldn't help her smile. Still, she couldn't put into words why she'd called Nan. It was part she thought the baby needed his family there, even if his daddy wasn't, and part Nan had never pressured her to tell the truth—Layla could count on her not to make her fill in a name for 'father' on the birth certificate. Nan would just let her be, exactly who she was, exactly how she wanted—a lot like Nate was right now.

"Okay, I'm nosy, but *you're* a superhero."

His hand left hers, slid over her waist, and tugged her the short distance that separated them on the bed, pressing her flush against his chest as his fingers landed in the small of her back. She pressed her smile against his neck. His next words took her by surprise.

"I wish I had been here."

A flutter of panic burst out of her heart, but fizzled when she told herself there was no way. She was the only one who knew; he would have asked already if he had any suspicions.

"Why?"

"*Now* who's nosy?"

She shifted her head back to meet his eyes in the dim light of the bedside lamp. Pressing her lips together, she watched for a sign, any sign he knew he was a father, and that *that* was why he wished he'd been here. His teasing expression changed, and he reached up to touch her cheek softly.

"I just think you shouldn't have had to be alone."

"I wasn't alone. I had Nan."

He shifted, pressing a gentle kiss to her forehead, so she couldn't see his eyes, only hear the emotion in his voice.

"That doesn't count. You shouldn't have had to be alone, Layla. I wish I had been there to see how brave and strong you were. To see how amazing you did."

Those tears were back, now, and there was nothing she could do to stop them. Her heart ached to tell Nate the truth. They were so deep into this now, she couldn't see how she could. And if it was going to go down in flames anyways, she could hold on for just a little while longer, couldn't she? Draw all of the warmth and comfort and love out of whatever this was, so she could at least have something to remember when she was alone again.

As she drew a shuddering breath, Nate tipped his head back, catching sight of the tears.

"Hey...hey, I thought I was saying something nice." He brushed at her tears gently. "Don't cry, Lay. I'm just being nice."

"I wish you'd been there, too."

He held her for a long, quiet moment, stroking her hair and murmuring softly to her. For the first time, she admitted to herself she wished things had gone differently. All this time, she'd told herself she was happy to raise Mason alone—having Nate with her would only complicate things, but now she felt differently.

Nate could love her. He didn't right now, but she felt like he could, someday, if she worked hard at it. He was so good with Mason. They could have maybe done it the right way, not this backward, deceitful way that was only going to end in heartache for two thirds of the equation.

"Well, I'm here now," he finally said. And that was almost as heartbreaking as the idea he had wanted to be there in the first place. Letting out a slow breath, she shifted, pressing up to taste those words on his lips.

It wasn't long before Nate took control of the kiss, easing her back onto the bed and moving over her. The weight of his body pressing her into the mattress was a comfort; his hard steadiness against her soft vulnerability. He was here now. For now. And that was enough. But she needed more of this, more of his skin against hers, more of their bodies melting into one another like they were designed to fit together. Her fingers curled into the hem of his t-shirt, her knuckles brushing his warm skin underneath as she drew it upward, craving that heat against the places he'd just had his fingers.

To her delight, he shifted backward, discarding his shirt before he started on hers, exposing what he'd been touching just moments before. He inched the fabric up over her stomach.

"An honest-to-God superhero," he murmured, shaking his head as he dropped his mouth to the spot just below her navel. "Amazing. And beautiful." He punctuated his words with kisses, until he'd worked his way up, past the band of t-shirt just under her arms, and took her mouth again for a hot, intense second before he slid her shirt the rest of the way up over her shoulders and over her head.

"You're not half bad yourself," she said, tracing her fingers over his abdomen, the ridges of muscle firm under her touch. He paused, closing his eyes as her hand moved upward, splaying her palms over the taut muscles in his chest that held him hovering inches above her. Finally, she closed her fingers around the nape of his neck and drew him back into the kiss.

When she was soundly kissed, he made his way back down, trailing a wet line of kisses along her jaw, down the side of her neck, between her breasts, and down to the waistline of her panties. Carefully, he slid them down, following the exposure of her skin with kisses, to her hips, her knee, and when her thighs fell open because she had no other choice than to offer herself to him, he started back upward. The arch of her foot, the soft, ticklish spot at the back of her knee that almost earned him a kick in the chest, and then time stopped as he moved, finding softer, damper flesh, until his mouth stopped at the apex of her thighs.

Her heart felt like it would burst when his hot breath hit the most sensitive part of her, her hips pushing up toward the touch that hadn't even come yet. The first slow, warm slide of his tongue against her heated flesh reduced her to a puddle. When she might otherwise have been self-conscious about her body, the angle, the intimacy, pleasure flooded her senses and pushed any doubts out of her mind, reducing her stream of consciousness to her heartbeat thudding wildly, her breath rasping out in long, harsh exhalations, and where Nate's tongue would touch her next. And then her orgasm, a vague idea in the distance at first, snowballing into something greater, quicker; a bright, hot burst of pleasure that made her call his name, her fingers grasping at the sheets by her hips, just trying to find purchase, something to ground her. And then he did, shifting up her body and anchoring her with the weight of his, pressing into her with one sure, easy stroke that made her sigh with relief.

Nate paused then, brushing her hair off her forehead, and gave her the chastest of kisses, as though they weren't one body, an easy smile tipping up one corner of his lips.

"Look amazing, *feel* amazing. I'm an idiot for staying away so long." He slipped his rough fingers behind her knee to draw it up, changing the angle without moving at all and making Layla pull in a sharp breath.

She tightened her fingertips into the muscle of his shoulder, pleasure blurring the edges of her vision with a warm fuzziness she welcomed. She'd never asked for what she wanted before, never felt confident or cheeky enough to encourage a partner—the words always came out wrong—but she felt it rising up in her chest, pushing past her vocal cords. Easier than last time.

"Why don't you make up for it, then?"

One of his eyebrows shot up, that smile widening, and he wedged a hand under her hip, drawing her up tight to him, applying pressure in all the right spots. A little chuckle came out of him when her head dropped back on the pillow, electric shots of pleasure coursing through her when he made contact with her already-sensitive flesh.

"Needy girl," he breathed out a second before he shifted his hips, withdrawing, then pressing into her again. "You don't have to ask twice."

She sure as hell hoped not, because she couldn't find any more words once he started moving, finding a rhythm within her that felt so natural, so perfect, she could have easily been convinced it was a dream Nate Montgomery was here, loving on her body in a way nobody had before.

Well before she'd had her fill of him; the way he smelled, the way he tasted, the way he felt, right down to that little line between his brows as he focused, she felt another orgasm rising up, her blood rushing in her ears. Her fingers scrabbled against his skin as her hips rose, pushing into him, her breath coming out in hitched sobs. It was entirely too much and never enough all at once.

"Easy, Lay," he breathed out, the strain of his wavering control reading loud and clear. "Come with me."

And she did, because it felt good to let go. Of the bare shreds of control she had over her life, of all of her secrets and her belief that she didn't deserve anything good. Because this was good. Too good. Her head fell back against the pillow as the first wave washed over her, and he followed her, his mouth leaving a wet trail up along the column of her throat before his teeth raked lightly back down, and he let out a groan, his movements stilling as his body tensed, his fingers digging into her hip where he held her.

When he finally moved, he lifted his head, once again brushing the hair off of her forehead, his eyes tracing along her features as if he was memorizing them. The emotion in them scared the hell out of her. She knew *she* was edging into dangerous territory but it was so much worse if he was, too. She could handle disappointment; she'd lived with it her entire life, she knew how to manage it. But the big blow Nate got with his accident was enough for a lifetime. This time it wouldn't be a bull; *she* was going to let him down.

"As good as Denver?" she asked, trying to lift her voice beyond that same crushing emotion she saw mirrored in his eyes.

"Hell, better. Ten times better," he said with a laugh as he rolled onto his side, bringing her with him, their damp bodies still just as close. He wrapped her up in his arms, resting his lips against her forehead. "Layla Sullivan, I'm falling in love with you."

His last words were barely a whisper, but they sounded loud, like a megaphone right over her shoulder. Her first instinct was to laugh it off. Because that was the safest thing. Because this was the thing she feared the most. But she couldn't. She swallowed hard, her mouth suddenly dry. Even if she'd had words to respond, she couldn't have forced them out over a tongue that felt like lead, all of her afterglow ruined by those eight words.

THIRTY-THREE

"THANKS AGAIN FOR letting me stay to study," Kerri said, punching a couple keys on her laptop distractedly. Clearly, the studying portion of the evening was over. "It just gets crazy at home with the kids."

Layla smiled, drawing her knees up and wrapping her palms around a mug of chamomile tea. "With two kids under five and a ten year old boy? No way."

The younger girl glanced up with a smile.

"Besides, I don't mind the company."

"Where *is* Nate anyway?" Kerri's eyes drifted back to her laptop as she scrolled through a block of text.

"What do you mean 'where's Nate'?"

"I mean he's normally here. When he's not at the ranch, making rodeo school plans."

Layla let out a breath. Right. He *was* normally here. And she was starting to enjoy his casual presence in her life. Which was what made the next step suck so badly. Her heart hadn't stopped pounding since he'd used that word. The 'L' word. The word she'd promised herself she wouldn't venture toward, no matter how right it felt. And then *he* had turned around and used it. Okay, so he hadn't come straight out and said he loved her, but he was *falling* in love with her, and that was just as dangerous. She had to tell him. She couldn't put it off any longer. She had to tell him or this bridge wouldn't just burn, it would incinerate.

"Hey, can you keep a secret?"

"Depends on the secret," Kerri said, twisting her lips as she focused on the screen of her laptop.

"No, I really mean it."

The younger girl drew in a long breath, then dragged her eyes away from the laptop. Once she took in Layla's expression, she slowly closed the computer.

"Okay. Sure. You know you can count on me, Lay."

Blood rushed in her head and she uttered words she'd never said. Not to *anyone*.

"Mason is Nate's."

Kerri's jaw dropped and she jumped to her feet, nearly dumping her Macbook on the floor.

"What!" her voice was high and thin. "Are you sure?"

Pressing her lips together, Layla nodded.

"Lay, does anybody know? Does *Nate* know?" Her eyes wide, Kerri took two steps toward the door and then turned tight, swinging back to Layla. "Does Nan know? Does anybody know?"

Layla shook her head this time, swallowing hard. This felt more vulnerable than being open and exposed on the delivery table. More vulnerable than Nate seeing all her stretch marks and extra jiggly bits for the first time. This was the secret she'd worked hard to hide for nearly two years, and she'd tossed it out casually on the table. Judging by her babysitter's response, *nobody* was going to not make a big deal of this.

"That's the first time I've ever said that out loud," she mused quietly, twisting her fingers together. "Nobody knows. Except you, now."

"Oh my God, why would you tell *me*?" Kerri's eyes went wide as she threw her hands up.

"Because I needed to test it out before I tell Nate. I should have told him before, but I promised myself this wouldn't amount to anything, and now…"

"It's something." Kerri nodded. She folded her arms over her midsection and took the seat at the other end of the couch, visibly making at least an *attempt* to rein in her reaction. "So you're going to tell him now?"

"Well not right *now*, but soon. Tomorrow, probably, when he comes over after work." Now it was Layla's turn to get up, crossing the floor anxiously before doubling back and doing it again.

"You look like you're going to throw up," Kerri supplied unhelpfully.

"I *feel* like I'm going to throw up."

"Okay." Kerri paused for a moment, her lips pursed in thought, her brow furrowed in concentration. "Do you remember what I said about Nate being a decent human being back before he met Mason?"

Layla's pacing paused and she let out a long breath through her nose. This whole thing, in theory, inside her head, seemed much less daunting before she'd actually said the words.

"This is different, Ker. This isn't just something I was hiding because who wants to tell a hot guy that wants to take you on a date that you have a kid. This is something I intentionally kept from him. Something that affects *him* directly. Because I didn't..."

"Because you didn't what?"

"Because I didn't want him to think I was only going out with him because I wanted something from him."

"*There* it is." Kerri got up and crossed the floor to where Layla was standing. She was young, but she was an old soul who had experienced a lot before she and her sister had settled in Three Rivers. Her warm fingers closed around Layla's forearm and the shorter girl caught her eyes. "You work hard to provide a nice life for Mason. It's not as if you're sitting back with your feet up, expecting someone else to take care of you. You're doing the right thing *now*. I'm sure Nate, decent human being that he is, will see that. He might have a tough time at first, but he loves Mason as if he was his own already, and he doesn't even know. So that counts for something. I'm sure that love will overpower any disappointment he might feel about you not telling him to begin with."

She wanted to believe what Kerri told her, but the truth was she knew the sting of rejection all too well. She barely had anything worth him wanting, and when she added dishonesty to the mix...well, she wasn't a betting woman, but even *she* wouldn't have put money on Nate sticking around.

"Sit down, I'll get you more tea."

She did as she was instructed, curling in on herself while Kerri moved around the kitchen, then came back, settling on the other edge of the couch. She packed her computer carefully and set it aside.

"I'm sorry, I shouldn't have dumped on you. I know you need to study for finals."

Kerri shrugged, smiling kindly. "Sometimes a friend needs someone to listen, and that's more important than studying."

She was as much a friend as her sitter, at the end of the day. Maybe the only person she really shared her day-to-day stresses and troubles with...until Nate. He was her friend. Maybe she didn't have to ruin all of this because they were friends...but no, he'd used that word, and it had screwed everything up. And it was the right thing to do. That would be her new mantra until she saw him tomorrow and confessed.

"You know how much I appreciate you, right? You are so much more than a babysitter."

The girl just shrugged with a smile. "I just can't believe you never told me before this. You've never been a good secret keeper."

"Well, I've been holding onto this one for a long time."

"And even Nan doesn't know?"

"I think Nan might know, in her heart, but you know Nan."

"Right, she'd never let it cross her lips unless it was common knowledge. But do you think she might have told Nate her suspicions?"

Layla shook her head.

"Wow..." Kerri brushed a hand over the top of her head. "I just...I guess I've wondered before. But it's none of my business, right? Nate was definitely not on the top of my list of guesses, though."

"Who was?"

"Cutter Anderson." Kerri grinned broad and Layla rolled her eyes, the tension slowly working out of her. Cutter Anderson as a father was laughable in itself, but *her* and Cutter...that was almost worth a belly laugh.

"Uh, no."

"It would explain his quick break to Denver."

Layla laughed, shaking her head. This felt normal, it felt good. She knew it would be chaos by this time tomorrow, but she could enjoy this for what it was now.

THIRTY-FOUR

NATE SAT BACK in his favorite booth at Hinkley's, his legs stretched out under the table, a mug of coffee in front of him. Across from him, Lily was still jabbering about a new sponsor for the rodeo school. Shit was starting to get real; whether he was in it or not, there were clearly lots of gears turning he didn't have a thing to do with. He let her go for a minute or two, his lips pursed like he was listening, but really, he was thinking about Layla, across the street and down a block, manning the desk in Dr. Fields' office. When they'd first reconnected, he'd thought maybe a few dates and she'd be out of his system, but the opposite had happened. The more time he spent with her and Mason, and at her quiet little love-filled house, the more time he *wanted* to spend with her. And it was escalating pretty quickly beyond just a little crush or a way to pass the time. So much so that the thought of hitting the rodeo circuit again, going out on the road to rope and drink and row, just wasn't appealing anymore. Hell, he'd even used the 'L' word the other night. It might not have been the right move, but there was definitely something there, something simmering just under the surface of his heart, and it just might have been love. He wasn't sure he even knew what that was supposed to feel like, but it didn't feel like anything he'd ever felt before.

"And maybe once you're back in the scene again with the rodeo school, you can head back to Denver. You could work your way back up the ranks." *That* caught his attention. He snapped his gaze to his friend across the table.

"Lilypad," he interjected. "I don't *want* to rodeo anymore." The idea formed as the words came out, and as it hung in the air between them, it even felt *good*. He would have preferred to retire with a nice bankroll to span him out, raise some stock, and love a woman on the nice little spread he'd owned, but when it boiled down to it, the end result was the same. Even if he could have scrounged up the money, somehow, to traipse all over the Midwest to ride the country's rankest bulls, he didn't *want* to.

"Oh come on now, that's like me saying I don't want to ride endurance anymore because of my accident."

They'd both had devastating injuries, sure. She and her horse, Encore, had been struck from behind by a texting driver during a training session. Lily's pelvis had been broken and Encore, while he'd recovered physically, had never recovered mentally, and was turned out as a pasture puff at the Baylor ranch. But it hadn't been the very sport she was trying to participate in that had hurt her, it was just an asshole in a Toyota. His bull riding career tried to kill him every time he wrapped the bull rope around his hand, and this time, it had damn near succeeded. He was still walking and he wasn't addicted to painkillers, and he counted both of those as a resounding success. Quit while you're alive. It was a good policy.

"I really mean it."

Lily watched him with sharp eyes—they'd known one another for a long time; from the time he'd first spied her hanging over the gates at the rodeo, with a camera half as big as her head. At the beginning, he'd fancied her a romantic interest, but they'd turned out to be great friends—something he'd been grateful for when she showed up at his hospital bed with her eyes full of tears but an encouraging smile on her face. If he was lying to himself, she'd know.

"Nate Montgomery."

Rhonda Sullivan interrupted their serious conversation with a holler from halfway across the diner. He sat up a little straighter. He hadn't heard the full story from Layla—it was clear she had an interesting relationship with her mother—but either way, a man was a fool not to try at least a *little* bit to impress the kin of the woman he was *falling in love* with.

"Mrs. Sullivan," he said with a smile as she approached.

"Hi Mrs. Sullivan," Lily said, lifting her hand in greeting.

Ignoring Lily altogether, Rhonda leaned against the table, turning her back to his dining companion.

"Nate," she started, her voice sugar-sweet. "I'm so glad to see you by yourself. I just wanted to have a chance to say how impressed I am."

He ducked his head. "Nothing too impressive here, I promise."

"It's just, there are so many men that just *shirk* their fatherly responsibilities, and it's nice to see you stepping up. Even if it *did* take you a while."

Right now, Nate's heart was in the back of his throat, and he swallowed hard a couple times to try and come up with a response but nothing was coming.

He fumbled for a minute, sounds coming out of his mouth that didn't form words, Lily's surprised stare boring holes in him. The walls of the diner suddenly felt awful close.

"Uh, Rhonda...Mrs. Sullivan...I'm not sure what you're talking about."

The woman tipped her head as she looked down at him, like she'd just knocked him down and was trying to find the softest, most vulnerable part of him to kick. It sure as hell felt that way, too.

"Oh you know what I'm talking about. Lord knows Layla works too hard trying to keep that baby fed and clothed. Hopefully you can find it in the goodness of your heart to start living up to your *financial* fatherly duties, too." Her voice rose octave by octave until he was sure people *outside* the diner could hear her.

And just as quickly as she'd appeared inside the door of the diner, she was gone—without even stopping to talk to Tina behind the counter, who had stopped midway through wiping down the counter and was staring in his direction with her jaw hanging open.

Suddenly, the diner was tiny. Nate couldn't draw a breath; his throat felt like it was closing, his chest constricting. He was sure every eye in the place was on him, waiting for him to say something. But all he could think about was Layla. In his mind, he combed over every conversation they'd had, every minute he'd spent there, every feature of

Mason's face. He hadn't asked. So she hadn't told. A lie by omission. *But she would have told me, wouldn't she have?* After seeing how much he cared about Mason, wouldn't she have said something? They'd become so close in such a short time, imagining Layla as being deceitful was a tough pill to swallow.

He could hear every swish of his heartbeat in his ears, and his cheeks were blistering hot.

Lily's voice cut through the din.

"Nate?" He focused on her face, her lips set in a grim line, her hand waving in the space between them to try and bring him down to earth. "Breathe."

Was this what a heart attack felt like? He could imagine the obituary headline now. 'The bull didn't kill him, but the baby did.'

Not *the* baby. *His* baby. *Jesus.*

He got to his feet and bolted out of the diner.

THIRTY-FIVE

BY LAYLA'S ESTIMATION, the best part of the day was in the evening when everything was quiet and still, and she had a few moments to herself where she didn't have to do anything. She was just settling into that moment with a mug of tea in the kitchen when she heard the familiar rumble of a diesel engine in the yard. They'd made plans—she would tell him tonight—so her heart jumped a little, knowing it was so close. But she'd made peace. Whatever happened would happen and there was nothing she could do about it.

She picked up her mug, turning just as the screen door slammed loudly behind him. She thought to remind him he'd come late enough Mason was already in bed, but when she looked up and saw him standing in the middle of the floor like a thundercloud, she drew in a tight breath. Something was really, really wrong.

"Is Mason mine?"

Three words. Her heart dropped to her toes. It wasn't supposed to happen like this. It was meant to go the other way. She'd spent the afternoon considering how she'd soften the blow, and now she'd waited too long. Everything was ruined.

She stumbled over words, trying to say something, *anything*, that would make it okay for her to cross the floor and touch his jaw, kiss him, and draw strength from his arms. She stopped, steeling herself.

"Why don't we go outside and talk?" It was an effort to keep her voice even when all she wanted to do was cry. This would be much more painful than she'd anticipated.

She breathed a sigh of relief as he stalked back out the door he'd just come in and she caught up just in time to stop the door from falling shut, trying to assemble words into some kind of an explanation.

Taking a seat on the bench they'd spent so much time on this summer, she motioned for him to sit, but he stood, arms crossed, leaning his hips against the rail of the porch across from her. *This is bad.*

"What's this about, Nate?"

"Why don't you just answer the question, Layla?" His dark gaze pinned her, and she wrapped her hands around her mug, every part of her body tense, her jaw clenched so tight her teeth ached.

She dropped her gaze, unable to look him in the eye when she answered. "Yes."

"Fuck."

Maybe she *was* just like the family she'd tried so hard not to be like. Manipulating good people for their generosity. Except this wasn't about money. This was about love. And she'd still end up empty-handed in the end. Hot tears prickled her eyelids.

"I'm sorry, Nate. I just..."

"Why'd I have to hear it from your mama? In front of everyone at Hinkley's? Why didn't you call me in Denver? Why am I just finding out *now*? Were you *ever* planning to tell me?"

Overwhelmed by his rapid-fire questions and feeling like her whole body was being held in a vise, she let out a short breath through her nose. Of course, her mother. As hard as she'd tried to hide their relationship from her, she'd clearly failed, because Rhonda had been sure enough to act on her hunch. The woman was something, but family wasn't something she could be considered anymore.

She swallowed a big ball of emotion in her throat that wanted to come out as a sob and lifted her chin. It would have been easier if he just left, walked away, nursed his anger on his own. But here he was, demanding answers—answers she *owed* him, and nothing she could say wouldn't sound selfish and awful and silly now the tables had been turned on her.

"I didn't think you'd stick around when I said I wasn't interested in the same thing we had before. And then things went quick..."

Nate wiped a hand over his face, letting out a long breath. When he spoke, his voice was filled with emotion, insistent. "If you'd told me when you first found out, I could have helped you, Layla. I could have sent money—"

At that word, she found her voice, and the strength to bring herself to her feet. "No. I didn't want money. *That's* why I didn't call you in Denver. *That's* why I didn't tell you here. My *mother* wanted money and that's why she made a guess at you being Mason's father because *I* sure as hell didn't tell her."

He could think of her however he wanted, but that was one thing she *wouldn't* let him think about her.

"You didn't think I would want to have a part in my *son's* life?"

"I didn't want you to feel like you had to."

"What about what *I* want?" He ran a hand through his hair, clearly getting more agitated. He'd told her over and over during the last few weeks he was around because he wanted to be—it never occurred to her maybe he would have wanted to be a part of Mason's life from the beginning. Somehow, she'd imagined his life in Denver so far removed from what happened here in Three Rivers there was no way he'd want to be tied down to the girl from the wrong side of the tracks who had been too stupid not to get pregnant during a one night stand.

This couldn't get better. How could he trust her again after she'd misled him? Now that her mother was involved? The best thing to do was let him cut his losses and walk away. She hadn't considered, when she had played this out in her mind, that he would resist. But it was the only way. Her heart was breaking, but she'd have to cut deep. It was better to hurt now than later, when Mason would be old enough to experience the loss, too.

"You don't want this, Nate," she said, crossing her arms over her midsection in an attempt to hold herself together. "You might think you do, but you don't. And it would have been easier for you to walk away when you didn't feel any obligation."

"You don't know what I want. You have no clue. You haven't since the beginning. You just never believed me." Nate's voice got progressively louder. Not shouting, but she could feel his anger simmering just under the surface, just beneath his words. "And even if you knew, would you even care? Would it even hold a candle to what *you* want? When do my needs get to be considered in this equation?"

"They don't." Something flitted across his features, barely registrable, but it was what she was looking for. It was the severed tie.

He scowled, took a step toward her like he had more to say, but then shook his head, turned on his heel and stalked away. She didn't try to stop him.

THIRTY-SIX

"ALL RIGHT, THAT'S enough."

As Nate was securely in his bed with the blankets pulled over his head, Nan's voice had to be a hallucination. Maybe he was still a little drunk. It *had* been at least six hours, judging by the daylight piercing his cocoon, since the empty beer on his bedside stand had been consumed. But it might have ganged up on him with all the other beers before it.

When the blankets flew off of him from the foot of the bed, he knew it wasn't a hallucination.

"For the love of God, Nan! What if I'd been naked?" He scrambled for the blankets, but she was quicker than he'd expected.

"I used to change your diapers," his grandmother said, winding the blankets up in her arms so he couldn't pull them back over himself. "And besides, you aren't."

That was true. He was still in last night's jeans and he was pretty sure *they* were the source of the stink he'd just noticed.

"How did you get in here?" He knew he'd locked the door.

"This is my house. You think I wouldn't have a key? And don't even *start* about tenant's rights to 24 hour notice. I had to make sure you were still alive. I haven't seen you in days, and if you weren't talking to me right now, the *smell* alone would make me think there was a corpse in here."

"I've seen Banks. You could have talked to him."

He squinted in the late morning light streaming in through the window above his bed and rolled onto his back. He should have known Nan wouldn't let him wallow for long. It wasn't her style. She was always the first to move to action in difficult situations. She usually did the right thing, with good intentions. He couldn't really say the same for himself.

"Your brother has been known to lie for you."

"*And* rat me out. So which was it?"

He didn't remember much after Layla had taken the bar at Danny's, but he *did* remember Banks pulling up on him, lights flashing, and the tense ride back to Nan's.

"None of the above. Get up and take a shower. There's a pot of coffee and two Advil waiting for you upstairs."

With that, she turned and marched out of the room, taking his blankets with her. And, because he knew she wouldn't give up until he did, he got up and took a shower.

Twenty minutes later, he was sitting at her kitchen table with the promised painkillers and coffee and a no-nonsense Nan sitting across from him, her eyes trained on him.

"I don't wanna talk about it, Nan."

"Well, you're gonna. Because everybody else in town is."

"Did you know?" Suddenly, it occurred to him maybe this hadn't been only Layla's secret. Nan had been spending a lot of time and energy on the pair, she had to have known.

"No," Nan said, shaking her head. "I had my suspicions, but she didn't tell me. Not my place to ask. Did you ask her? Or did you just listen to her mother's poison?"

"I shouldn't have *had* to ask. I shouldn't have found out from her mama, either. *She* should have told me. Called me in Denver when she found out she was pregnant. Or at least been up front when I started hanging around."

Nan nodded slowly, twisting her coffee cup in place thoughtfully.

"Yes, she should have told you."

He'd expected a fight, or at least a more defensive response from Nan. She didn't want to fight. And neither did he. Dropping his elbows on the table, he put his head into his hands, fisting his fingers in his damp hair. This monumental shift in his life didn't feel better no matter how he tried to approach it—drunk, sober, sleeping, awake. His heart hadn't beat at a normal pace since Rhonda walked into Hinkley's. Every second felt itchy and uncomfortable. If it had been *anything* else, his first instinct would have been Layla. Lose himself in her; her big heart, her fragrant skin and soft body. But what he wanted most for comfort was the very source of his discomfort. Hardly seemed fair.

"She should have told you, but I understand the reasons why she didn't." Nan's voice cut through his fresh rush of anguish. "That girl has had one hell of a hard go. From the time she was little. Half the people in this town won't even look her in the eye, and it got worse when she was pregnant and there was no father around. But she made a happy little life in that old house for her and her son, regardless. I think she was trying to protect herself. And she might not have done the right thing, but I understand why she did. That's the first real peace she's had in ages."

"She could have protected herself without lying to me."

"She could have, but I imagine this was the path of least resistance. For a girl who's been fighting for her whole damn life for a fair chance...I can see why she'd take the easy way out."

He shook his head, clenching and unclenching his fist on the table in front of him. Talking about it opened it up like a fresh wound. Drinking had definitely been the better choice.

"I *still* can't believe she lied to me," he said more to himself than to Nan.

"Have you been completely honest with her?"

That one stuck. He hadn't. While he'd talked about the fact he'd never go back to the rodeo, he *hadn't* been entirely truthful about the true state of affairs. The fact that he had nothing to offer her. He supposed that was a lie by omission just like Mason's paternity.

When he didn't answer, Nan pressed her lips together. "Well what do you want to do now?"

"I don't know." And if he had his way about it, without Nan prodding him, he probably would have been frozen in action for the foreseeable future.

"Well, this is how I see it." She leaned back in her seat and Nate knew she was probably going to say something he didn't want to hear. Because that was Nan's way, cutting straight to the heart of the matter, regardless of what comforting platitudes you wanted. She was always frank, but kind. "You were game to be a part of their lives before this all came to light. I saw the way you looked at Mason the other night, Nate. You were gonna be his father whether or not you *were*, biologically speaking."

"I have no idea how to be a father," he said with a scowl. "I didn't exactly have a shining example to follow."

Across the table, Nan let out a long breath, folding her hands together the way she always did when this topic came to light. It was less and less frequent as he and Banks had grown older, but this was a predictable move, like she had it hidden away in a compartment in her brain and her heart and needed this particular sequence of behavior to get it out to talk about it. None of it could have been easy; the act of raising her grandchildren when their parents just simply *wouldn't*, and further, never saying an impolite word about it.

"No, you didn't. Nate, your parents...they weren't bad people. My son wasn't a bad person. They were just selfish. And overwhelmed. That happens sometimes; and yes, there are days I wish they had stood up to their responsibilities...but my life was richer for having you two boys to take care of, so in a way, I'm *glad* they went east without you. I know that's probably something you've never come to terms with."

He shook his head. No, he hadn't come to terms with that. He'd been bitter about it growing up; every birthday card with a five dollar bill in it fueling his adolescent frustration—but then the cards came less and less often, and he hadn't heard from them in a decade now, and while he hadn't come to terms with it, he'd been able to bury it...until now. He cared about Mason so much already he couldn't imagine abandoning him, no matter how well he knew Layla could take care of him. And yet, cutting ties with Layla was exactly what that meant.

"You didn't even *know* Mason was yours and you were already a significantly better father figure than your dad *ever* was to you," Nan continued. "You're not selfish. A little overwhelmed, maybe. But you're also still in Three Rivers, so that counts for something."

He let out a breath. If he was truthful, the one thing he'd wished for over the last few days was that things would go back to the way they were before he'd uncovered her lie. Without having Layla and Mason to look forward to, his time spent in his grandmother's basement was as dismal and depressing as the time he'd spent laid up in his house in Denver, except maybe a little worse, because what he wanted was only ten miles and a serious conversation down the road.

"What do *you* think I should do, Nan?" He expected she'd be on Layla's team here—she was still helping her out as far as he knew.

"I think you should have a conversation with the girl. A serious one. Hear her out. Tell her what you want. And if you feel good after that, do what feels right. You know she doesn't expect anything from you, right?"

"Yeah," he breathed, pressing his fingertips to his eyes. Maybe that was the worst part.

THIRTY-EIGHT

LAYLA WOKE WITH a jerk. *Something's not right.* She reached to the bedside stand and turned up the volume on the baby monitor. Everything sounded normal, but she couldn't shake the feeling something was wrong. Carefully, she slid out of the bed, and pulled on her robe, illuminating the light on her phone to check the time. 3 a.m. With the device still clutched in her hand, she tiptoed to the door of the bedroom, but by the time she was there, the icy dread that pulsed through her veins moved her feet faster, until she was sprinting to Mason's bedroom door.

By his change table, she flicked on a soft-light lamp and peered into the crib. Her heart stopped. Eyes half open, Mason lay on his side, his body stiff, face and hands twitching.

Layla picked the baby up and cradled him gently to her chest, supporting his head and fixing her gaze on his. When she finally found her voice, she repeated his name in a whisper, trying to keep his focus on her. He was trying to cry, but the breaths got cut short as he seized. Tears rushed her eyes, but she somehow managed to find her way into the gliding rocker in the corner before her knees gave out. She picked up the 'just in case' cordless phone she kept on the dresser beside the chair. Things that weren't supposed to happen. She'd never thought she'd have to use it.

She stroked her baby's hair back off his forehead and focused on a repetitive tremble in his cheek, trying to temper the panic that made her heart beat a double-time staccato at the base of her throat as she fumbled to punch in the first number that came to mind.

It rang three or four times before Nate's groggy voice answered.

"Nate..." Layla choked on her words, pausing to take a breath. She hadn't planned to call him—she was pretty sure she was the last person he wanted to hear from, especially if it was concerning Mason—but it had been instinctual. He'd been such a huge part of her day-to-day over the last few weeks.

"Layla, is everything okay?" Suddenly, his voice was sharp and clear and filled with concern. The tears that had been building up spilled over and her next words came out on a sob.

"S-s-something's happening with Mason."

"I'll be right there," he said, and she heard movement, fabric sliding, jingling. "Just sit tight. I'll be right there. Stay on the phone. Just put it down beside you. If anything changes, talk to me, okay?"

"Okay," she said, following his direction, then pulling Mason to her chest, hoping he couldn't see her tears or scared face. She heard doors closing, footsteps, an engine roaring to life, but none of it really registered.

There had been another time she'd felt this way, and for a long time it felt like it was a million years ago. And now it felt so close. Too close. She hadn't known that baby for long, never felt him in her arms or kissed his soft hair. She'd never stared at his face wondering what sort of man he'd grow up to be. And she'd mourned for him for months, afterward. The circumstances that had produced *that* baby might have been even more complicated than these, but she'd wanted him. Badly. And she hadn't been allowed to keep him. She had Mason...*had* had him for eight months, and that wasn't nearly long enough. *I'll trade anything to keep him just a bit longer.*

After what felt like an hour, Mason finally relaxed with a whimper and a couple quiet sobs, curling his fingers into the lapel of her robe. This she could handle. This was normal. A baby upset in the night, wanting his mother. She swallowed hard and tried to soothe him with quiet babbling but her tears didn't stop, and then Nate was kneeling in front of the chair, with one big hand on Mason's hair and the other on her hand, meeting her gaze as he squeezed her fingers. Though all she could think about was Mason, she noticed Nate's shirt was on inside out, his hair messed fresh from sleep. Tiny details that didn't matter, but she hung onto them because it was less scary than thinking about the image of Mason struggling.

"Lay, what happened?"

She shook her head as she tried to put it to words. "It was like a seizure. He couldn't breathe. He seems okay now, but...I didn't know what to do."

Nate brushed Mason's hair back off his forehead with a tenderness that made Layla's heart ache. The baby's eyelids drooped and panic made her pull her hand away from Nate's to touch his chest and make sure he was still breathing.

"We're going to go to the hospital. I'll hold onto him and you go put some clothes on."

She blinked slowly, terrified at the idea of handing Mason over. His little body was now heavy and limp, but thankfully breathing, at the very least. It took a minute, but Nate helped her to her feet and gently pried the baby out of her arms, cradling him in the crook of his elbow while he drew her close with a hand on the back of her neck and kissed her forehead; a gentleness she'd didn't expect or deserve.

"I got him, Lay, I promise." The gentle rumble of his tender words brought a new rush of tears and a twist in her heart.

Though she felt like she was moving through glue, Layla propelled herself to her bedroom and dressed. She could hear Nate and Mason moving through the house, the clarity of Nate's voice as he talked to what must have been Nan, on the phone, and then quieter, a deep rumbling of words she couldn't make out. She emerged to find him waiting by the door, murmuring quietly to the baby he'd swaddled protectively against his chest. He met her eyes and she saw a thread of the fear she felt in her heart mirrored in them. He ushered them out to the truck.

"You ride in the back with him, Lay." Nate tipped his head toward the passenger side and she rounded the truck and climbed onto the tiny bench seat while he strapped Mason into the car seat he hadn't removed yet, despite what had happened. When he finished, he made eye contact with her again over the baby, his lips pressed together. "I got you both."

~

Nate guided his pickup through the sleepy streets of Three Rivers to the highway with a confidence he absolutely didn't feel in his heart. He didn't know a whole hell of a lot about babies, but the sleepy, barely-conscious baby he'd just strapped into the back seat and his frenzied mother scared the shit out of him. The unadulterated panic he saw in Layla's eyes had to keep him calm somehow—if he didn't do it, nobody would. Nan's soothing talk had helped, assuring him not to worry, it was something that happened sometimes, and usually there was no damage done, but it was hard to let those words override the concerning things he'd seen.

He caught Layla's eyes in the rear view mirror. She'd been babbling at Mason, talking about him staying awake, promising him he was all right and she was right there.

"How's he doing?"

"I think he's sleeping." Her brow furrowed with what he assumed was a frown, but he couldn't see anything but her frightened eyes in the mirror. He folded down the convertible middle seat and slipped his hand over it to find her knee, giving it a gentle squeeze.

"How about you?"

"I'm scared," she said, her voice cracking. He squeezed again, and then her fingers slid under his. "I'm just glad you're here."

There was a part of him that was angry. He should have been *there*, with them, not a ten minute drive away. If she'd been honest with him from the beginning, he would have been. But her soft fingers in his grip felt more right than he'd felt in the last seventy two hours or so, so that counted for something.

He couldn't have said no if he'd wanted to. Her panicked voice on the phone, the looming quiet in the background when she'd called. She could have been in Antarctica and he would have gone.

The drive to the regional hospital in Johnston that served the entire area was only twenty-five minutes, but it felt like a lifetime. Nate's attention remained divided between the road and glancing in the rear view mirror at Layla, who had a death grip on him with one hand, and the other on Mason. When he pulled up under the emergency door's covered entrance, he twisted in his seat to make eye contact.

"You go in and get started. I'll park and be right in." She nodded and climbed out the other side while he got out and unbuckled Mason from his seat. He looked like he was sleeping, like he'd seen him a dozen times, carried him in from the truck looking just like this a half dozen times. But this was different. Normally, he would shift, fuss a little. His little body was heavy, dead weight. He stopped for a second while Layla rounded the back of the pickup, watching Mason's chest in the neon light flooding over them, until he was sure he saw it rise and fall, and then handed him over to her. She looked completely and utterly lost as she cradled the baby to her chest and stumbled off toward the sliding double doors.

He climbed back into the truck and quickly parked in the mostly-empty parking lot, making his way back up to the building as fast as his legs could carry him. Layla was watching for him, still clinging to Mason like their lives depended on it. The wild look of panic she'd had in her eyes when he'd found her in Mason's bedroom was back. Fresh tears tracked her cheeks.

"They're just clearing an exam room for us," she said, glancing over her shoulder.

"Hey," he murmured gently, brushing a hand over Mason's hair. "We're really in the best place right now. Nan will be here any minute. Don't worry."

A short, anxious breath huffed out of her and she glanced behind her again. He followed her gaze this time to a sign indicating that outside of mid-day visiting hours, only immediate family was permitted.

"What if they don't let her in?"

"She's his grandmother. They'll let her in."

A nurse poked her head out of a set of doors, gesturing to Layla. "Come on in, mom and dad. We're ready for you."

Dad. Just like that, he'd stepped into a role he had no idea what to do with.

THIRTY-NINE

NATE CAUGHT HIS eyes just before they closed. His head jerked up and he glanced at the doorway, expecting to see Nan, but she wasn't there. She'd arrived not ten minutes after they were settled in the exam room, and as soon as she'd sufficiently fussed over first Mason, then Layla, she'd gone in search of coffee for all of them. By his estimation, she'd been gone at least twenty minutes—long enough to give him a chance to talk to Layla now that all of the urgency had drained out of the situation and they'd settled in for the long wait. But they hadn't—instead, Nate had convinced Layla, who was fading quickly as the adrenaline of the night drained out of her, to rest, and she was curled up against his chest as if the last three days hadn't excavated an enormous hole between the two of them. Mason rested in her arms. They were a family. *A family. His* family.

He barely knew what that was. Of course he called Nan and Banks his family. And even the Baylors and the Andersons were in on the mix. But the nuclear family—dad, mom, baby—that one felt so far out of his wheelhouse he didn't know what to do with it. More than once, he'd wished he'd had a little more time with his parents. Banks had memories, but he didn't have much more than an image in his mind to hold onto—and that he wasn't even sure of—it could have been from the little grainy photos Nan kept around. Not on proud display like the pictures of the boys growing up, of course, but around none the less. *Family is family*, she said. When he'd been a boy, he'd pressed from time to time but Nan simply said they weren't cut out to be parents and left it at that. Even though they'd burdened her with the raising of two small boys, she still wouldn't say a bad word about them.

And maybe being good at being a parent was genetic. Maybe *he* wasn't cut out to be a father. The urge to run had never been so strong as when Layla had confirmed Mason was his son. *Their* son. Maybe the only difference between Nate and his own father was he had nowhere to run to.

Layla stirred; her eyes were closed but he wasn't sure she was sleeping. Her soft, coconut-scented hair was so close, it would be just inches to drop his lips to the top of her head, and the temptation was *strong*. He was angry, had *been* angry for days, but all of that had paled tonight when he'd heard her panicked voice on the other end of the phone. And sitting here in this hospital room felt like the only place in the world he was supposed to be right now.

Unable to resist any longer, he reached down, tucking a strand of her hair behind her ear and sliding his fingertips over the length of it as it fell over her shoulder. Everything inside him was at odds. He wanted this—wanted her, wanted Mason, wanted to be all in—but it scared the living bejesus out of him. As he pondered how he could reconcile his fear with this deep-rooted desire to do the right thing, to do what he wanted to do, he heard a throat clear from the doorway and it shook him from his thoughts.

Nan stood in the door of the room with a magazine tucked under her arm and her hands full of coffee cups. A wide smile crossed her face as she surveyed the trio crammed onto the hospital bed; she looked *entirely* too pleased with herself. He raised a brow and shook his head. Layla was still quiet, so maybe she'd fallen asleep by now, but his grandmother still wasn't allowed to gloat within earshot. Crossing the floor, she extended one of the two steaming paper cups she carried to him.

"It's just vending machine drivel, but it'll have to do."

"Anything is better than nothing," he said gratefully, freeing one arm to take the cup from her. While he was beginning to fade, the gravity of his duty to keep watch over Layla and Mason kept him awake; the coffee would help.

Nan just got settled into the chair beside the bed when Dr. Fields appeared in the door. Nate had been surprised to find him here on duty, but the doctor explained in a small area like this one, all of the doctors took time away from their individual practices to take rotational shifts at the regional hospital. He couldn't have been happier, because it seemed to settle Layla a good deal. She had a great working relationship with the doctor, and it translated personally, it seemed. He ran his hand down over her shoulder and gave her a little squeeze. He hated to wake her—she had a shift scheduled at Danny's for the afternoon and she'd need all the sleep she could get.

"Lay, the doctor's here."

She shifted, drawing in a deep breath, and then straightened, wiping a hand over her face. He felt how she looked, but the coffee was helping. He offered her his cup, but she shook her head, her eyes snapping to focus on Dr. Fields. She'd been relaxed and loose but her body tensed against his now.

"Mason is going to be fine," he said, clearly and slowly, with eye contact, the same way Nate had been speaking to her most of the evening. The doctor probably had more practice communicating with scared people in emergency situations than he did. "Tests came back suggesting a low grade infection caused the fever. I'll prescribe some antibiotics."

Nate breathed a sigh of relief and he felt Layla's tense body relax just a little.

"And that caused him to have a seizure?"

The doctor nodded, perching near the foot of the bed. "Some children have febrile seizures. They're almost always completely harmless."

"So...will this happen every time?" Layla pushed herself into a sitting position, and Nate felt the coldness in the space her body had occupied.

The doctor shook his head resolutely. "It *could* happen again, but probably not."

Pressing her lips together, she rose from the bed, lying the still slumbering Mason on the bed beside Nate, who put his hand on the baby's back. Half to stop him from rolling off the bed, half to ensure he was still breathing. He watched Layla straighten her clothes nervously.

"Does it have an effect on him?"

Again, Dr. Fields shook his head. "Seizures because of fever aren't anything to worry about as far as brain or physical damage. If it happens again, keep an eye on him. Call an ambulance if it lasts for more than 5 minutes, and just make sure he can't hurt himself."

Nate cleared his throat then, because Layla's body language suggested she was getting ramped up going through the possibilities of this happening again, and that wasn't in her best interest by any stretch of the imagination. The doctor was being honest with her but with so much adrenaline still in her system and so little sleep, the best thing for her was to get home in her own bed.

"So can we take him home, Doc?" he intercepted, reaching to touch Layla's wrist.

"Yes," the doctor responded, and then turned back to Layla. "Layla—there's nothing in the bloodwork that indicates this is anything but an isolated incident. You can give him Tylenol for the fever and just keep an eye on him. If *anything* makes you worry, you know you can call me."

~

Layla let out a breath and nodded as she let the doctor's words sink in. She felt comfortable coming to her employer with any fears or concerns, but she didn't figure he'd be interested in getting a call in an hour when she was home alone again, standing over her baby's crib questioning every sleeping twitch or flinch. She had to get a hold on herself. Nan had told her when she'd arrived things like this happened from time to time, it was totally normal, and it didn't mean anything was wrong with Mason. And now the doctor had backed it up, but she still felt like she was bearing the weight of the world on her shoulders.

Nate picked up Mason and touched her waist lightly. Everyone was watching, waiting for her to gather herself and leave. But this felt like the safest place, especially with Nate here.

"O-okay," she stammered, letting Nate guide her out of the exam room.

"Thanks, Doc. We'll call you if we need you."

And then they were walking out through the waiting room, out the sliding doors of emergency, and into the cool night air toward Nate's truck. With Mason's seat in it. The seat he'd bought before he'd known Mason was his son.

He was a good man, and she'd been wrong to keep this secret from him. He was so good, in fact, that even though she was probably the last person in the world he wanted to hear from, he'd dropped everything in the middle of the night when she called, treated Mason with the tenderness of a father who had been present all along, and even been kind and warm to her. The exhaustion, the adrenaline, and the realization all threatened to swamp her in tears.

Nan followed along with them, and reached out to touch her back at the exact moment when Layla needed it the most.

"You want me to come with you, honey?"

"I got this, Nan. We'll call if we need you," Nate said as he pulled the door of the truck open and put Mason in his seat.

Layla turned to Nan while Nate buckled Mason in, a little bit dumfounded by his words, but touched. Nan's eyes asked the right questions—*is this okay? Are you all right with this?* Even though Nate was her grandson, Nan was still looking out for Layla.

She nodded silently. Even if he was angry, she felt safe with him, like he could protect her from the scary uncertainty motherhood had so suddenly become. It hadn't always been easy, but it had never been as terrifying as tonight.

"Okay, honey. Give me a hug." Nan wrapped Layla up in her arms—a funny sight because as tough as she was, Nan was tiny—and squeezed her hard, the way Layla wished her mom would. She felt tears pricking at her eyes again before the older woman released her, then vised Nate into a hug. This was Layla's family, blood or not. A little patchwork family she'd put together when she could no longer depend on her own. "You two call me if you need *anything*."

"We will."

Nan headed toward her car—a little slower than necessary, like she had one ear turned back for trouble, but they waited until she was in her car and the engine had roared to life and then Nate helped Layla into the passenger side of the truck for the long ride back to Three Rivers.

FORTY

LAYLA STRUGGLED TO keep her eyes open in the dim glow of the radio in the dashboard of Nate's truck as they turned in the driveway. He'd tucked her up under his arm in the girlfriend seat and the hard warmth of his body and the dull roar of the truck's engine were so familiar and comforting, she could have forgotten about everything and drifted off. Except she knew this familiar and comforting thing was also temporary. Nate wasn't going to just slide back into the spot where she'd grown so accustomed to him being just because she'd called him in a panic in the middle of the night. They had to talk. Sooner rather than later. She'd owed that to him even before tonight.

The kitchen and living room lights were still on, Layla noticed as she pulled herself into a sitting position, Nate's headlights swept over the front of the house. No porch light on. She was surprised the door was even closed; they'd taken off so quickly. Nate pulled up beside her car and put his truck in park, killing the engine. The quiet settled between them, and she could feel his eyes on her.

"You okay?" he finally asked into the darkness.

Layla glanced over. She couldn't make out his features. Right now? Sure, she was okay. But a deeply resonating feeling of *not okay* was just under the skin. Nothing was okay as long as he was going to get in his truck and drive away. That was what she expected—what she'd basically set herself up for from the minute she saw him in the bar that first night. But it wasn't what she wanted, and she'd do anything to change it. And she'd realized it too damn late.

"Yeah," she lied.

"Okay."

They climbed out of the truck and she let Nate retrieve the baby—it seemed like it meant something to him, and even though Mason wouldn't remember, it couldn't be bad for him either. She led them up the stairs of the house and opened the door for him. He went straight through the entryway and to the back of the house like he belonged there, with Layla trailing behind.

Nate settled Mason into the crib, the way she'd shown him one night when he'd run out of small projects to do during the bedtime routine, and then turned to her.

"You need to hit the hay, too."

She crossed one arm over her midsection, grasping the elbow of her other arm anxiously.

"I'm exhausted, but I don't know how I'll be able to sleep."

He touched her shoulder lightly and turned her toward the door, steering her down the hall toward her bedroom without a word. When they stopped, she heard his voice at her back, a deep rumble in the quiet of her dark room.

"Would it help if I stayed?"

Her heart twisted in a way she didn't expect. Of course it would help if he stayed. But would it really make anything better? She was lying to herself if she said yes. It would only prolong the inevitable. But she needed to lean on his strength just a bit longer. And he *was* offering...

"Yes," she said, barely above a whisper.

"All right." He moved through the room, flicking on the lamp on the bedside table, then shouldered out of his t-shirt. He'd done it a hundred times but it never got old. It took her a minute to shake herself from watching it, but then she slipped out of her pants and bra, leaving the t-shirt she'd been wearing and underwear, and climbed into the bed. It wasn't long before she felt his warmth at her back. Involuntarily, she shifted closer, and then she felt his hand close on her hip lightly, tugging her back toward him, in the familiar, intimate position they always slept in. She let out a soft sigh as his fingers dangled down across her belly and his breath heated the nape of her neck. Even if they were just going through the motions, it was the comfort she needed.

"Nate?"

"Mm?" he mumbled against her back. He'd nestled up close, his fingers absently stroking that soft, slack skin between her hip and the curve of her belly. It was half tickling and half a turn on, and something he always did. Something she loved. So many little things tonight had made her feel like there might be hope; and that tiny spark of hope was as dangerous now as it had proven to be at the beginning of the summer.

"Thank you for tonight."

He was quiet for a moment, and then he moved his hand from her hip and brushed her hair back from her forehead. She felt his breath close, and then pressure, like he was resting his lips against the crown of her head.

"Anytime. Now get some sleep."

It was the best sleep she'd gotten in days.

FORTY-ONE

NATE WASN'T SURPRISED to find Layla still fast asleep when he roused. He *was* a little surprised, however, to find his body had forgotten about any of the bad blood and secrets between them. Extra carefully, he slid his arm out from under her head and untangled himself from her soft body. It would have been easy last night, both of them hurting, to make her feel good—to make himself feel better about the whole thing—but that would have undone everything he'd worked so hard to lay out at the beginning of this relationship.

He shouldn't have cared about undoing it, but he did. And that meant he was going to have to figure all of this out sometime between now and when she woke up and found him still in her kitchen. He slid into his jeans, pausing at the door to make sure she was still asleep. She'd moved some, but her eyes were still closed and she breathed evenly. A right at the door took him down the hall to Mason's room. The baby was still fast asleep, and for just a minute, Nate watched his chest rise and fall in the dim morning light. Like nothing at all had happened last night, even though he'd managed to turn his mama's world upside down.

And his daddy's. Now he'd had a chance to sleep on it, everything made perfect sense. Layla was so used to shouldering the burden of her life alone—it was logical that her first instinct wouldn't be to share it, but to protect her ability to continue to carry it alone. It wasn't like she'd ever been able to count on anyone close to her to help her out. She hadn't lied to hurt him; she'd lied to protect herself. He could respect that. He hadn't exactly been forthcoming about losing everything, and that was to protect *him*self. But none of it really mattered; protecting yourself was useless because regardless of what precautions you took, life was going to hurt you one way or the other. What mattered most was lying right here in this crib, had filled this humble little house for the last few weeks. *Love. Family.* The loving little family they'd forged together against all the odds and circumstances. And he was a damn fool for letting an emergency like last night be the only thing that proved it.

It wasn't long before he felt her presence in the doorway. He didn't turn right away, but when he heard her take a few tentative steps into the room, he couldn't stop himself from looking at her. He'd told her not a week ago he was falling in love with her, and seeing her paused in the little wedge of morning light coming in through Mason's bedroom window, her long, bare legs and thick thighs poking out the bottom of the oversized t-shirt she'd thrown on, he knew it hadn't been lip service. Her hair was still rumpled, her eyes sleepy, but she was perhaps the most beautiful thing in the world. Nate nodded, and she joined him at the side of the crib, curling her fingers over the rail and peering in, looking for the same thing he had. Her whole posture relaxed when she saw it, and she rocked back on her heels.

"Hey," he said quietly.

"Hey."

"You want some coffee? I'll go put some on."

"Mm," she whispered.

Just like he couldn't stop himself from looking at her, Nate couldn't stop himself from reaching out to touch her jaw either, running his thumb over the crease on her cheek the pillow had left. She turned her face into his touch, a move that nearly broke him. He had been unkind to her, but she still trusted him, looked to him, wanted him. And he felt the same way.

He left her then, standing by the crib. She'd let the baby sleep, but he could understand why she'd want a few extra minutes just to soak in the fact that he was okay. In the kitchen, he assembled the coffee filter and grounds and set up the machine, grabbed two mugs, and the milk from the fridge for her coffee. She padded in just as the final drops of coffee were dripping into the carafe, her brow furrowed like something was on her mind. He'd had enough on his over the last twelve hours; it wouldn't surprise him that she did, too.

"Nate, I need to apologize."

He glanced at her; that hadn't been exactly what he was expecting. When he saw how dead serious her eyes were, he turned, leaning his hips against the counter as he watched her.

"I shouldn't have lied to you about Mason. I should have told you. I just..." she trailed off, brushing her hand over her face to push her bangs off of her forehead. "I was scared because it was getting real."

"It was," he said with a nod. "It *is* real, Layla. Don't you think I was a little scared too? I'm not exactly the settling-down type, and all of a sudden there's this ready-made family and I want it *so* bad. To find out it really was mine all along, that I wasted all this time for nothing...it hurt."

"I know." Her eyes flickered downward for just a moment before they came back to his, proud and strong.

"And I have nothing for you, Lay. Except what's standing right here. My truck's on its last legs, and I don't have fifty bucks in the bank. They took my house, my horses..." He let out a breath. He'd never been this honest, maybe not even with himself. "I don't know if this rodeo school thing will pan out. I can't provide for you and Mason the way a man is supposed to. And I think that's why it hit me so hard when I found out."

She leveled her gaze at him across the island, then she was on the same side as him in a few easy strides.

"You don't get it."

"What don't I get?"

"If I wanted money, I would have called you the minute I suspected I was pregnant. I didn't want to screw up your life. And then you were here, and I thought we were just having fun."

"We *were* having fun, weren't we?"

"And then when you...said that thing..."

"Said what thing?" He raised a brow, watching her with amusement.

"When you said it, I was going to tell you...I had plans. But then my mother..."

"Said *what* thing?" he pushed.

She pressed her lips together, her brow furrowed with her frustration. She didn't want to say it out loud, but she had to come to terms with it even if he had to drag her kicking and screaming to it.

"That...you said that you were falling in *love* with me, and I thought you ought to know the truth then. I was going to tell you."

"So you *did* hear it." He tipped his head down, watching as she blushed a bit.

"Yes, but..."

"But?"

"I know you didn't mean it."

~

Layla's heart beat a mile a minute when Nate set his eyes on her. Last night, and again this morning in Mason's room, he'd been gentle, kind. She'd all but forgotten about how angry he'd been on her front porch just a few days earlier. And he wasn't exactly *angry* now, but it was intense, whatever it was. It stole her breath and made her pulse jackhammer. If his fixing a few squeaky hinges and missing shingles on her siding felt *real*, this was something else entirely.

"Layla Sullivan, how many damn times do I have to tell you something for it to get through to you?"

She couldn't respond, just swallowed, watching as he got closer to her.

"I don't say things I don't mean. I *was* falling in love with you."

Was... Clearing her throat, Layla blinked. He was so close now she could feel heat radiating from his body. She was half tempted to grab him, half tempted to run.

"I *am* in love with you. And this little family. I'm all in, Layla. If you'll have me. I didn't know that before, didn't think you'd want me the way I am. But if you'll let me, I want to try to be better for you. And for Mason. I'll do the rodeo school thing and I'll sell wrenches on the side if I have to. Whatever it takes to make your lives better for me being here, not worse."

"Hammers," she supplied.

"Hammers, wrenches, tape measures. The whole damn hardware store. Whatever it takes."

Layla let out a breath. She didn't care about the money—she'd make it, no matter what...*financially*, anyway. It was the idea of having someone else in her corner. Someone to pick her up when she fell down, to share her secrets with, to lean on when times got rough...that was worth every dollar in the world. And to think that it would be Nate Montgomery wanting to be that person. Well, she wanted to pinch herself.

"It won't be easy," she finally said, a last ditch effort to give him an out.

"You think I need easy?" His lips twisted in a shit-eating grin, lightening the mood marginally. "If I didn't like a little challenge, I never would have ridden bulls for all those years."

"It's not a little challenge. It's the hardest thing *I've* ever done in my life, and I grew up with my mama," she paused, allowing herself a little smile. The weight of the moment was lifting— slowly, but surely. "It's exhausting until you think you can't even stand up anymore but you have to because you have one more shift, something breaks every time you think you've got something under control, and then there's a middle-of-the-night emergency just to remind you you're not in the driver's seat. It's a gut punch, and then another one, until you think you can't stand up anymore...but somehow you can."

Nate quieted her, sliding a hand over her shoulder and down her arm until his fingers threaded into hers and he gave them a squeeze.

"Now imagine dividing that by half."

She pressed her lips together.

"Let me shoulder some of that burden, Layla. It's the least I can do. You've been doing it alone long enough. And you've done a helluva job. But now you can rest a little."

His words hit her right in the middle of the chest, making her heart swell up with something somewhere between pride and love...yes, there it was. *Love*.

Nate shifted forward, his free hand gliding over her hair and bringing her close to rest her forehead against his. She closed her eyes and drew in the deepest breath she'd been able to take in months.

"I love you," she said, abandoning all the careful caution and anxiety she'd been feeling since he'd shown up on her barstool. She had nothing to lose now.

There was barely a breath before he responded, sending her heart soaring and bringing a fresh flood of tears to her eyes. "I love *you*, Layla Sullivan. And I'd be proud as hell to call you mine."

EPILOGUE

"YOU READY?" NATE asked from the door. He was leaning on the frame, all cowboy cool in dark jeans and a starched button down shirt, like he was ready for something important. A handful of butterflies took off in Layla's stomach when it dawned on her—that something important was *her*.

She let out a shaky breath, checking her reflection in the mirror one last time. Her long hair was loose, in soft waves over her shoulders. Kerri had come early to help her out because she was clueless about this sort of thing. They couldn't afford a stylist, or a makeup artist, or even a fancy dress, but she felt beautiful, and that feeling multiplied when she turned back around and saw Nate's face; his gaze all pride and love, and maybe hotter than was appropriate considering they weren't alone.

"I'm ready," she said, willing her voice not to crack. It was silly to be nervous, but the butterflies battering her ribcage didn't get that memo.

"Great," Kerri said, handing Mason to Nate. The baby's outfit was the mirror image of his father's, tiny Wranglers and matching plaid. "I'll let everyone know."

Layla watched her back as Kerri left the room, wondering how the heck she would manage to walk out of the house and to the little altar they'd made by the pond, and then Nate held his crooked arm out to her, balancing Mason on the other hip, and she knew exactly how she'd manage. The same way she'd manage the rest of this crazy life—with him by her side.

Nate leaned over, his breath moving the hair over her ear. "You're so damn beautiful, Lay."

She smiled and drew a deep, cleansing breath. "Let's not keep these people waiting."

Nate led her out of the house, down the porch steps and around the corner of the house. By the pond, the Baylor brothers had assembled a half dozen bales of hay and Nan had supplied old quilts to lay over them. Nan had also assembled flowers from her garden in jars at the end of each little row and a huge table arrangement next to Banks, who stood under an arch Nate had fashioned out of a fallen birch tree from their backyard. The sheriff's face split into a huge grin when they came into sight and all of their guests took his cue, rising and turning. She hadn't formally invited anybody but Banks, Kerri, and Nan, but the Baylor brothers and their wives and assortment of children, as well as the patriarch and matriarch of the family were scattered amongst the bales. And it was perfect. Exactly what she would have planned, if she'd had time to actually plan anything besides asking Banks to marry them.

The leaves were starting to turn but the sun was still hot enough for the little blush colored sundress she wore. Nate had told her to pick whatever she wanted, and she'd briefly looked at the bridal shop in Johnston, experiencing major sticker shock every time she turned over the tag on a dress she couldn't imagine herself actually wearing. This dress had been hanging in a second hand shop—just her size and exactly her style—with the right price tag.

They paused at the end of the row of hay bales to let Lilly Baylor step into the aisle and snap a few pictures; waiting until she checked the monitor on the camera and flashed them a huge grin and a giant thumbs up before they made their way toward Banks.

When they got to the front, Nate tipped Mason toward her and she pressed a kiss to his irresistibly chubby cheek; Nate mirrored her actions.

Banks nodded to the group still standing around them and they sat.

"What a special day," her soon-to-be brother-in-law began. "Now Layla and Nate didn't want anything too fussy so we're gonna do it quick and dirty so we can get to the part everybody's looking forward to—the celebrating.

"But I am gonna say one thing...off script, before we get started. You all know as well as I do how important family is. There's as much chosen family sitting here as there is blood family, and Nan always taught Nate and me the importance of choosing good family. We chose the Baylors. Nan chose us, and every other person in this town, and I think Nate is making a helluva good choice today. Layla, you're a good one. We all know how fiercely you love by the way you've taken care of that sweet little boy of yours. You're a hard worker and you've got a heart of gold, and I'm beyond happy my brother, who can, by the way, occasionally be a bonehead, has abandoned his bonehead ways and is making you a Montgomery today."

Banks had always been cordial, but Layla had no idea he felt this way about her. She took a deep breath, steeling back tears that threatened to overflow and shook her head. "Don't get me started already."

A chuckle moved through the group behind her and she turned to take them all in. Faces that reflected the same kind of love and joy that Banks' did. She hadn't invited her family—but right now, it didn't matter. From Nan to Kerri to Lilly Baylor and everyone in between, joyful expectation lifted their lips into smiles. This was her family.

"Oh he's just getting going," Nate deadpanned. "Now hurry up, Banks. I can't wait another minute for you to make this woman my wife."

ABOUT THE AUTHOR

Amity Lassiter lives in Eastern Canada with her herding dog, her barn cat, two horses and her Mister. She has loved telling stories her entire life and even before she could write could be found in her grandmother's basement, reciting fiction into an ancient cassette recorder.

The most influential author in Amity's life would be Peter S. Beagle, the author of The Last Unicorn, who introduced her to her first achingly impossible love story and made her believe in magic. She met, and shared the most surreal small talk with Beagle in May 2014.

She loves critters, coffee, and cowboys – and she still believes in unicorns.

You can find more from Amity Lassiter online at www.amitylassiter.com